THE ART OF UNPACKING YOUR LIFE

SHIREEN JILLA

BLOOMSBURY READER

LONDON · OXFORD · NEW YORK · NEW DELHI · SYDNEY

This edition published in 2016 by Bloomsbury Reader

Copyright © 2015 Shireen Jilla

The moral right of the author is asserted.

Bloomsbury Reader is an imprint of Bloomsbury Publishing Plc

50 Bedford Square, London WC1B 3DP

www.bloomsburyreader.com

Bloomsbury is a trademark of Bloomsbury Publishing plc

Bloomsbury Publishing, London, Oxford, New Delhi, New York and Sydney

ISBN: 978 1 4482 1594 2
eISBN: 978 1 4482 1519 5

Visit www.bloomsburyreader.com to find out more about our authors and their books.
You will find extracts, author interviews, author events and you can sign up for
newsletters to be the first to hear about our latest releases and special offers.

You can also find us on Twitter @bloomsreader.

Printed and bound by CPI Group (UK) Ltd, Croydon, CR0 4YY

For my mother

Contents

'Every family has its joys and its horrors, but however great they may be, it's hard for an outsider's eye to see them; they are a secret.'

Anton Chekhov

Chapter 1

The sociable weaver bird nest splayed across the acacia thorn tree like an ancient, sun-damaged headdress. Teeming with over three hundred inhabitants, this nest weighed over a ton and had broken most of the lower branches. Brown-capped heads whipped in and out, shrill with gossip. Past weavers had poked in each individual straw in a communal effort to create a dense, cool apartment. This generation had merely moved into their century-old home without even doing renovations, the guide Gus explained to Connie who was eager for every detail.

The reserve had turned this classic Kalahari feature into their airstrip reception. A thatched roof slid protectively over the nest, leaving the top of the trunk jutting up into the deep blue. Connie had only seen such an unblemished block of sky in children's paintings.

A blonde South African, whose badge labelled her a Kimberley, was under the roof, sheltered from the bleaching thirty-five-degree glare. Her make-up was flawless, despite the heat she must have endured to get to the airstrip. She held out a wooden plate of icy face towels neatly wrapped like swaddled babies. A jug of home-made lemonade and two black bowls, one of watermelon cut into cubes and another of glistening date and coconut balls, were on the table beside her. The china was arranged on a silver platter on the yellowwood table. Connie was grateful for the towels, the nibbles and furniture chosen to transition unnerved guests like her friends into this remote environment.

Connie lowered her camera and nervously reviewed her photo. It was extraordinary to see her five dearest university friends together in the Kalahari. They were all just about in shot. She hadn't asked them to pose as a group, because every one of them appeared to shrink from the ferocious heat, the wilderness of high spring grass and deformed thorny trees marked by blood-orange Namibian sands. They were nearly at the reserve, yet they seemed to have had enough of travelling and waiting. No one bothered to talk.

It was her idea to bring them back together on this holiday, yet Connie was stunned. She had imagined herself cool in white cotton like Kristin Scott Thomas, light among an eye-watering desert of dunes. Her MP husband, Julian, was hardly up to the role of Ralph Fiennes. Watching him rub his forehead with one of his vast white handkerchiefs he usually employed on his blocked sinuses, Connie suppressed a smile. He could have been taken hostage from his desk in the Treasury in his work shirt and brown suede slip-ons. His collapsed chinos were the only sartorial marker that he was on holiday.

Connie looked down at the camera screen again. She knew Julian's slight sneer masked his extreme discomfort, which Connie could see was mirrored in Sara's expression. Sara had come straight to Heathrow from her chambers, 2 Bedford Row, in a black suit and off-white silk shirt. Her tailored barrister's jacket was neatly folded into her large handbag, but the blouse clingfilmed her. She was distracted: alternating between staring at her BlackBerry, eyeing the reserve and hoovering up the date balls.

Only Matt's American wife, Katherine, refrained from exhaustedly bingeing. Matt's marital bulk was coiled around her wicker chair, as she sipped lemonade. True to her title, London editor of *Women's Wear Daily*, Katherine had changed at the hangar in Jo'Burg into a barely grey pair of cotton combats, cream canvas shoes and a diaphanous silver shirt. Her translucent face was partially armour-plated by enormous black Chanel sunglasses. Spying the sun darting through the open sides, Katherine sprung up and strode to the centre of the reception. Matt silently followed, carrying her chair.

His over-protectiveness irritated Connie, because it made her, in turn, feel protective of Matt. After his ex-wife had brutally upgraded him for a partner in their law firm, he had come to dinner at least once a week. Until he met Katherine. Considering he was one of Connie's old friends and not in politics, Julian was unusually fond of him.

Connie was abruptly distracted from Matt and Katherine by Lizzie's voice, which snapped into the silence.

'I had no idea it was going to be this hot. I'm like a beef Bourguignon on a hot stove. Am I red, Luke? I feel purple. I might actually be allergic to this kind of heat. Knowing my luck. How unfair would that be?'

A blotchy heat rash had formed a patchwork across Lizzie's neck and face. Luke didn't reply. Lizzie fanned herself with her rumpled scarf, the fringe of which flicked into her left eye.

'Ow. Have I got a piece of my scarf in my eye? Can you see, Luke? It's hurting in the corner.'

Lizzie hadn't been hopeless when they had all shared a house in their second year though she now moaned to Connie that she would never live in such a lovely house again.

Lizzie didn't wait for Luke to examine her eye. 'I wonder whether Sara's got a mirror in that gorgeous Mulberry Bayswater handbag of hers. She is lucky to be able to afford it. Eight hundred and ninety-five pounds. You must know that: I haven't got the money to buy a sock on your website. I can't believe one of my best friends owns such a posh online shop.'

Luke stretched his left bicep across his body. Even in this extreme heat, he had this new nervous energy that surprised Connie. Freshly divorced from Emma, Connie was concerned that he might be unhappy on this holiday. Instead, he appeared to have extricated himself without a scar and with custody of his children, a fact that shocked Connie. She hadn't expected it from him.

He stretched both his arms above his head, forcing his sporty top to glide up a few inches. Connie couldn't help staring at the muscles that bound his torso. She had forgotten how handsome he was. She turned away.

There was no relief. Dan was ignoring Alan, his partner for over a decade. Their silence seemed to be the tail end of an on-going argument. Alan created a second tower of coconut and date balls, before rapidly demolishing them, as if he was determined to upset health-conscious Dan, who ignored him. He meticulously applied suncream to his face from a neat black tube, using the silver platter as a mirror to re-check his coverage, before opening the sketchbook and tin of pencils beside him. Looking up occasionally, Dan started assiduously drawing.

Connie was worried that there was a distance between all of them that hadn't existed yesterday at Heathrow, where the excitement of their extraordinary holiday and Sara's famous case had made the conversation flow easily. The whole of the UK was gripped by the Jade Sutton trial: a photogenic, middle-class couple accused of murdering their only daughter. Sara's team had successfully got the wife, Joanne Sutton – if Connie remembered her name correctly – off. And the group had been eager with questions.

Time had become elongated on their overnight flight from London. The slow way it passed reminded Connie of sleeping on the floor under Hector's bed, on Neptune Ward in Chelsea and Westminster hospital, after Flora had absentmindedly dropped that yellow Irish fishing buoy down the stairs on to his head. They flew to Johannesburg, fast tracked with the reserve's 'fixer' through frenzied passport control at O.R. Tambo airport, and then drove in an air-conditioned Mercedes people carrier to a depot-style building, which housed the check-in for their private ten-seater plane.

The plane was burnished with San bushmen's watery illustrations in earthy tones of northern Kalahari eland, springbok, abstract shapes and dancing figures. The bushmen's stories described their landscape in practical terms, though they engraved images from dreams and trance-like states.

'Therefore we are the Stars we must walk the sky,
for we are the Heavens things Mother is Earth's thing, she walks the earth
She must lie sleeping in the ground, we are which must not sleep
for we walks around, while we sleep not, we are the Stars which sleep not.'

Connie wanted to absorb everything about this adventure. But the others seemed reluctant to let go of their lives in London.

After a short flight they had been released into this Kalahari reception. Feeling uncertain and unnerved, Connie looked towards their guide, Gus, who was standing beside a cream safari vehicle with another man, presumably their tracker. Connie had developed a shorthand with Julian and her children, and without it she felt rusty, staid and gauche but she did what she always did: she smiled broadly and talked through the tension.

'We're here. Really we are. Wow. Can you believe it? We're in Africa. Well, the Kalahari. How incredible. Unbelievable even.'

Julian interjected, 'Self-edit button, Constance.'

Lizzie giggled. Luke turned away. Dan pursed his lips.

Julian's jokes were acerbic, but Connie knew Julian would sense his mistake and quickly re-establish equilibrium. It was what they did well together, what made them a potent husband-and-wife team.

Julian tucked Connie's hair behind her ear. 'Sorry, campers. I appreciate it's too bloody hot to joke. Can someone please switch on the fucking air con?'

They all laughed, except Luke.

Lizzie unhooked the outsized woven bag weighing down her shoulder. 'Oh, I almost forgot.' Leaning the bag awkwardly on to her hip, she delved inside, struggling to take out a large royal blue photo album. 'You are all going to love this photo.'

Nothing measured up to their time together at Bristol University for Lizzie. She hadn't moved on. Connie looked over at the photo. They were drunk and laughing. They were always drunk and laughing.

Lizzie dropped the bag on the ground and flicked the thick plastic-covered pages. 'Look! It's all of us that weekend we moved into Harley Place. Can you believe it really is us?'

'Who else might it be, dizzy Lizzie?' Sara said.

'Okay, Sara, but I had this amazing idea.' She waited dramatically but no one took Lizzie's obvious bait. 'We could take the same photo of us in the same position. Twenty years later.'

'Do you have to keep reminding us,' Sara murmured.

Lizzie didn't appear to register her reluctance. 'Katherine or Alan, maybe one of you can take it? I'd love one of just the six of us back together again.'

'Yeah, course, Lizzie darlin',' said Alan, pretending to frame them with his fingers. 'Shall I airbrush out the decades?'

Lizzie laughed, 'If only. Can you airbrush out the fat as well?'

'Lizzie, don't be banal,' snapped Sara.

Katherine looked back at the album. 'Matt, honey, I can't believe that's you with long hair.'

Matt ruffled his dark, thick hair now layered into a sensible solicitor's crop. 'I was always built for comfort not for speed. No change there.'

Connie looked at him and then back at the photo. He had been an unusually broad, solid man in his late teens.

'You're not larger,' Lizzie stated.

Connie knew she intended it to be a reassuring comment.

Lizzie continued, 'Look at me, I was skinny. Do you remember? What I would do to get that body back.'

In the photo, Lizzie was thin with long straight blond hair, if the same hotch-potch clothes. Lizzie's arms, legs, bust, hips and waist had inflated, while her hair was frizzy from schizophrenic cutting and colouring sessions, ranging from deep mahogany to bright blond.

Thankfully, Connie noticed Katherine taking control of the camera. 'You guys, I need you lounging. Not necessarily on the ground, Lizzie. We don't have to go that far for authenticity's sake.'

She was drawn back to the photo. Connie, Sara, Luke, Matt, Dan and Lizzie on the roof terrace at Harley Place one hazy Sunday afternoon in early September of their second year.

Alan spoke. 'What is that?'

'Haven't you seen photos of Dan's canary before?' Lizzie asked.

Squashed next to Matt, Dan looked minute and compact in that vivid yellow V-neck jumper he had always worn, an unsubtle attempt to signal to them he was gay. Connie caught Luke's eye. He smiled, doubtless remembering how they had dumped it in a bin outside the student union. She couldn't remember whose idea it was. In those days, their thoughts were interchangeable.

Sara folded her legs over one of the reception's wicker chairs. 'I can manage to strike that pose.'

Sara had been perched in one of her many A-line vintage wool dresses, on the only chair on the terrace. She was more curvaceous these days, though still beautiful with an old-fashioned elegance that, coupled with her sharp wit, was undoubtedly the reason she intimidated men. Her face was like Grace Kelly's: liquid green eyes framed by the dark, permanently questioning curve of her eyebrows and her thick wavy blond hair matching her perfectly white complexion.

Luke caught her eye again. In the photo, their long, lean bodies were parallel; their legs were like chopsticks criss-crossing each other. Luke was tauter then, though he still had the same mid-brown hair cropped close to his narrow head. His brilliant blue eyes made his immaculate face unmissable. Connie felt awkward.

Sara was on to them. 'Yes, it would be great if you two could possibly stay unwrapped for this photo. Please.'

Connie and Luke laughed lightly.

'Okay, guys, let's take this picture,' said Katherine impatiently. 'Ready?'

They finally moved together, in position.

'One, two, three. Say safari.' Katherine scrutinised the photo she had taken. 'Great. One more, for luck. Okay, we're so done here.'

Julian was still looking at the original photo. He could hardly be jealous. It was all so long ago.

Connie, Sara, Luke, Matt, Dan and Lizzie had been residents at Wills Hall in their first year. Connie had a room on the same floor as Lizzie and Sara. Twenty-two years later, their friendships had equity that only time can give.

The Kalahari? Julian looked incredulous when Connie first tested out the idea. Why? Julian needed a strong argument for any plan that diverted dramatically from their norm, which was, Connie was the first to acknowledge, lovely and fortunate: four teenage children, weekdays in London and weekends in the constituency in Oxfordshire. Julian forcefully pitched for a birthday party at their country house in Adderbury. They could invite everyone they knew, including her university friends.

Connie's grandfather had built this hunting lodge, which was currently a privately owned safari reserve. She had known this fact for years and had never acted on it. She had been so busy with the children. Now Connie yearned to experience what her grandfather had created. Once she had thought of the idea, it was impossible to let it go.

The second time Connie had suggested the Kalahari, Julian gave way. By then, their housekeeper Sally had announced that she was pregnant and Connie wondered whether they would practically be able to go. Julian had suggested the holiday would give Sally some space to pack and get organised for the baby, before leaving to stay with her parents. While they were on holiday, Sally would obviously be in sole charge of the children, so Connie was surprised, but secretly relieved. She wasn't going to employ another housekeeper – she couldn't replace a close friend who had lived with them for over a decade. This was her chance to get away for a week without the children.

Gus approached the group, playing with his brown leather bracelet. 'Welcome to the Gae. I'm Gus – if we haven't already met. And I'll be riding out with you this week.'

It was time for them to go. Sara slipped her BlackBerry into her bag and Matt put his arm protectively around Katherine's shoulders.

'I can honestly say that Gae is the most beautiful place on earth. One hundred thousand hectares of the most undisturbed wildlife. George Sanderson's inspirational vision.' Gus nodded towards Connie. She was touched he knew about her grandfather.

'Oh, I must tell you. We have been to the Kruger,' Katherine interrupted, 'I was covering it for my magazine.'

Gus nodded. Connie wasn't sure whether it was in agreement, or merely a reflex.

'Hand on heart that's a zoo compared with what you will see here. We have only six vehicles on the whole reserve. You will experience something like no other safari. Trust me, eh. This evening, we'll take our first proper orientation drive out – see some action with the Southern Pride.'

'Southern Pride?' Julian interjected.

Connie caught Luke eyeing Julian.

Gus smiled more easily than they did. 'The Southern Pride are our young lions, who were spotted this morning at a water hole.'

Already, Gus seemed able to bind them together in this adventure in a way that Connie had so far failed. His rebellious blond-brown hair had a laid-back shapelessness that reminded Connie of her eldest son, Leo. She wondered how Gus saw them. A lost, pale lot.

'This is Ben, our tracker. We are lucky to have him, eh?' His slight nod and direct gaze made it clear that 'we are'. 'Ben was born here on the northern part of the reserve. He worked in the mines, but made it back here a couple of years ago. Nothing out in the bush escapes him. I trust him with my life.' Even broader grin. 'I *have* trusted him with my life.'

Ben gave a slight smile of humble acknowledgement that didn't risk exposing his teeth.

Julian leaned forward politely to shake his hand. 'Ben, great to meet you. Julian.' His long white fingers were engulfed by Ben's deep coal palm. 'We can't wait to learn from you.'

'Ben understands English, but it is his third language. His first is Tswana and we speak in Afrikaans.'

Sara jumped in. 'You speak Afrikaans? Isn't that rather un-PC?'

'It's still an important way of communicating, eh? Let's go for a drive.'

They hovered politely, clearly no one wanted to be the first to grab the front row of seats. Matt held Katherine's hand, though she nimbly swung a lean leg up to the step above the wheel and into the front seat. Matt struggled to follow her, grunting heavily as he grabbed frantically at one of the vertical metal bars supporting the tarpaulin roof, before lurching into the seat behind the driver.

'I haven't seen my bag,' Lizzie said anxiously. 'It's got my photo albums in it. They're irreplaceable.'

Gus touched her arm gently. 'They'll bring them on afterwards.'

Cameras were removed, handbags placed on the floor. They shifted shoulders away from the sun. Ben sat on the metal tracker's seat out on top of the bonnet. Gus reversed aggressively down into a ditch. The vehicle lurched, fell. Lizzie and Sara clutched at a bar, Connie thumped against Julian, who took her hand.

9

'Aardvarks. Their holes are everywhere,' Gus explained cheerfully. 'The word is Afrikaans for earth pigs. Too right, eh?'

Ben half-inclined his head towards Gus, speaking in low Afrikaans. Gus halted the vehicle abruptly enough for them to be thrown, yet again, towards their hot crossbars. 'Look. There.' He swung his arm out to the side. 'A roan antelope. After eland, they are the second heaviest of our antelope.'

A single animal with backward sweeping ridged horns moved lazily through the long sour grass, no more than a couple of metres from the vehicle, unperturbed by Gus's driving. Strawberry blonde, it moved with the weight of a large animal, but the grace of a fawn.

The group turned paparazzi, snapping away even when its haunches were barely visible behind a thorny bush.

'Look at the size of its ears.' Gus turned round to talk to them. His reddened tan was shiny in the light. 'Great for detecting danger, eh?'

He started the vehicle again, driving one handed and leaning round. 'A roan female. Very rare. Great first spot.'

Julian was smiling. He squeezed Connie's hand.

Gus grabbed his radio. 'Gus to lodge, over.' After a long pause. 'Gus to lodge, over.'

A sleepy voice like a faint echo drawled, 'Abraham to Gus. Where are you?'

'Approaching the lodge.'

Connie saw the lodge two wide sweeps of road away. It was a collection of a half-dozen squat primitive buildings in the armpit of a sweeping mountain. Great swathes of this wilderness encircled and enveloped it. Orange stone buildings hid under grass-thatched roofs like Vietnamese farm girls under their conical hats. Connie grinned at the strangeness of their holiday accommodation.

As the vehicle pulled up, a rotund black man in a gleaming white uniform, presumably Abraham, was positioned on a wooden path raised above the thick Namibian sands and grasses that weaved towards the lodge. He held out another plate of iced towels.

'Welcome to Gae,' he said with a broad smile.

Chapter 2

Sara hadn't brought her camera to Africa. She hadn't packed her own bags. She had left her cleaner instructions on the sweep of kitchen granite. She only agreed to come earlier this week, just a few hours after walking out of the Bailey on the last day of the trial of Joanne Sutton.

Sara quickly concluded that the holiday was not what she expected. It was her own fault: she hadn't even looked at the website. She hadn't had time. Or the desire. She had been totally focused on the case. Connie, delighted that she could make it and sensitive to how exhausted she must be, had arranged it all.

Sara regretted delegating her desperately needed holiday.

'I feel deeply uncomfortable,' murmured Julian. 'The *Guardian* would have a field day.'

'Too right. Christ, the blatant social inequality. How smug rich do you feel, Julian Emmerson?'

The pounding heat made Sara desperate, trapped by her own instincts. She wasn't going to be the one to impose their white wealthy Western authority on the laid-back smiling Abraham. Lizzie slumped down on the path; Alan sat fanning her; Connie more effectively used her brochure. It took Katherine's New York chutzpah to get them moving. 'Really, I do need to lie down, Abraham. Could we go to our rooms please?'

As the others followed Abraham down another exposed path, Sara made a beeline for the nearest conical building. Inside, the open plan sitting room was cosy with cream sofas and cushions and photo books about the Kalahari stacked by a stone fireplace. A spiral staircase led up to a balcony, which was filled with museum-style cabinets. Above, the thatched roof was un-ornamented. The combination of primitive materials and European sophistication reminded Sara of a ski chalet.

Sara's eyes were drawn back outside. She moved on to a veranda sheltered by a flat roof. Out beyond the comfort of circular wicker chairs, the terrace and the swimming pool, white butterflies moved rapidly between the sour grass and wild yellow flowers; countless impala grazed; miniature beige birds dipped their toes into the pool, where the lone swimmer was a vast black beetle backstroking in ever more frantic circles.

Sara was exhausted. Her body started to ache as if she was getting flu. Since the trial ended, she hadn't been able to shake off the tension that cracked through her temples.

'It's unreal, isn't it?' Connie was at her elbow, her eyes shining with excitement. 'I feel proud that my grandfather built it. It's crazy I've never been here before.'

'Amazing.' Sara squeezed her arm. 'How did he end up here of all places?'

'I have no idea. My mother wasn't a keen traveller – his story doesn't interest her. I'm hoping to find out. There's a small library of Kalahari artefacts in the gallery upstairs.'

Connie led her across the swimming pool deck down another wooden path towards three more conical houses. She opened the first heavy wooden door that scraped the stone floor before revealing an elegant sitting room. They looked straight back out to the Kalahari through the sliding glass doors that took up all of the back wall. There was no getting away from it.

Sara felt the tingle of air conditioning. Thank God.

'Girls, hello.' Lizzie had tipped the entire contents of her two bags upside down, straight on to the floor. 'Can you believe it? We're sharing a house again, Sara. It's like being back at Bristol.'

Sara had always found Lizzie's disorganisation trying. After everything she had gone through, she needed a relaxing holiday.

There was nothing relaxing about this chaos. They might as well be camping.

'I had forgotten that you're such a slob, Lizzie Gibson.' Sara instantly regretted her tone. After all, this was Lizzie. She was one of her oldest friends.

'I know, I have put on three stone. I have a middle-aged spread already. God knows what's going to happen when I hit the menopause.'

'Lizzie, don't be silly,' Connie immediately answered, which made Sara smile. Ever-protective Connie.

'Do you remember how skinny I was at university? I was as thin as Connie.'

Sara couldn't remember. Unlike Lizzie, she didn't look back. Whereas Lizzie was always talking about the past – what they looked like, what they said, where they went – Sara had a powerful but short-term memory.

Lizzie couldn't afford this trip, Sara was certain of it. Sara imagined that Julian and Connie had paid for Lizzie's whole holiday. They were extremely generous, though their act was bound to make Lizzie envy them more.

'You're lucky to have lots of clothes,' moaned Lizzie, surfing through hers to unzip Sara's Mulberry holdalls and coo over the contents.

Sara stared at Lizzie's mountain of crunched clothes. 'Volume isn't your problem, Lizzie.'

Lizzie looked up. 'Mine are old. You will recognise every single one.' She lifted up a once-white linen shirt, cropped short for her eighties midriff. 'I loved it when we were living in Harley Place. You must remember?'

How could Lizzie possibly think that Sara recognised her clothes? She was artless sometimes. It was, perversely, what Sara most adored about her. These days, who did she ever meet who was like Lizzie?

Connie darted in. 'Didn't you buy it in that charity shop in the centre of Clifton? The one run by that crazy punk with green spiky hair and the black poodle?'

Connie was brilliant at life's details, particularly other people's life details. Sara had missed her without realising it.

'Yes! It was twenty pence. Do you remember? Can you believe that?'

'Yes I can,' Sara murmured. 'Really Lizzie, I need to get you to a personal shopper the moment we are back.'

Connie shot her a warning eyebrow. 'Sara, come and see the shower.'

She led her through to a mercifully modern bathroom into a cylindrical brick courtyard with a high curved wall. In the far corner was an outdoor shower with a hole in the brick through which Sara spotted another impala.

'Look! They've created a window – you can look out at the Kalahari while you shower.'

Sara couldn't think of anything less appealing. She wanted to escape from the outdoorsyness of it all. She rarely went outside in London. The Jade Sutton case, from brief to the end of the trial, had taken six months. She had cabbed in and out of Chambers. It was one of her few extravagances, which she defended to her mother: in a cab she could work, take calls and sort out her admin.

Connie and Lizzie's incessant chatter moved back inside. Sara stood in the sliver of shade taking stock. This place made her feel intensely uncomfortable. She was drawn back to the last time she felt in limbo: after her bar exams she took a year off to study French law in Grenoble. It was a twelve-hour journey from Calais to Grenoble. The coach was zinging with sweat and stale food by the time it lurched nauseatingly round and round up into the mountains. She weakly stepped out into a town that assaulted her with its foreign voices, shops and architecture. She was insecure. Of course, things changed. Grenoble and its small town elegance became her home. She met Jean Philippe: wise, intelligent with an airy beamed apartment up a narrow cobbled street. He was her gynaecologist. He made a pass while he was examining her.

'Outrageous. Do take care,' Connie shouted indignantly over Lou's colic-ridden screams. Sara spent a handful of her limited cash calling Connie for a debrief. It was profoundly irritating to be competing with a newborn for her attention.

Jean Philippe's parents were at right angles to Sara's mother. They were artists, whose wooden chalet-style house was wedged on the side of the mountain outside a picturesque hamlet, ten kilometres outside Grenoble. They lived as full and chaotic a life as her mother lived a quiet, industrious one. Every Sunday, Sara and Jean Philippe would join his three siblings, their children, neighbours and friends for a massive Sunday lunch. Before the end of her university year, Jean Philippe asked her to marry him.

Sara was in love. She didn't hesitate. She hadn't slogged at a shit school, watched her mother suffer extra night shifts at the airport, to give it up for the first bloke who turned up. She left on the next coach back home to Manchester.

She never looked back, precociously taking silk at thirty-seven, and then every barrister's dream: 'the life-enhancing brief'. The Jade Sutton case: complicated, high-profile, impossible. Every silk worth their salt wanted it.

Sara was drawn inevitably back to Joanne Sutton's mercury stare. She had to pull herself together. There was nothing she could do about it now. She sighed again. She only thought about Jean Philippe when she was shattered and stressed.

She hadn't fallen in love since. So what? There was something fundamentally wrong with the men she dated. Too talkative, too vain, too stupid, too nasal, too egotistical. Christ, she didn't need to be with anyone. She didn't have time.

Sara gave herself a slight shake. Look at Connie's life. Practically a teen bride and four demanding kids. No one had four children any more. Connie had a people-carrier-load of children to compensate for Julian's antics, Sara was sure of it. Not that she ever discussed it with Connie. It was an unspoken agreement: Julian's affairs were out of bounds.

Sara escaped back into the bedroom, where Lizzie's debris was the only sign of her. She reminded herself she had come on this trip for Connie. She would feel better after a sleep. She slipped under the delicate pear-shaped mosquito net, lay on top of the sheet, reached beside the bed for the British Airways eye mask and ear plugs in her handbag, and lay down fully clothed flat on her back. The bed was comfortable, if a little narrow. These days, she only slept in a single bed when she went home to Manchester.

Sara gave way to sleep.

Chapter 3

Connie was first back at the bar. She hadn't been able to lie down. Every detail was heightened as if she were wearing 3-D glasses. It was so exciting. Recently, Connie's life felt empty. Of course, it was busy and absorbing until her baby Hector started secondary school last September. Every morning at seven thirty, Hector disappeared with the older three. Connie was left behind, marooned in his early childhood, only knowing the answers to primary school questions that were no longer relevant. After school, Lou's long-standing boyfriend Rolo took sulky ownership of their open-plan kitchen. Connie lurked upstairs, lost and lonely.

She had their housekeeper, Sally, who had lived with them for a decade since Leo was seven. Connie spent more time with Sally than anyone else, even the children and Julian. Only Sally was party to the intimate details of Connie's life. She had been her best friend. Sometimes, when Connie was feeling low, she felt that Sally was the only close friend she had left.

Initially Connie imagined Sally, a trained nanny, would move on, but she stayed. They shared domesticity, trivia about the house, the children's timetables, endless meals, shopping, organising and sorting.

Over the years, Connie and Julian talked about Sally's desperate desire for her own child and the notable absence of any boyfriend. When Sally announced she was pregnant without revealing the name of the father, Connie was hurt. By Sally's standards of passivity, it was a shock. What's more, she hadn't confided in Connie. Who was the man? A one-night stand? A sperm donor? A friend?

Sally made it clear the subject was off limits. It seemed that there was a boundary between Sally's 'work' and her personal life that Connie didn't previously know existed. Sally was the only person she confided in about Julian's affairs. Her pregnancy made Connie realise that Sally didn't share any intimate details with her. The intimacy that Connie felt they had shared was an illusion; it turned out that they never had been really close.

Connie glanced self-consciously in the large mirror behind the bar. She allowed herself a couple of date balls from the bowl. As she popped the third into her mouth, Luke appeared. His lime-green T-shirt and running shorts were soaked with sweat.

'We are leaving shortly, Luke,' she was anxious the group would never be ready in time.

'I'll have a quick shower and be ready in fifteen,' Luke swiftly drained two glasses of water without looking at her.

'When did you start exercising?' It was a stupid question, which she instantly regretted. It wasn't what she wanted to ask him.

He dabbed his neck with the towel coiled around it and smiled optimistically. 'It's a great way to get some control of my life, Connie.'

Luke hadn't explained to her what had happened to his marriage. With their history, Connie had no right to ask.

Luke continued, brightening to his subject: 'I'm working towards an Iron Man in September,' he added confidentially. 'All I'm aiming to do is complete this one.'

How like Luke. Big confidences about work and sport, but not about the important things.

'It's all change, all change, Connie,' he added, as if trying to convince himself.

Connie couldn't think of an appropriate reply that wouldn't be too personal. Luke left the bar to get changed. She glanced at his retreating back and wondered if he ever thought of their past.

Connie lived with Luke in Harley Place for two years. Every morning, he made her breakfast in bed, climbing three flights of stairs to bring her coffee, eggs and toast on the metal tray he had bought for the purpose from IKEA. They shared the largest bedroom in the house. They were both immaculate and minimal. Luke was practical. He built ceiling-to-floor wardrobes and bookshelves along one whole wall, painting them and the walls dove grey. They each had half of the vast wardrobe. Luke merged their books and ordered them alphabetically. They had an old desk each in front of the two long sash windows. They were both reading history and always worked together. If one of them finished first, the other would read on Connie's grandmother's purple velvet chaise longue. It wasn't only their degree they shared. They were physically alike – long and lean – and sexually at one. When she made love to Luke, Connie used to feel as if she was in a movie. Sara loved to describe them as: 'Siamese twins, joined at the groin.'

The obvious next move after Bristol was for them to get a flat together, before getting married. However, they were both reserved. Neither of them ever said they loved the other. It was not a deliberate or manipulative move, rather a reticence they both shared. Yet their unexpressed emotion created a big question about what was going to happen next. They drifted through the summer term. Connie, who loved stability, became nervous because their domestic bubble was about to pop – the others were going their separate ways – Luke and Connie couldn't stay on at Harley Place. Luke was determined to set up an Internet business, which would mean he would need go home to save money. It was a mad idea, which Connie couldn't understand. The Internet was only in its infancy at the time, who knew what impact it was going to have on society. Connie worried that was an excuse for not getting a proper job. Well, her father said as much. Connie was inclined to believe him, though she didn't say anything to Luke. Their relationship had been straightforward. Suddenly, it was complicated in a practical sense, and neither of them were experienced enough to untangle or, crucially, prepared to take the initiative. They both waited for the other to move them forward.

One night, Lizzie went out on a date and Connie couldn't sleep. Instead of gliding to their bedroom chaise longue, she decamped to the sitting room downstairs. A week later, she would see it as fate.

She was asleep on Matt's old russet-red sofa bed, when the doorbell woke her. She was hardly conscious. She opened the door without looking at Lizzie or her date, and curled back into the foetal position on the sofa. She remembered looking up to see a man looming over her. What she saw in his dark eyes was decisiveness and purpose.

'You must be Constance.'

She nodded without speaking or sitting up.

'Why are you sleeping on the sofa?'

'I couldn't sleep and I didn't want to wake Luke,' she hesitated. 'My boyfriend.'

'Oh, what's he done?' There was no missing the playfulness in his eyes.

'Nothing, nothing at all.' She sat up quickly, keen to get away from him. 'I couldn't sleep.'

Lizzie reappeared. 'Much better. I was desperate for a pee.'

They stood awkwardly, the three of them.

'Connie, you really shouldn't wear that nightie downstairs,' Lizzie said sharply. 'Luke loves to see you semi-naked, but not the rest of us.'

Connie instinctively wrapped her arms across her breasts. 'Sorry, I'd forgotten you were out. I'm off to bed.'

'Have you two introduced yourselves?' Lizzie relented.

'No. Rudely, I haven't. Julian Emmerson.' He held out his large hand, which Connie reluctantly shook, keeping her other hand across her nightie. He held on to it. 'Wonderful to meet you, Constance.'

Gus was taking them in search of the Southern Pride, which had been spotted by another ranger near a northern watering hole. It would mean they didn't have time to stop for every animal they spotted along the way. They were keen. Lions gave purpose and excitement to their first drive.

This time, they climbed swiftly into the vehicle. Matt, Katherine and Luke in the first row, while Connie sat between Julian and Dan in the middle, and Sara, Lizzie and Alan in the back. She gratefully noticed that there was an ease to their movements as they placed their cameras, suncream and water bottles in the leather pouches behind the seats in front.

Luke shuffled a large rucksack from between his legs. 'I've got something for you all.'

He brought out a pile of dark grey tissue wrapped items. Each one had a handwritten name tag dangling from a purple ribbon.

'Matt.' Luke tossed a package to him.

Matt tore it open and stretched out an elegant taupe-coloured shirt in exquisite cotton. 'Luke, you're great, mate.'

'I don't believe it.' Lizzie exclaimed as she opened hers. 'It looks expensive. Wow, thank you, Luke.'

On the left-hand breast of Connie's shirt in olive embroidery as if hand scribbled were the words: *The Group*. On the back was an olive-sketched map with cartoon-style buildings showing Harley Place, Connie's house in west London, and Adderbury and Gae in the Kalahari.

Connie squeezed his shoulder. 'You are brilliant. Have you all seen this?' Connie held up the back of the shirt.

'That's great,' Sara lifted up her shirt. 'Super-styley. And the right size. Luke, you are a gorgeous boy.'

'Very thoughtful,' Dan said.

'Thanks, Luke. If I ever get lost getting home...' Julian said.

Luke nodded. His awkwardness was so familiar, it made Connie smile.

They drove through a locked gate in the boundary fence. They left the lodge side of the reserve and drove across thirty metres of no-man's-land scrub, and then out through another gate into the lions' side of the reserve. Lions had been introduced relatively recently to Gae, Gus explained. They were segregated to protect other species. Gus shared these details as they drove. He kept up a running commentary, which made Connie feel more involved than the average tourist.

The group of delicate golden antelopes, half-hidden in the grass, were steenbok, he explained. 'Delicious – similar to your venison. You'll probably have them on the barbecue tonight.' He stopped abruptly. 'A secretary bird taking off up there.'

Connie leaned up and out to the right, not sure what she was looking for. Without moving even his head, Ben murmured to Gus.

'Ben, thank you, look, another, look. Two secretary birds together about to fly.'

Matt and Katherine sighted them first. 'Beautiful,' Katherine cooed. Julian's rapid camera clicks showed he had spotted them.

Gus turned round. 'They are carnivores, eh. They kill their prey by stamping them to death.'

The secretary birds had a fantastic orange splash across their heads. They were four-foot tall, like hawks with long legs. Fanning their wide grey and black wings, they took off at speed. Connie had never seen any bird like them before. Watching them was like meditation, she thought. She stared until they were faint dots in the sky.

Everyone seemed transfixed, except for Lizzie, who was bending down in between Alan and Sara, trying to pick up her species checklist from the metal floor.

'They are vast aren't they?' murmured Luke.

'It's hard to believe that they are real,' murmured Sara.

'Extraordinarily huge,' Dan agreed.

'They were incredible,' Connie added.

Connie smiled. It reminded her of how skiing holidays bonded people together. It was the shared experience. Only here, what they were sharing was exciting and extraordinary.

Lizzie squeezed back up as the birds disappeared. Alan had picked up her species checklist.

'Thank you, Alan. You are sweet.' Lizzie smiled. '*Sagittarius serpentarius.*'

They headed up over a sand dune densely packed with grasses and thorny bushes, which reminded Connie of a Norfolk beach. She checked herself: there was no comparison. The track was brightening to an angry orange in the last light. From the top, they could see three hundred and sixty degrees of vastness. The grassland filled most of the picture: green, patchy and dead flat. Two bronzed hills folded behind it, pencil outlines of half hexagons. Against the blue sky, they were stark and lunar.

As Gus drove on down the other side, he gave them the 'lion rules'. Lions weren't bothered by the vehicles: they were bulky nuisances, no more. They saw the whole vehicle and the guests inside it as one object, but that didn't mean that they were tame. Any sudden movements, or body parts out of the vehicle, or shouting could annoy or threaten them.

Gus stopped at the shaded water hole, where the lions had been spotted early that morning. Julian swung nonchalantly out of the vehicle with his vast camera and long lens.

'Julian, you need to get back in the vehicle,' Gus insisted.

'Hey, Julian. What are you doing?' Katherine added. 'Get back in.'

'Julian, mate,' Matt said, 'get back in, for God's sake.'

Julian ignored them. Gus looked annoyed.

'One second, Gus. Please, Bristol babes and boys, quick can you look this way. Say carnivore,' said Julian grinning.

As they looked obediently in Julian's direction, willing him to take it and get back in, Connie saw three lion cubs under the Camel Thorn tree a few metres behind him. She was anxious, but she would never command Julian back into the vehicle. Ben silently slid from his seat on the bonnet and into the vehicle beside Gus.

'Get in,' Gus voice was authoritative.

'Julian! Lions,' It was Dan, who was first to articulate what they saw. He sounded petrified. 'Behind you. Lions. Get in quick.'

Dan's voice was usually calm, though Connie knew underneath he was more turbulent. Instinctively, Connie wasn't frightened, though she realised Julian had taken an unnecessary risk.

'Stay calm, Dan,' stated Gus, 'It's okay, eh?'

His words were designed to be soothing, but Connie sensed Gus was irritated by Julian and the unnecessary issue he had created. Julian moved quicker than Connie ever remembered. His face coloured with excitement. 'Really sorry, Gus. Close shave. I had one this morning. No need for another.'

Without acknowledging Julian's apology, Gus started the engine, turned into a crooked three-point turn and then crept backwards towards the Camel Thorn tree. Dan squeezed her hand – he was drained of colour. He seemed genuinely terrified, whereas Julian looked exhilarated.

'Let me get my species checklist out. One big tick: lion.' Lizzie sounded louder in the now silent vehicle. '*Panthera leo.*'

'Lizzie, shush,' insisted Dan, turning gently towards her. 'Please, sweetheart.'

Sara whispered, 'They are devouring some animal's brains.'

Lizzie poorly stage-whispered, 'Look, everyone, look.'

Katherine, Matt and Dan hissed at her.

Connie smiled. She wasn't scared. She was comfortable with all animals, even these lions. She hadn't been on safari. She hadn't travelled much. She got married at twenty-one and had Leo when she was twenty-two. So she savoured this experience.

'They have a fresh kill,' whispered Gus, stopping the vehicle three metres from the tree under which they were sheltering. 'It's a... Ben?'

Ben murmured with a slight nod of his head.

'It's a warthog,' Gus translated. 'They are eating the head.'

Their silence intensified the moment. Normally excitement would have made them chatty and loud in their appreciation. Instead they snapped away, looking up periodically from their cameras, as if undecided whether photo memories or physical ones were more powerful.

The lion cubs had their front legs stretched out in front of them. Hector's cat Rolo – who was an established member of their family before Lou's boyfriend of the same name appeared on the scene – adopted the same pose. Well fed and shaded, they looked happy. One of the lions had had more than his share of warthog brains. The other pawed his head in a not unfriendly cuff, before grabbing the remaining warthog chunk and moving a few feet away to assert his ownership of the rest of supper.

'They are male lions about two and a half years old,' Gus explained. 'Still not fully grown.'

Mere babes. Connie felt a longing she quickly dismissed. Her family had a largesse, which delighted Connie. Each child added more. Connie loved being pregnant. Her bump had pressed up against her ribs forcing her body to widen, generously expand to make space for the new person pushing its way into their family. The larger she became, the more significant she felt. She became greater than the sum of her own shy, skinny parts. She was born to have children. It was her happy contribution to this world. She couldn't get enough of it until she had Hector. Four was her number. Connie couldn't imagine having another baby. Not now. The time had passed.

'It's great to see them after a fresh kill, eh?' Gus said. He appeared to harbour no grudge about Julian's behaviour.

Connie echoed her appreciation. 'It's amazing. How extraordinary to be so close to lions. We are lucky.'

She felt a warmth towards Gus, who had brought them here.

'Julian,' Dan called, as Julian leaned a whole arm and lens out. 'Could you possibly not do that…'

'Julian, please. I made it clear you need to keep your limbs inside the vehicle.' Gus stated.

'Hold on, getting a thirty-second video. Okay, gang, a soundbite on seeing a large cat eating warthog brains for tea?'

Sara instantly spread her arms for the camera. 'It is extraordinary to be feet from such powerful animals. Hugely grateful they show no interest Sara Wilson *au vin*.' She raised her eyebrows.

Julian moved back inside the vehicle, nodding to Gus to acknowledge his point.

Gus relented and smiled. 'An American tourist freaked out.'

Connie smiled back. She was proud that she wasn't that American tourist. She was drawn to these magnificent creatures and trusting of Gus and Ben's instincts.

Gus spoke in quick-fire Afrikaans, Ben replied. 'Over there?' Gus responded.

They turned to look. A large female lion was standing a metre from the back of the vehicle, walking slowly but deliberately towards them.

Lizzie burst out, 'Gigantic beast alert.'

'Thank God for you, sweetheart,' Alan teased.

'It's okay, Lizzie,' Gus said immediately. 'She's absolutely fine. If I thought there was any danger, I would get you out of here, okay?'

The female lion strolled nonchalantly along the side of the vehicle. Connie believed that she was looking at each and every one of its occupants, contemplating their features. Dan shrank away from the side, pressing in against her. His leg shook convulsively. She stroked his hand as she did with Hector when he was tiny. He squeezed hers back.

'She is waiting until her cubs have eaten,' whispered Gus. 'Then she will have her dinner.'

'What a fantastic mom,' murmured Katherine.

Luke twisted round to face her. 'This is incredible, Connie,' he whispered. 'Thank you.'

Connie grinned back. 'It's great.'

'Shush, shush, shush,' Dan repeated. The mantra seemed to reassure him.

Connie looked at him sympathetically. She glanced into the back seat at Alan, who seemed oblivious to Dan's meltdown. She couldn't believe that he hadn't noticed Dan's state. If so, did he not care?

Alan had met Dan on a job six years ago. Dan was restoring a walled kitchen garden near Chipping Norton, where Alan worked as a gardener. The group never believed that Alan was good enough for Dan. Connie reasoned with Sara that no one would match up to Dan. Sara didn't agree, insisting he had compromised.

When they were living together, they had seen compromise as the cardinal sin. Their life at university was predicated on the principle of never compromising over anything. Not sex, love, fun or friendship. They were dismissive of everything they believed wasn't worthy of their efforts. Perhaps that was why they loved each other. Their friendship was representative of this time when only the big things mattered. The small things had yet to grind them down.

'Alan, it's amazing isn't it?' She turned, conscious she didn't make enough effort with him.

He nodded, 'Yeah.' She waited for him to add more, but he didn't.

She sensed that, along with Sara, he was the most reluctant to be here. Then she caught Sara's eye. She smiled broadly and stuck two thumbs up at Connie.

Connie was elated by her reaction.

Chapter 4

The sun was blistering behind a zigzag of soft peaked hills folding across the horizon. Gus had 'parked' bang in the middle of the track. No meter men, no traffic, Matt thought with a wry smile. Gus and Ben meticulously laid out a white pressed tablecloth over a small wooden foldaway table, twenty feet in front of the vehicle. Matt expected to be offered a warmish beer. Forget that. Out of a canvas holdall came half a dozen tall metal containers. They lunged for drinks, no longer self-conscious. They were all keen to process what they had seen, celebrate and savour it. Everyone had a slightly different take on seeing the lions: their proximity, the thrill, the fear. Cameras were out; photos shared; Lizzie insisted on replaying Julian's video several times. They rapidly ate all the canapés: mozzarella and tomato balls on tiny cocktail sticks, and mini spicy meat kebabs.

Katherine looked enthusiastically at the bottle of vodka. 'Hey, Gus, I would love one more. Only a little vodka though, please.'

Katherine gave her girlie smile that made Matt happy. Happy to be here, and above all, happy to be with Katherine enjoying herself after all the stress of the last few months.

'Oh yes please, Matt, same as Katherine,' Lizzie smiled enthusiastically. 'I can't believe it: a full complimentary bar in the middle of nowhere. What about you, Alan?' She linked arms with him. They seemed to have struck up an odd sort of bond.

'Lizzie, mine's another large one. Same poison as you, love.'

'We're like twins, aren't we?' added Lizzie enthusiastically.

'Too right,' Alan grinned back.

'Is that gin?' asked Connie.

'Mother's ruin, Connie,' mumbled Luke, as he grabbed a bottle of South African Castle lager and the bottle opener from the holdall.

'Luke, are you saying I look ruined?' Connie eyed him.

Matt was irritated. A classic Luke comment. He wasn't aware of the effect of his words on their audience. Katherine insisted he lacked 'emotional intelligence' and that he only got away with it because he was handsome. She had met hundreds of Lukes in New York: socially stunted, Internet goofballs.

Privately, Matt disagreed with Katherine. He believed Luke had never got over Connie splitting up with him.

Lizzie started taking photos. Connie and Luke posed like storks on the roof of the vehicle, Lizzie and Alan wrapped their arms round each other and took a selfie in their sunglasses, while Sara twisted her head to glare coquettishly over one shoulder.

Katherine moved decisively to stand beside Matt, the ends of her long hair touching his left shoulder. 'Hon.'

Matt wanted to stall her somehow. He had prevaricated about telling his friends and family for months. But Katherine had had enough. She wanted to share their news. He didn't. He couldn't tell her that, to be honest, he was embarrassed, although he knew that she sensed his reluctance. He was a straightforward, uncomplicated bloke. He wanted a life that conformed to the norm, which he took to mean mirror the life of his stockbroker father and housewife mother. When he married his first wife, Annabel, a fellow solicitor at his law firm, Clifford Chance, he had thought his life would mirror Connie and Julian's with a large family and a nice house in one of the Home Counties.

The group would know Katherine had put Matt up to it. It could never have been his idea. Connie would disapprove. Worse would be Julian's vocal disbelief and Sara and Lizzie's concern about poor Mattie beholden to his East Coast princess.

He sighed. He didn't want to ruin the start of his first holiday with his oldest friends for decades. The last few months had been stressful. Katherine was exhausted by it. She was highly emotional and complained of constant headaches.

All he wanted to do was enjoy his friends against this stunning backdrop. Forget the drama for one night.

What could he say to stop her? Why had he never been able to stop her?

A number of lawyers from his solicitor's firm were downtown at the end of a week of team bonding in New York. One of the partners' PA had got them a dinner reservation at Minetta Tavern in Greenwich Village for their last night. They had had dinner and were revving up to cocktails, when Katherine appeared, like a modern-day mermaid. Her eyes matched her gleaming green chiffon dress with its tiny waist. Long glittering earrings set her red straight hair on fire.

'Hi, I am Katherine,' She gently handed him her white slim hand.

Unbelievably, she seemed to have singled him out from the dozens of suits out of sync with the lush setting, the red velvet curtains, flamboyant customers and dark Prohibition-style bar. Matt believed he was averagely attractive – a full head of hair and good skin – but he wasn't remotely like the body-beautiful men you saw in London and New York. Men appreciated him for that; women didn't tend to fancy him.

He offered her a drink, yet imagined she must be waiting for some handsome buck. She ordered a rhubarb martini. Even her choice of drink made him feel like an aged brown bear beside a young magpie. All paws.

'I'm Matt, by the way.'

'Hi, Matt.' She was glistening.

'Do you live in New York, Katherine?' Christ, was that the best he could do.

'Yeah, for now. Where do you live, Matt?'

'Accent's a bit of a giveaway, I'm afraid.' What was he saying? 'London.'

'Great.' She looked him directly in the eye. For a moment, he wondered if she was keen, but immediately dismissed the idea.

'Do you need to talk to your co-workers? Feel free.'

'No, it's okay. We've been living in each other's pockets all week.'

'Are you married, Matt?'

Matt ruffled his hair nervously. He was unused to such a direct question and the answer was too complicated to share with a complete stranger. 'Errr…I was. Divorced.'

She gently combed her hair with her fingers. 'I'm dealing with this situation with my long-term ex-boyfriend. He didn't want to get married and have a family. And I do. I want to have children. It is the only thing that will complete me.'

Katherine sighed in a way that was familiar to Matt. The outward sound of a broken heart.

'I'm sorry, Katherine. Sounds shit,' he paused. 'He's a fool. He'll realise that and come back begging.'

She looked up at him with a slight smile. 'No, he won't. But thank you.'

There was a stillness between them, broken by Katherine turning to wave at a petite blonde girl, who stood looking lost in front of the curtained doorway. She turned back to Matt. 'My girlfriend. We're having dinner here.'

'Great. Have a wonderful evening, Katherine.' Matt turned away.

'You don't want to take my card?'

He turned back quickly to catch her expression. Her eyebrow was raised in that definite way he would come to love.

'Of course,' he said hastily.

She opened up her handbag, produced a purple leather card holder and slipped out a white card, holding it for Matt to take. He wondered if he should offer her his card, but wasn't sure what the American etiquette was.

'Are you going to call me?'

He blushed. 'Well, I'm only here until tomorrow.'

Her friend was beside her. 'Hey, Katherine.'

Katherine hooked her arm into her friend's. 'Hi, Nancy.' She continued to stare at Matt. 'Okay, we are having a light dinner. Then I'll come back to the bar. Wait for me.'

Of course Matt did. Women didn't ask him to wait; they didn't make a move. He was stunned. He was sure that he was missing something. She saw him as a sympathetic male with which to share her frustrations about her ex-boyfriend. No more.

In an attempt to re-bond with his colleagues and calm his nerves, he drank too much beer. When she returned, he was feeling positively cavalier.

'Katherine, I have to say that I have never been chatted up in a bar. Actually, I don't think that I've ever been chatted up before.'

'No?' She looked surprised.

His ego soared.

'I thought that you were probably waiting for some incredibly good-looking guy.'

She smiled. It was like a conversion to some cult. 'No, Matt, I was waiting for you.'

Even now, Matt couldn't quite believe it.

'Ladies. And gentlemen.' Katherine stated with the East Coast old-fashioned politeness that had attracted Matt to her when they first met.

Lizzie and Sara continued chatting to Connie in a tight triangle to the right of the table. Matt liked to believe that they hadn't heard Katherine. He put his arm around her protectively. She looked elegant in her beautiful taupe safari dress and deep olive scarf. She was fragile and feminine compared with his English women friends.

Lizzie and Sara helped themselves to more drinks, while Julian insisted that Gus and Ben have one.

'No, thank you,' Gus said firmly. 'I don't drink while I'm out with guests. Got to stay alert.'

'I can understand that,' Lizzie lurched over to him. 'What would you have done if the lions had attacked us?'

If Lizzie sidetracked everyone, Katherine might never get out their news, Matt hoped. Maybe she would be prepared to wait until after the holiday…

'I'd have got you out of there,' Gus explained earnestly.

'What if you couldn't get us out of there?' countered Sara.

'I'd have had to shoot the lion, though it's the last resort. We are taught rifle competency. We have to be able to fire three rounds in nine seconds.'

They all stopped talking. It was a sobering thought.

Gus turned round to the vehicle behind them on the track. 'I've got a single shot rifle in there and five extra rounds on me,' he tapped his belt, which had bullets hanging vertically along the leather strap. 'Listen, I would never choose an animal's life over a human life, eh.'

Katherine edged away from Matt and raised her voice unchar-acteristically, her hands held out. 'Lovely friends, with all this talk about life and death, I think that this really is an appropriate moment...'

Sara and Lizzie eyed each other and Matt eyed them anxiously.

'...for Matt and I to share with you, our dearest friends, some awesome news.'

Katherine, with all her charm, smiled broadly. 'This is a wonder-ful holiday that Connie has planned for us all. Thank you,' she ges-tured elaborately to Connie, before bringing her hand back up to her heart. 'And it is particularly poignant, special and important for Matt and me, because it will be our last for some time.'

She paused. Matt knew Katherine wanted the group to guess, to burst out congratulations. He started to feel uneasy and queasy. He wondered if he should interrupt Katherine, get it over and done with.

Katherine seemed to be growing uncertain, thrown by the lack of reaction from the group. Luke wandered away, grabbing another Castle lager from the table, before throwing his empty bottle into the canvas bag.

Matt could see Katherine reacting from her gut. 'I'm sure that you have sensed our excitement and happiness.'

She was going to confide in this spirits-soaked group. He winced with embarrassment.

'Not to overstate it, our acute anxiety. Anxiety and not uncertain pain, for me. Undoubtedly, reinforcing my certain inadequacy as a woman.'

Sara muttered under her breath to Connie and moved to grab the last two kebabs, which she slid off their skewers and ate together as a sandwich. Katherine pursed her lips together. God, get on with it, he thought, feeling mean towards Katherine, but desperate to protect her from Sara's, not to mention Julian's, short attention span. Katherine smiled at him, looking for his encouragement. He couldn't give it. Right from the beginning, it was his role to give her emotional support. He was her rock, she never tired in saying. Now he was back with the group, he was failing her.

Without him, Katherine looked lost. She rubbed her hands together. 'It has been a really, really anxious time for Matt and me. I have suffered. I've had to take a lot of rest, because it has been such a draining experience. Physically and mentally.'

Matt couldn't help it. 'Katherine and I are having a baby in eight weeks' time. A baby girl.'

Katherine frowned briefly at him and then rearranged her face into a smile, leaning into him. 'Truly, in our hearts, we are happy. Aren't we, honey?'

'Oh, Matt and Katherine. That's fantastic news. Congratulations,' Luke said, holding up his lager.

'What great news.' Connie hugged Matt and Katherine in turn.

It took Matt a few minutes to notice Julian and Sara were both staring at Katherine's taut pelvis peeking through the hugging cut of the safari dress.

'Oh, are you having one of those adorable Asian babies?' Lizzie said with visible warmth.

'Really? Seriously?' Alan was such an overgrown child.

He saw Katherine pale and he desperately tried to interrupt. 'Lizzie, Alan—'

Lizzie flowed on. 'My friend adopted the cutest Vietnamese girl. She's a single mother. She said, "If I get to forty and I haven't had a baby, I'm going to adopt." I admire her. I couldn't do it. But I'm happy for you both.'

'Lizzie. For God's sake,' Matt was flustered. It hadn't come out right. They should have waited and told everyone when the group were calm and sober. 'Listen, everyone. It's not the kind of thing I ever thought I'd do. We employed a surrogate, you know, after trying the usual avenues.'

Katherine looked angrily at him. 'Matt, I take exception to that. Employing doesn't come into it. Dawn, our surrogate, is a wonderful lady from Manchester. This is a highly personal relationship, it's not like employing a housekeeper. We are doing a lot to support her and her kids, I mean, far beyond what is legally required.'

Matt knew Sara too well. This comment was bound to unleash her complicated defensiveness about her own roots. She didn't disappoint him.

'Mancunians are good northern gels with wide child-bearing hips. Thankfully, some are still poor enough to carry some spoilt Southerner's child.'

He heard a certain truth that he knew would come from his female friends. He was cornered. 'Sara, that's unfair. Please, you are being judgemental, not to mention disloyal.'

'Sorry, Matt,' Sara said. 'But I don't believe it's right.'

Sara never wavered from her principles. Matt was bitterly aware he would have agreed with her a year ago. Still, he said defensively, 'We were desperate for a baby. What could we do?'

Luke spoke up unexpectedly. 'Exactly what you have done, Matt. You deserve a family – you would make a great dad.'

Matt was overwhelmed by Luke's support.

'It's really good, Matt,' Luke said. 'The love of your children is as good as true love.'

Matt looked at him, trying to read that perfect face, which gave little away. 'Both is best.'

Luke nodded and tapped him gently on the chest. 'You are going to have both, Matt.'

He wished he could take Luke away from the group and ask him what exactly had happened with Emma. He hadn't made the time to find out. He had been so wrapped up in Katherine and trying to have a baby that he had forgotten his old mate. Equally, Matt was desperate to confide in Luke about the bloody circus, from IVF to this horror show.

Katherine was focused on Sara. 'You don't need to believe in surrogacy. You are a principled spinster with no experience of loving relationships and the desire for children.'

Matt winced. Sara seemed angry more than hurt. Matt knew she had no desire for family. No one spoke for a while.

Katherine started what sounded like a conversation with herself. 'I feel extremely close to Dawn. I don't have a single girlfriend that would do for me what she has done.' Her eyes were wet. 'In the face of her sacrifice, I feel totally inadequate. You cannot imagine. She has given me hope and the possibility of my own child to love. I don't know how you can mock me for that...'

The others looked mortified. He moved to hold Katherine.

Finally, Julian spoke. 'I have to ask: how much does a surrogate get paid?'

Matt knew he was asking purely out of curiosity, he was a politician, after all. Though it would inflame Katherine.

'Excuse me, Julian,' Katherine whitened with anger. 'I am sorry, but I find that a totally inappropriate question. Dawn isn't doing this for the money. You underestimate her. She is a great human being. Anyway, we are looking after her. We are paying what are reasonable expenses.'

Sara was on her. 'Oh please. Why else would you carry some unrelated person's baby, except for the cash? How much is she getting for carrying your baby for nine months? A few grand?'

'Excuse me, Sara. Dawn and I are close friends. We speak every day. You know, if you share something this monumental with someone, it goes beyond any friendship you can ever have with anyone else. I will always love her like a member of my own family for what she has done for me.'

'How do you find out the going rate for a surrogate?' Lizzie asked. 'You can't exactly ask around, can you?'

'Good point,' Alan stated.

Connie intervened. 'Lizzie, Sara, Julian, please. This is such exciting news. Big news for Matt and Katherine. Having babies is such fun.'

'Don't you mean making babies?' quipped Sara.

That was the issue. Katherine couldn't make a baby. It made her question who she was. As for Matt, he was weakened by all of it.

Julian ploughed on. 'Is it thousands?' Julian held up his hands. 'In case I ever think of sending Connie out to work.'

Matt felt defeated and deflated. Clearly, Julian wasn't going to stop until he had his answer. 'Fifteen grand, which is considered very generous compensation. It's not in any way a payment. It's completely confidential. It's a slightly murky area, legally.'

Murky to him. Dank and depressing.

'The courts don't want a "market rate" for human incubators,' intoned Sara.

The vodka fought with the mozzarella and meat kebabs in Matt's stomach.

'Anyway, do tell us exactly how it works,' Connie interjected.

Matt could deal with the plain facts.

'Yes, please do.' Sara's wickedness was unmistakable. 'Did you have sex with Dawn?'

'Oh God, Sara,' he groaned. 'Listen, let me explain it. Once and for all.'

Katherine looked away.

'Right,' he cleared his throat nervously. 'There are two types of surrogacy: "traditional" and the more common: "gestational".' He raised an eyebrow to show he was embarrassed by the jargon. 'With traditional surrogacy, the surrogate's egg is fertilised with the man's sperm. Since we are lucky that Katherine produces wonderful eggs…' he tried to catch her eye '…we opted for gestational surrogacy. IVF, if you will. Katherine's egg was fertilised with my sperm in a lab and then placed in the surrogate, Dawn.'

He waited, wondering if he could risk cracking a joke to lighten the atmosphere, or whether Katherine would explode.

'Let me tell you, we have had some real issues.' Katherine was down and fighting. 'I've said to Dawn that she must rest and eat more,' Katherine's well-practiced worries were like arrows bouncing off their targets. She wasn't going to stop. 'I mean our life and happiness is quite literally in her hands. She understands that. Totally. She is a very caring person, but I don't think that she takes her own health seriously enough.'

Matt felt terrible and went to wrap his arms around her.

'When our baby girl is born, she will legally belong to Dawn. Can you believe that?'

Her green eyes were watering. Only her pride prevented actual tears.

'Really?' Sara's fascination was unattractive.

Katherine continued. 'We are obviously the "intended parents", but our baby girl won't be ours legally until the parental order goes through. There was a case a few years ago where the surrogate decided to keep the twin babies. Not that Dawn would ever do that to us. I mean, I trust her. Not because I have to, but because I do.'

They were silent as they digested that fact.

'You ladies, you cannot imagine the pain of knowing...' Katherine turned on Sara and Lizzie, '...knowing the only way you can be complete is by another woman carrying your child.'

'I wouldn't know,' interjected Lizzie. Matt knew that she hadn't intended to upset Katherine, quite the opposite. Her face crumpled. 'In case you've forgotten, Katherine, I'm single. I'm not lucky enough to have a Matt in my life.'

Matt closed his eyes and then slowly opened them. He turned to look over Katherine's shoulder at the hills darkly silhouetted by the burnt out sun. Rescue me. He sensed a gentle arm on his shoulder without looking, he knew it was Dan.

He had actively missed Luke and Connie, his best friends, when they all moved on – Connie in with Julian, Luke home to his parents, Dan staying in Bristol to do a garden design course, Sara to bar school in London and Lizzie backpacking round South America. It took Annabel's abrupt departure for Matt to truly appreciate his friendship with Dan. After she left, he texted Matt every morning. *Hi Mattie, how are things? Dan xx.* Every night, Dan called him as the third beer hit the Tesco tikka masala, twisting him from bullish to maudlin. Matt found himself confiding in Dan about Annabel's previous affairs, how he had ignored them hoping they were a passing phase, how humiliating it was at work, where everyone knew Annabel had left him for Jim, a senior partner; how damaging it was to his career, having to re-establish himself in a new firm, not to mention how destructive it had been to his self esteem.

Matt couldn't have survived that first year without Dan's kindness. He appreciated exactly what an old friend was: someone whom you could trust and talk freely to without losing face.

Dan lightly held his arms. 'Mattie, this is great news. I'm happy for you both.' His arm moved round Matt and Katherine's shoulders, drew them close to him and the group. 'Come on, everyone. We back each other up, whatever happens, remember.'

Dan was the quietest, but when he spoke up, the group always listened. Dan reminded them of who they were, before life's complications got in the way.

'We're going to toast Katherine and Matt.' Dan was firm.

'Matt and Katherine,' Luke was there first.

'Matt and Katherine,' echoed Julian hastily.

Sara was the loudest. She tried to catch his eye, but he studiously ignored her. She sidled up to his right side. She linked arms with him, giving his forearm a light squeeze. An intimate gesture from her. 'Sorry, Matt. You know I get out of control, but I don't mean it. I love you,' she whispered. 'And if you're happy, I'm happy.'

He nodded rapidly. He was desperate to move on to another subject.

Chapter 5

The restaurant was hidden under a thatched grass roof behind the sun loungers. It was nine thirty by the time the group noisily sat down to dinner. The candles flirted out of glass jars, casting some of them into shadow. The dining chairs were covered in pale orange cotton, a nod to their surroundings. The long rectangular table, hidden under a deep white tablecloth, was as shiny as any London restaurant. Her wobbly high-heeled sandals clacked like fallen skittles over the decking. Sara had helped her yank off her walking boots earlier – her feet were swollen. She slumped down more awkwardly than she intended. She wished she had brought some dressy evening clothes. She was wearing her sparkly purple top with jeans, the sort of boho chic, which worked when she was out with her two local friends, but her old girlfriends had become more stylish with age. And money, of course. Sara had offered to lend her a dress, but Lizzie couldn't fit into anything of Sara's, which was depressing, because she was hardly thin.

Connie's impossible legs were emphasised by her white skinny jeans and aquamarine silk top, which slipped below one shoulder, leaving it bare. Katherine was in a leaf-green silk shift dress with a loose tie. She probably only ate because Matt loved cooking. Sara looked like Grace Kelly in that super-expensive white Joseph shift with a cream and orange wrap over it. Lizzie looked ruefully again at her heavy sequins, which emphasised her sagging breasts.

Sometimes she looked in the mirror in disbelief. How had it happened? She didn't feel like a fat person. She had to take the Tube into work, she reasoned, and didn't have time to exercise – work was too busy. Channel 4 had a bar on the ground floor, the bar snacks there were, admittedly, her weakness. And she didn't want to rush home to be on her own.

Feeling uncomfortable, she diverted herself by mentally devouring the wine tasting menu.

GAE TASTING MENU

Starter

Goat's cheese fritter with blueberry & apple salad.
Iona Sauvignon Blanc

Entrée

Treacle duck salad with fig tapenade and fresh fig
Sijnn Rose

Main

Grilled beef medallion with buchu potato crumpet,
gemsbok lerito
courgette and red onion
Thelema Cabernet Sauvignon

Dessert

Baked chocolate mousse with raspberry paint,
vanilla ice cream and macerated berries
Beaumont Goutte d'Or

It would be a sacrilege to continue the Dukan Diet here. Lizzie had stuck rigidly to it for over eight gruelling weeks – well, on and off, there was the inevitable cake every Friday. It was always someone's birthday and Lizzie, who knew everyone in the whole building, was always included in celebrations. She had been at C4 since she graduated from university. She couldn't quite believe it had been that long. She distinctly remembered every detail of how she got her job at C4 from the advert in the *Guardian*. She had the cutting framed in her bathroom.

Of course she applied. She was an English graduate with a good 2:1. She was passionate and creative. It was her dream job. She imagined herself commissioning drama programmes from a steel-clad office, all of her own. What fun. She clicked with the Deputy Head of Drama, Simon, who interviewed her. He was gay. Gay men always loved Lizzie. She couldn't quite believe it when she got the job. She was the first of the group to start a proper career.

She obviously intended her programme coordinator role to be a stepping stone to commissioning editor. She worked hard. It was always busy. The job was all-consuming. And Lizzie loved the social life. Channel 4 was like being back at university – lots of friends, lots of fun and parties. Of course, she didn't think that she would be there forever, because in the back of her mind, she was going to get married soon. When a commissioning editor's job came up, Lizzie thought of going for it, but she didn't want to work even harder. She enjoyed having time to talk to her friends in the building. She didn't want to miss out on her social life. She didn't apply. Nor did she fill out the application for the next few positions that came up.

Time passed. Her thirty-fifth birthday was miserable. She broke her thumb in the loft door of her rented flat and rushed to casualty, forgetting the Prosecco she had loaded into the freezer, which had exploded by the time she returned. All in all, it made her realise that her life wasn't as good as she thought. She was thirty-five, single without children and in a dead-end job. She applied for the next commissioning editor position in drama. She was turned down for a younger, more ambitious, external candidate. It was such a shock. All this time, Lizzie assumed her promotion was there if she wanted it. She was stuck.

Lizzie focused on the menu again. Rather frustratingly, none of the group had noticed she had lost almost half a stone. Well, she might have already put it back on. She hadn't weighed herself since she got out here – there were no scales in their bathroom. She shouldn't have eaten those sandwiches in the Jo'Burg hangar this morning, not to mention the date balls on the bar.

'How are you, lovely Lizzie?' Jules nudged playfully at her elbow.

If it had been anyone else round the table asking the same question, undoubtedly Lizzie would have spilled out the truth. She didn't have a man, or own her own flat and her career was going nowhere. Instead, she daydreamed about how attractive Jules was. He was charming, flirty and fun. An important man in politics: chief secretary to the Treasury. She could see herself as a wife of an MP living in a nice house in the country.

Lizzie squeezed up against him, imagining they were flirting on a first date. 'I feel great. How is life at number ten, Jules?'

'Lizzie, you know I don't work at number ten. I'm not the PM.'

'Though you might be one day, Jules. Play your cards right. Knowing you, as I do, you can do anything.' She risked touching his arm. 'I've always believed in you.'

She was spinning, diving, rocking. A full-body roller coaster. She wasn't sure if her shoulders were actually rolling forward. She usually shared one bottle of house white with her local friends Sasha and Julie on a Thursday night at the pub at the end of Sasha's road.

'Thank you, Lizzie. I do appreciate that.'

His soft brown eyes were focused on her.

She couldn't help thinking that she should have been Jules's wife instead of Connie. He was attracted to her first. He had come to Bristol to take her out, taking the train after work on Friday. They had got on really well: laughing non-stop, easy and playful. On the doorstep of Harley Place at two in the morning, Lizzie was sure that he was going to make a move. Lizzie couldn't find her keys anywhere. She rang the bell. Connie had answered it in that flimsy white nightie she always wore.

Lizzie flicked her hair out of her eyes. 'Well, you know Jules, it's all your fault. You let me get away.'

She had said that to him back then. The way he narrowed his

eyes at her meant that he believed it too. He was lost in thought. He looked slightly anxious. He must be thinking of their moment together. He sighed.

It could have worked out so differently!

The goat's cheese fritter was posh – a tiny colourful work of art on a vast white plate that seemed designed to make Lizzie feel hungrier. When the treacle duck salad arrived, it consisted of two weeny slices of duck with a dessertspoon of fig tapenade. She scooped some on to her finger and licked it.

Jules was back with her. 'Where are your manners, Lizzie Gibson?' He laughed heartily.

'I can't help it. I'm starving and it is delicious,' she smiled. 'But tiny!'

'Shall we ask for two portions next time? You and I love proper food, proper portions.'

They were partners in crime. Both fun-loving and spirited. She thought ruefully that she used to be as skinny as Connie. If only she was, she would be living this lifestyle.

The wine was also gorgeous, clearly expensive. 'Don't you love this wine, Jules?' Lizzie could imagine that it was just the two of them here. She could hold his attention, hold on to him.

Jules leaned closer. 'You know, this is real discovery for me. I'm a French wine snob, but I am really savouring this Iona Sauvignon Blanc. It's complex for a Sauvignon.' He produced his phone. 'Lizzie, excuse me, I'm going to see what they say about it.'

He had such a spontaneous curiosity.

'Look at that. Iona,' he showed her an aerial shot of vivid green vineyards in front of blue lake, close to the sea. He was absorbed by the tasting notes. 'I could certainly taste the ripe gooseberry and kiwifruit. I missed the lime marmalade, though. Did you?'

'Yes. I missed it all, I'm afraid, Jules.' She leaned back, happy in her drunkenness, watching him reading through all the notes on their website.

Suddenly he put down his phone, got to his feet, moved to the end of the table and tapped his glass with his fork to get the group's attention. He was great with a large audience.

'Never fear: what goes on safari, stays on safari.'

They were loud, raucous. The group together again. She was proud that they were her friends.

Alan slipped into Jules's empty seat. He smiled and squeezed her hand, before whispering. 'You are dressed to party.'

She grinned at him appreciatively as Jules continued, 'A few slurry words from me. Then I promise to shut up.'

'Unless we heckle from across the House,' Matt roared.

Laughter. Chairs rubbed back. Katherine smiled and moved round the table to sit on Matt's lap.

Lizzie always sensed she was one of those women who used to weep into her Chardonnay or, knowing cool Katherine, Grey Goose vodka. Until she met Matt. She relied heavily on him. You could see it in the way she leaned into him.

'No, you are far too easy an opposition,' Jules whipped in.

'You wait, Julian Emmerson.'

'Matt's interruptions aside, I wanted to say a few words about you lot, Connie's oldest friends – so put your Zimmer frames aside for a moment.'

There was a slight hush. Lizzie knew Jules was bound to say something playful.

'We've lost one, but we are about to gain one.'

Lizzie's eyes were on Katherine as Jules was going to say the unsayable and get away with it.

'Luke has parted with the delicious Emma – no accounting for taste – pared down his life and his waist size.'

Luke gave his self-conscious smile. Lizzie had always found it hard to understand his attractiveness. He was too handsome to be sexy. And he could never stand up and give this speech. He wasn't a man like Julian.

'So to Luke's compactness.'

'Hear hear,' Matt shouted. 'Luke, give us a few tips please.'

'Please, Luke,' Jules leaned down mock-solicitously. 'We beg you, don't wither away.'

Lizzie laughed loudly; Sara clapped. Luke glanced at Connie.

'To our eight-week-away new addition: Matt and Katherine's baby girl. Congratulations. I've never seen a mother to be with such a gorgeous bod. Surrogacy is the way forward.'

Only Jules would get away with saying that to Katherine.

'Our dearest Dan keeps his considerable lights under an elegant box hedge.'

Lizzie smiled at Alan. He didn't smile back, nor did he look at Dan.

'Might I add, he is always the first person of your gang to shine light on everyone else's achievements.'

Lizzie was deflated, unappreciated. Dan was always seen as the most loyal person in the group, which wasn't fair. She was the one who remembered everyone's birthdays, she always called as she walked to work from St James's Park Tube station.

As the others laughed, Lizzie frowned. Their lives had moved on without her.

Alan leaned into her. 'Are you all right?'

Lizzie nodded.

'A white hydrangea tells me that you have won an award for your latest garden outside Florence.'

They started to cheer. Dan blushed. He had that kind of modesty that somehow attracted more attention, Lizzie thought. She veered between feeling upset he hadn't told her about the award, and resenting the fact he had won it.

'And Sara Wilson QC. Counsel in the trial of the decade: the Jade Sutton case. Joanne Sutton acquitted.'

It was unfair. Their lives were fast-forwarding. Lizzie turned to look down the table at Sara.

'This afternoon, I've been reading the pages of coverage of her spectacular success. A profile of our own very dear QC in *The Times* legal section. Brilliant barrister brings clarity to a highly charged, high-profile, complicated case. The Jade Sutton case will never be forgotten.'

They clapped, laughed. Connie went over to Sara and gave her a big hug, but Sara extricated herself clumsily. Her white silhouette swayed past the pool, heading for the bar. Only Sara would get away with walking off. The others didn't seem to notice.

'It's been an exciting year for all of you.'

Did he have to rub it in?

'Constance's madcap idea to drag you halfway round the world,

I am the first to admit, now feels like the right plan, at the right time.'
He held out his hand to Connie. She moved to his side. He held her
close. 'A celebration at a certain point in all our lives.'

Lizzie was jealous.

'We are on the cusp of great things I feel.'

What about me? Lizzie wanted to scream.

'To Constance, for making this happen. And for being my beautiful, bright, best friend and partner in all things. I couldn't live
without you. I love you.'

'Yeah, Connie,' Matt howled before clapping his hands. 'We love
you.'

'We do,' added Dan warmly. 'We really do, Connie.'

'And,' Jules added. 'To greatness.'

Alan put his arm around her shoulders. He was the only one
who noticed her. Connie and Luke were first up dancing to the
music, louder in the bar. They were wiggling away, as they always
did in Harley Place, only without touching. Matt was galloping
round with Katherine. She looked as crazy a dancer as he was.

Jules leaned over her shoulder. 'Lizzie, cheer up. What's wrong?
Come on, you know I can't dance with you – I have two left feet.
I'm going to introduce you to this sumptuous Thelema Cabernet
Sauvignon instead.' He lifted up an amazing smart black bottle
with a phoenix as the only decoration on the label.

Lizzie was reminded, yet again, how sexy she found him.

'Imagine: you are on a date with a sophisticated, intelligent man
with a bone-dry sense of humour but a rich hinterland underneath.
How can you resist? Thelema Cabernet Sauvignon, 2009, Lizzie
darling?'

Lizzie smiled.

Chapter 6

Luke coughed a breath out. His chest hurt. He felt nauseous. His legs ached. His feet waded through the sand track as if it were deep, fresh snow. It was surprisingly cold out on the reserve. He was running in shorts: he should have worn his tracksuit bottoms. Some of the rangers ran this two-and-a-half-kilometre circuit out of the lodge, through their 'village' of bungalow homes and back, Gus had told him. Luke loved the connotations. Africans were top athletes, the result of generations of bare-footing it through the bush. He imagined doing the run without trainers. But he was worried about snakes.

Luke and Sara were the last to go to bed, around three in the morning. He couldn't leave earlier. He had savoured his first full night with his friends, laughing and joking with Sara, a woman who was simply a close friend. Who didn't demand of him something he couldn't begin to understand, let alone give.

Still he set his alarm for five. They were riding out at six and he had to get in a run before it got too hot. When he ran, he focused intensely on his technique. His hands lightly curled, imagining he were holding a pair of baby sparrows with broken wings; his forearms at ninety degrees to his body; the soles of his feet ping ponging to his buttocks; his hips staying in line with his body, not over-striding as he had a tendency to do.

He was too cold and hungover to do more than distract himself from his growing discomfort by leafing through the debris of last night. He spluttered and slowed to a gentle jog as he replayed Sara's rant.

'Emma was nothing but a PA, Luke. A fucking PA. You never should have married her.' Sara was vehemently protective of him, which Luke found reassuring. 'I should have stopped you.'

Emma wasn't clever, which made her easier initially. Luke concentrated on his Internet business. His luxury goods website was the first of its kind and had set him up for life. He came home late every night and had a delicious meal. Emma was a great cook and she created a stylish, modern home. She loved shopping and decorating. He loved that, having grown up in a disorganised house. And he wanted to force himself to move on from Connie. Even now, Connie unnerved and unbalanced him. He couldn't help visualising pulling off those tight white jeans. Those narrow hips flaunting her long slender legs.

He was profoundly in love with Connie though he never told her, a fact that haunted him long into his marriage to Emma. Yet after three years together, Connie unceremoniously left him for Julian, marrying him soon after. She hurt him more than he thought it was possible. Since then, he avoided educated women, convinced unintelligent women were less likely to cause him pain and demand emotional commitment that he didn't have it in him to give any more.

Luke knew he was awkward with most women – Connie was the exception. He might have blamed his parents. They didn't share confidences. The silence between them wasn't obvious to Luke until he was married to a woman who never stopped talking and interpreting sinister motive into his every move. He had yearned for the simplicity of his own family life on Dartmoor when, during the relentless farm day, which steamrollered over every summer holiday, he had been able to retreat to his attic room.

It was there he had taught himself how to use a computer, eventually how to programme it. When he went back home now, it was a relief: his bedroom had remained the same: his LEGO stuck with Blu-Tack; his athletics shields old-fashioned and dusty; his posters of Debbie Harry wallpapering the sloping dormer ceilings of the loft conversion his father had built. Whether his parents had left it out of laziness or as a shrine to their only son, he would never know. Emma would have re-decorated to erase his early life, before she was in it.

The sky was starting to blush. Through the dawn grey light, an outline of hills was gently forming. Luke was drawn back to Sara's other slurred comment. 'You do know that I always thought you and Connie would get married?' Sara's hand slapped the mahogany bar. 'You don't mind me saying that, do you, Luke?'

He wondered why Sara had the need to spell out the painful fact. Sara had been more aggressive than usual. It must be coming down from this Jade Sutton case. It was a big deal. Luke couldn't imagine sparring in court. After his divorce, he did everything to avoid confrontation.

Last night he was upset. He had stuttered that Connie was part of a past life he barely remembered. He wished he had the temperament to bang the bar, but he wasn't that kind of man.

Luke struggled to breathe evenly and lift his sledging feet. He gave in to wondering whether Sara was right. Would Connie have married him, if she hadn't met Julian? He never understood why Julian, whose stomach shaped his shirts, got away with his affairs. It made him hate Julian with an even greater passion.

The last time he skulked out – another fictitious meeting – to meet up with Sara, she blurted that she had seen Connie with a very good-looking civil barrister in the bar at the Athenaeum. At an hour when Connie was normally with her army of kids. Connie was having an affair, she pronounced.

Luke felt a crazy tug of jealousy. Not that he wished he was Julian. Definitely not. He was financially dependent on Connie's inheritance. Luke's only comfort was that he could divorce Emma and afford custody of his children, making sure that they were properly cared for while he was at work, though in the holidays, he largely worked from home. It was his own business and he wasn't going to miss out on his children's childhood.

The sun was stretching up and Luke started sweating. He had been mistaken about Emma. She had been a far greater challenge than Connie ever was. Initially unbothered by his reserve, Emma and her effervescence had helped him to navigate the emotional minefield of other relationships, more than Connie, who had been almost as private as Luke. He had believed that he had found a woman who truly loved him.

After Finn was born, Emma ballooned. Her thirty extra pounds made her aggressive and critical. He hadn't been able to do anything right. All he wanted was a night out with friends occasionally. Not much to ask. But she waged war against him going out with anyone, male or female. She hated Connie, Lizzie and Sara. She insisted that they looked down on her. Perhaps they did. She slagged off their clothes, their taste, their homes, their behaviour. Luke took to seeing Matt and Sara covertly. Then he stopped seeing all his other friends. It was easier to stay at home.

Still Emma wasn't happy. She fought over everything: maddened by his silent shrugs, she resorted to throwing things, often heavy, breakable things. He was too ashamed to tell anyone that Emma hit him. He went to casualty many times. At the hospital they asked, of course. What could he say? My wife hits me. Sara would have been outraged. You let the bloody PA hit you? Hit her back. Luke never did. He hadn't got it in him to hit anyone.

Luke finally left her, taking the children with him. Emma's violence meant there was no question of her getting custody of the children. And Luke couldn't risk it – even though she had never hit them. Yet. Though no one except Luke's lawyer knew about Emma's abuse. And he had to absorb the unspoken disapproval of his parents and all their friends, accepting that he might lose Matt and Connie. Matt viciously said he was worse than his ex-wife. How could anyone take a mother's children away from her? What could Luke do? He could never tell anyone the truth. He never would.

He sighed and slowed down as the track wound round towards a small cluster of pale grey functional bungalows flanked by safari vehicles. Emma cornered him and he gave into her. That hurt. It all hurt, if he was honest. He had been destroyed by her. He had Finn and Ella. Yet she shipwrecked them. They were lost and incomplete.

He was jogging, barely faster than a walk, hoping he wouldn't face the embarrassment of bumping into Gus, when his left ankle gave way. It slid feebly sideways down an aardvark hole. Luke lurched, madly jerking his arms. Desperate not to fall, he fell awkwardly, agedly. The shock made him shake. His chest was screaming. He lay, face smothered by warm sand, afraid to move, terrified he was injured. He didn't budge. He gingerly lifted himself into a low crouch, hips down. He waited for a stab of certain pain. There was none. He stood up with bent knees. Was his left ankle hurt? Slightly. He felt a stiffness, which could be from lack of sleep. Maybe the after-effects of the flight.

And yet. His body was strong. He would get back into his stride, shake off this feeble morning-after lethargy. His legs started to loosen up, despite the fall. Luke sped up a little as he spotted Gae. Running was the answer. Running from middle age and its total lack of room for manoeuvre. Running marked the freedom for him to start again. As his body performed, the truth dawned on Luke. He loved his children and every moment of their time together. They had a great relationship. But his marriage had masticated him, vomiting out his remains.

He needed to concentrate on himself, not to mention his health. Get back out into the world. Luke glanced at his watch. He had twenty minutes – he would whip into the gym for a few stretches on one of those black mats. He ran straight past the pool to avoid being dragged in by the others for a coffee and doubtless more food. He walked the last few yards past the thatched fence into the oval enclosure that held the one-room gym and massage area.

Kimberley, the girl who had greeted them at the airstrip, was bent over a massage bed on the grass to the right of the gym. Wind chimes rang in the tree above her head. She was covering a blue leather bed with two pristine white towels. Her calves were slender and brown under her white uniform. He could see the outline of her narrow hips inside her dress. Kimberley immediately unfolded her body and turned towards him with a whitened, uncomplicated smile, which propelled her full, young face towards him. 'Morning, Luke. Good run?'

Easy and warm with possibility, Luke thought. Could this be the answer?

Chapter 7

Connie watched Luke running past the bar where they were meeting without looking in her direction. Even from a distance, he appeared angst-ridden. She wanted to ask him about his divorce and why he had taken the children away from Emma. She disapproved of the way he had behaved. It was out of character. He never did anything to hurt anyone, Connie thought, even when she deserved it.

She reached to pour another coffee from the flask positioned on the bar. She felt horrendous. She never drank more than half a glass – she wasn't relaxed enough at the kind of events Julian endlessly circled in London. The buzz of being with her true friends in Gae made her overeager to reach for her glass. When Julian and Connie swayed back to their house, she was desperate to get horizontal and sleep. She stripped off her clothes and left them in the cone shape they made on the rug beside their bed. She struggled to find the opening to the mosquito net. She lay down flat on her back, her body spinning on a roundabout with her head tipped back to feel the breeze. She heard Julian on the phone in the sitting room, but it didn't matter. For once, she was drunk and truly happy.

'Connie, darling, are you awake?'

'Mmm…'

'It was really fun tonight,' he bent down to whisper in her ear. 'The whole holiday was a stroke of genius. Well done you.' He kissed her on the lips. 'Sleep well.'

There was no sign of Sara, who was sleeping, according to Lizzie, who appeared wearing her sunglasses, before removing them dramatically to display weeping, red-rimmed eyes. Gus pronounced it was hay fever caused by the flowering Kalahari sour grass. The lemon scent of these swaying, hip-height grasses had been fragrant in the air. Gus went in search of another guide, who had wrap-around sunglasses that would seal Lizzie's eyes from the pollen adrift in the air.

Connie was shifting off the bar stool to wake Sara, when Matt sidled in on his own. She automatically asked about Katherine, sensing the answer was going to be another knock to their first early morning drive.

Matt looked forlorn. 'She's not going to make it, I'm afraid. She needs to rest.'

She made a soothing sound that stuck somewhere deep in her dry throat. She touched Matt's arm, because she couldn't come up with anything more concrete.

'Phantom pregnancy?' Sara appeared in ivory thick-rimmed Chanel sunglasses and a khaki safari dress with a narrow cream belt. She was clutching a thick olive wrap.

How could Sara be so sharp after a late night? Connie wondered. Matt paled, running his fingers through the front of his thick hair. 'A migraine. It's the stress of it all…'

'Migraine?' Sara snapped back. 'What – not a common headache?'

'Are we a woman down?' Julian interjected from the other side of the bar, where he had been hunched over his BlackBerry. He was checking it out here more than he usually did, or maybe she was more conscious of it on holiday. 'Has delicate Katherine abandoned us for the comfort of the chaise longue?'

This morning was going to be challenging. They would be tetchy, snapping at each other until their hangovers lifted. She could predict it as surely as she could her children fighting the morning after a late night.

Luke strode up to the bar in a grey tracksuit. 'Morning all.' He looked buoyant. Connie wondered what had changed in the last ten minutes. He reached for the water jug, poured a glass right to the rim, and drank it in one continuous gulp.

Julian lifted his head up from his BlackBerry, 'Have you already been self-flagellating on the perambulator?'

'I love it,' Sara laughed. 'I must write that down.'

Connie gave a compromising smile, hoping that Luke didn't notice.

'I was out running in the bush.' There was no mistaking the uncertainty in Luke's voice.

Kimberley, the girl who had met them at the airstrip, appeared in a doorway. She stood, legs slightly too far apart. They politely stopped talking. Sara eyed her critically over the edge of her coffee cup. Julian was staring at her.

'Luke, I've got a slot at 10.30. Doesn't that work for you? You'll be back by then, eh?'

'Perfect. Thanks Kimberley.'

She smiled for too long as women did in front of Luke, before turning back outside. Connie couldn't believe it. She swivelled away from Luke.

Connie could hear Luke nervously swing from foot to foot, banging his trainers together with each move 'I'm having a massage. I've been working out too much. My muscles are stiff. It's all there is to it.'

'Not the only thing that's going to be stiff,' Julian said.

Connie turned away from them. Her mind was empty.

'Julian, for God's sake,' Matt grimaced. 'There are ladies present.'

Sara snapped in. 'What? Matt, give us a break. We're not in corsets. I represent men who nail their victims to floorboards for fun.'

Julian flashed his eyes. He was loving every minute. Intrigue, political or sexual, brought his world alive. 'Isn't there an unspoken gentleman's agreement not to fuck the staff?'

Connie was more upset by Luke than she was by Julian. Why did he never speak up? There was a pause in the conversation that held like a long inhale in her yoga class.

'Luke, take some advice from your uncle Julian, Kimbo looks a little tame to me.'

Connie dreaded what was to follow. She had to stop herself from reaching for Luke's hand.

'The perfect night is more Pippa Middleton and Keira Knightley. With Tracy Emin in there, to spice it up.'

Connie closed her eyes. She would have laid her head on her forearms, but she didn't want to draw attention to herself. There was a heavy inevitability to her marriage. She could feel Luke moving instinctively closer to her.

Connie was drawn reluctantly back to last week.

Nothing extraordinary. An intimate evening for about fifty in Winfield House, the Georgian red-brick American ambassador's residence inside Regent's Park. A cursory stop at the security gate, invitation and passport shown, down the short drive to the front door straight to the guiding arm of an elegant fixer. She led them into an eighteenth-century French panelled drawing room towards the jovial midwestern ambassador and his skinny, vivacious wife. Introductions. Julian got straight into politics with the ambassador, no small talk required. Connie's role was to instantly find common ground, which could be hard despite what Sara might think. She commented on the ambassador's wife's beautiful grey sequin dress. She always searched for a genuine compliment, it was her shortcut to getting on with anyone. She was in: the ambassador's wife had a new grandchild. She loved London. Did she know that Barbara Hutton had built Winfield House and had given it to the American state for the price of a dollar? How fascinating. When another member of the Cabinet arrived, the ambassador moved on. They did too – moving systematically round. It was what they did.

After forty minutes, Julian suggested they leave. A curvaceous columnist from the *Daily Mail*, as recklessly ambitious as the smirk under her neon red lipstick, tottered over, squeezing her plunging V-neck stretch dress between Julian and Connie. No ceremony: flattering chat, a few raucous jokes and straight to intimacy without paying even two hundred pounds to pass Go. She pressed her heavy left breast on to Julian's right arm. He pressed it back. His eyes danced. He knocked into a passing waiter; he forgot he had said they should leave. He forgot Connie.

She played her own game many times. How long could she stick it out before she left? At Winfield House, it was thirty-two minutes. A personal best.

Of course she knew that she was being publicly humiliated. It had never mattered as much as it did right now.

Gus re-emerged with wraparound glasses for Lizzie. As they collected their shawls and scarves, an arm squeezed her, gathering her up. 'Good morning, sweetheart.' Dan's face was awash with warmth and concern. It was too much. Connie wanted to push him away. 'You know, I woke up feeling awful. I never asked about the children. How is my god-daughter?'

Connie's upper lip twitched. The sheer comfort of her children. Leo, Lou, Flora and Hector.

It had rained relentlessly last weekend in Adderbury. On Sunday afternoon, they set up a Risk game on the low table in front of their fireplace. Julian built a great fire – a ritual that delighted him. Flora and Leo masterminded toasting hot cross buns on skewers, while Hector dripped marshmallows into the hearth. Flora lay with her arms outstretched on the rug in front of the fire, her hot pink hoodie almost covering her golden ringlets. Connie made a vast pot of tea.

They squatted around the coffee table. The cards Leo dealt himself made him certain to take Africa, which the whole Emmerson clan evangelically believed guaranteed winning the game.

'Are you sure you didn't cheat?' Hector complained.

'Excuse me, babe-teeno,' Leo played pompous with Hector, only half as a joke. 'You offend my honour. I don't need to cheat to win.'

Julian groaned as soon as their soldiers were arranged. 'I'm going to get murdered by my first-born son. Oedipus.'

'Dad, I have a name, remember you had me christened? Hello, I'm Leo.'

'I hate your mock-defeatist charade, Dad,' Lou turned on Julian, 'It means you are going try harder to win.'

'Lou, you, Dad or Leo always win. I don't know what you are complaining about,' Hector moaned.

'Oh Hector, I'm sorry,' Julian said giving him a large bear hug. 'You know we can't let you win. Then you would really hate us.'

Flora murmured, 'You are all obsessed about winning. It's really not what life's about, you know.'

Lou piped back, 'Flo, our resident love-and-peace peddler.'

'What about a hot cross bun?' Connie suggested.

Lou, Leo and Julian all simultaneously groaned. Flora and Hector giggled.

Julian smiled in Connie's direction. 'LOL, Mum,' he said with an exaggerated teen drawl. 'You always say don't niggle, have something to eat.'

'Did you say tickling?' Hector asked with a gleam in his eyes, which had made Connie smile. He was eleven and alternated between boyish tumbles and teen strops, not sure where he belonged. Connie was always thankful when the boy returned.

Hector launched on Leo, who at seventeen was old enough to be childish, though, of course, he had a dig at Hector. 'How old are you, Hector Emmerson? You are in long trousers, you cannot do this with dignity anymore,' said Leo, before he rolled out from under Hector and landed heavily on him to his half-screams, half-laughs. 'You're going to crush me, you ape. Aah, Leo, you've eaten too much KFC this term.'

'Excuse me, I am master of this universe and certainly the official tickle monster,' Julian lurched on his two boys.

Seconds later, Flora was on top of Julian trying to extricate him from the boys. Only Lou held back. There were howls of laughter and shrieks of half-pain.

Julian sat up. 'Okay, get Mum now. One, two, three. Charge!'

Chapter 8

The black-backed jackal on the track turned to look back at them. A switched-on fox, more barrister than scavenger. The group was huddled under the dark tan, fleece blankets when Ben made this first spot, exposed as a barely perceptible nod in Gus's direction. It was a rare close-up, Gus translated with unwavering enthusiasm that perversely Sara couldn't help wanting to deflate. The jackal was uncannily similar to a domestic dog. Even its howls were canine, Gus explained. He had told them he was a trained zoologist and Sara was grudgingly impressed. Overqualified for driving zoological voyeurs round the reserve, Gus and his observations became instantly more interesting. It made her look harder. She wanted to recognise what Gus could automatically see. She had been gripped by Channel 4's *Inside Nature's Giants*. She wasn't passionate about animals, it was the steep learning curve that the series represented for her. She prided herself on her inexhaustible knowledge on every subject from *Mad Men* to Dawkins' view of reality.

She couldn't help being quietly triumphant when she made the second spot.

'Look, Gus.' She leaned forward, tipping her hat back. The cord hung close to her neck. 'Thirty degrees. A warthog mother and her babies.'

'Good spot,' Luke said.

The warthog was leading an immaculate line of four little warthogs in a gentle trot parallel with the vehicle. Julian, Lizzie and Luke went for their cameras. Lizzie shrieked, 'They are gorgeous, look at them.' She immediately squeezed her head and shoulders down between her legs and started to churn through the contents of her bag. Matt and Dan were both obliged to inch away from her towards the edge of the vehicle.

'God, they hold their tails up like they do in *The Lion King*.'

Julian laughed, 'Sara, please tell me you aren't planning to base your entire safari on a comparison with Disney.'

'Popular culture, Julian dear boy, listen and learn,' she smiled. 'Now, Gus, sing for your supper. Feed me some interesting warthog facts.'

Despite this preposterously early start, Sara was glad to be here. It was a distraction. Julian's speech last night potently reminded her of how serious her situation was. She was deeply ashamed her close friends were toasting her success. What would they think of her if they knew the truth? Their supposedly brilliant friend had been blinded by her dogged determination to win this case. Nothing new there. Only this time, she had been seduced by her client into making a fundamental and fatal mistake.

In the dining room at the Bailey, where the humour was generally post-coital and non-confrontational, she could hear the dig: women get too close to their clients. Only Sara never acted like a woman. She didn't have that excuse. She had to stop thinking about it. It was over. She would have to live with a guilty itch. No more.

Gus grinned easily. 'They are holding their tails up so the ones behind can follow them through long grass.'

'Keeping going, Gus,' she insisted thankfully. He was exactly the type of person who could never second-guess what was plaguing her.

Gus blushed slightly, then faced the group and sat on the steering wheel. 'Okay. They move around in matriarchal groups called sounders: a mother and her young. Young males move away until they are adults. Then they rejoin sounders, but only ones with oestrus females.'

'What the hell does oestrus mean?' Sara cut in. 'Queen's English please.'

'On heat,' stated Luke.

'Thank you, lovely Luke,' said Sara hastily. 'Stupid me.'

'Got it,' Lizzie sat up clutching her species checklist. 'Anyone got a pen?'

Dan immediately bent down and delved into his canvas bag and produced a sketching pencil. 'Here you go, lovely.'

Gus said, 'They feed on their knees, which are actually their wrists.'

'Sara, I'm wondering if your insatiable desire for encyclopaedic knowledge of the feeding habits of the warthog is ever going to be satisfied?' asked Julian. 'Are we going to track the black rhino this morning?'

'Patience, Julian,' soothed Dan. 'Enjoy the moment.'

'When are we stopping for a coffee?' Lizzie mumbled. 'I've got a stonking headache.'

'I wouldn't mind a water,' added Luke. 'I'm feeling a little dehydrated.'

'Luke, it's down to that punishing regime of yours,' Julian interjected. 'Walking into rhino is the ultimate safari experience.'

'I'm looking forward to it,' insisted Luke.

'They don't do that in the Kruger. It isn't considered safe.' Sara knew that Matt was simply echoing Katherine.

'We'll be fine,' Luke insisted.

'They have too many vehicles, which mean the rhino get harassed and become a lot more aggressive than here,' said Gus.

His streaked blond chunk of hair flopped forward. It wouldn't look amiss in Chelsea, Sara thought wryly.

'Here we have a strict policy of not worrying the animals.'

Sara's pale green eyes gleamed. 'Gus, don't panic. We're not suggesting you are recklessly endangering our lives.'

'Look, I would never put a guest's life at risk, eh? We won't do it unless the conditions are absolutely right. Ben has to be happy. And you all comfortable, eh.'

'Gus. We're not suggesting you're trying to lose one of us – though Matt implied it. It was his wife speaking via him. Like the devil through Damien in *The Omen*.'

'Sara, stop it,' said Dan.

Gus started to laugh. It dissolved first as a snort and then a sneeze, which made him hastily reach for a white cotton ironed handkerchief that weirdly reminded Sara of her granddad, a miner for forty years in Seaham Colliery, County Durham. Every day, granddad William went to work in 'The Nack' with a pristine white handkerchief pressed by Sara's nan into a square and tucked carefully in the pocket of his trousers. He had retired before they closed the pit in 1994. Sara's nan insisted that the closure killed him.

Matt laughed easily. 'Sara, how could I forget how incorrigible you are?'

'All of which I'll take as a compliment,' she said tapping Gus on his shoulder. 'Let's go.'

Gus started up the vehicle, cracking along the narrow track over the bumps at a pace. Ben pointed towards a hillside far away to the left. 'A troop of baboons on the move,' Gus yelled over the noise of the vehicle. They bent in a synchronised movement, down and over each other towards the left. Three dark baboons were loping horizontally across a bushy hillside.

'A troop of baboons, eh?' Sara teased. 'We get a literacy lesson thrown in.'

Gus interpreted her literally. 'I have a great list of collective names of the animals. Shall I photocopy it for you, Sara?'

'Please do, Gus,' Julian interjected. 'Sara, learn it by tomorrow and enlighten us all.'

Ben murmured to Gus, creating a V-shape with his arms before flapping his fingers against his palms like he was playing castanets. She barely heard him speak, let alone made out actual words. Gus veered violently off the track straight into the rampant veld grasses, skirting a Camel Thorn tree. As they careered round it, Lizzie and Connie shrank to protect their arms from its three-inch thorns. The contents of Lizzie's bag slid forwards and then backwards two rows along the floor of the vehicle.

Still Connie was silent. Sara was worried about her after Julian's outrageous display this morning. She knew Connie wouldn't want to talk about it. She never did.

Gus shouted without slowing down. 'The thorns grow on the side the animals feed on to protect the tree, eh?' He picked up the radio. 'Gus to Gae, over. We have picked up black rhino tracks due east of Gosa.'

She shouted above the vehicle, 'I hate to make a statement of the bleeding obvious, Gus, but you are driving straight into thick thorny bush.'

It was like standing up in court on the first day of Joanne Sutton's trial, even after the mind-numbing pre-trial review. A wobbliness deep in bottom of her womb: part fear, part excitement, neither quite upstaging the other.

Gus turned and gave her a quick grin. This time Sara got the distinct impression that he couldn't help being delighted that he had the upper hand. 'Sara, the cat family use the road, so you can track them along it. Not the black rhino, they stick to this thick bush. We call it African acupuncture, eh?'

He careered down and up a deep hole round another Camel Thorn tree, while talking continuously. 'Ben spotted a black rhino midden near that Camel Thorn. They are in this block.'

'Block?' Luke asked.

'Between where we saw an earlier track on the road. The roads are in right angled grids – it's easy to track.'

'Rewind boys. What the hell is a midden?' Sara was put out she was unable to keep up with safari speak.

'It's a giant toilet, which black rhino use to mark their territory. Black rhino dung is brownish in colour and has evidence of the twigs they have eaten in it. And they tend to kick over it.'

'Perhaps more dung detail than strictly necessary,' Julian stated, before standing up in the vehicle, holding on to the roof bar. Not known for his physical prowess, he had to cling on while pretending not to, Sara noticed with amusement.

They veered through dense grass that was higher than the bonnet, circuiting Shepherd's Trees, the name Gus gave to the short sturdy evergreen with white bark and scant green leaves underneath where antelopes and other grazers had eaten. He pointed out a bushy shrub called a Raisin Bush with straight branches, apparently popular with the bushmen for making bows and arrows. They bounced back on to another road, where Gus stopped as abruptly as he had taken off. He consulted Ben.

'Okay. Ben has picked up a male black rhino chasing a female rhino and a baby around in this block.'

'Really?' said Julian instinctively curious. 'How did he do that?'

'From their tracks,' insisted Gus, who held his own with Julian to Sara's delight. 'Ben's getting out here to do some more tracking on foot and see where he gets to. We can have some coffee, eh?'

'Yes, please,' Lizzie groaned. 'Alan, back me up.'

'I would love a coffee too,' Luke smiled that bloody gorgeous smile.

Sara reflected Luke didn't feel the need to masticate his words into smart sound bites. He didn't shout, even when she howled at him in the bar last night. She blushed thinking about it now. She missed their drunken nights out together. She wondered whether she might suggest another bender with Luke when they were back in London. She missed what he represented in her life. A male friendship woven together with time and trust rather than a contact built like Meccano. Luke somehow managed to be a highly successful entrepreneur, navigating a high-powered global career, without being tainted by it. Out here, Sara was conscious of the harshness to her tone, and the aggression and bite in her comments. The result of years of rubbing up against belligerent colleagues and clients.

She moved up beside Luke and linked arms with him. 'Lovely Luke. I think that I gave you a horribly hard time last night.' She lowered her voice. 'You know, about Emma and Connie. Forgive me.'

He slowly smiled with his lips closed. 'I don't know what you are talking about, Sara Wilson.'

He was a really decent man.

'I've missed you, Luke, a lot,' Sara squeezed his arm. 'Can I get you a coffee?'

They stood close to the cotton clothed foldaway table, not quite as blue as the sky which opened up the landscape. Their dawn start was a semi-conscious dream for Sara. It was now full-blown morning and she was hungry and thirsty. Sara opened the white plastic screw top jars: coffee bags in one, tea bags in another and three with chocolate muffins, croissant and watermelon chunks. She unceremoniously grabbed two deep metal mugs, chucked a coffee bag into each one, some hot water from the leather-clad flask and took three brownies, before adding a mini-croissant as an after-thought. She passed two brownies and a coffee to Luke, who gave her his Colgate smile in return.

Despite the warmth she was feeling for Luke, Sara felt a certain coming down, as she sensed the others did. They were all tired, though their talk was still focused on the morning's ride and the project in hand: the black rhino.

Sara didn't listen to Matt's question, only Gus's answer. 'Yes it's the Chinese. They use the rhino horn for alternative medicine.'

'How much do the poachers get?' Sara instantly joined in, moving between the two of them.

'One hundred thousand pounds sterling per horn.' Gus looked up from the coffee he was making for Lizzie. 'They can afford helicopters, eh.'

'Can't the government stop them?' she asked.

Gus shook his head emphatically. 'They don't even try. A ranger shot a poacher up near here and he went to prison for manslaughter.'

'You are joking?' Sara was outraged for the first time in a long while. It made her pause. She could hear the hoots of derision over the daily bottles of Chablis, invariably opened in her room in Chambers. 'What do you want a moral compass for, Wilson? Psychopaths and barristers are the same: they leave their feelings at home.' Only she hadn't, had she?

'Here, we wear these boots. Standard issue, eh?' Gus turned over a boot to show the deep, distinctive tread. 'We know if anyone else's out here.'

Connie asked, 'How many are there left?'

Gus raised his thick eyebrows. 'There are four thousand rhino left, eh.'

'It's terrible,' Connie said with emotion. 'It's a crime against nature. My grandfather would turn in his grave.'

'They've got to be stopped,' Gus agreed.

Lizzie took her coffee and wandered off to lie flat in the grass beside the track. She was completely invisible from the table. Matt and Luke, who noticed her position first, nudged each other and grabbed their cameras. It didn't take Luke long to climb on the roof of the vehicle to get an aerial shot. Sara walked slowly over to take a look at her. Lizzie was asleep in dense grass, where there were probably snakes, spiders and every manner of itchy thing. She was even snoring. Luke took another photo.

'Leave me alone, horrid people,' Lizzie moaned, raising one arm like a flagpole with her hand barely visible above the grass.

'Don't move, Lizzie,' said Dan. He went back to the vehicle and emerged with his sketch book. 'Stay still. This is going to be a great picture.'

The move over to Lizzie shifted their conversation on.

'There has been an amazing amount of twittering about your case, Sara,' Luke gently commented.

'Oh yeah?' Since it ended, Sara studiously avoided the coverage. It was like she had binged on ice cream and had no desire to face the empty tubs.

Julian joined the conversation. 'Thousands of people think they did it, plus there are a fair few cranks.'

Sara smiled easily. 'Male, I presume? They either insanely fancy her, or don't believe her.' Sara was drawn back to the contents deep in the bottom of her left-hand mahogany desk drawer at home. 'The fate of the attractive female co-defendant.'

Sara noticed Connie walk away towards Luke, who was back at the table, grabbing another muffin.

'One can't help wondering if the Suttons got off because they are telegenic and middle class?' Julian mused.

Sara answered automatically. 'No bloody evidence. The facts say they didn't. We don't have trial by media in the UK, despite what the papers may think.'

It was the right answer. It had been right at the beginning. Sara had finessed the case out of Reading Crown Court into the Bailey, claiming local media feeling would create prejudice. She knew everyone at the Bailey. She always won on home turf.

Julian pursued, 'What about her DNA in the boot of Nigel Sutton's Range Rover?'

'The strands of her hair could easily have come from a piece of clothing, or her teddy. Jade Sutton took it everywhere. It was supported by the expert witness for the defence.'

'Not likely?' Julian shot back.

'The judge would say that's a matter of comment, Julian,' Sara said with a patience she didn't feel. 'Not fact.'

Why wouldn't anyone let her forget this case? Move on. She needed another brief and quickly. She must call Pete, her clerk.

Luke interjected. 'What was the mother's name again?'

'Joanne Sutton,' Sara said her name too quickly. She was exposed, as if the group could see her drawer heaving with press cuttings from the case. She grabbed a croissant and wandered away from Julian towards Luke and Connie.

Even in Africa, she couldn't escape the images. She had cut out every photo she could find of Joanne Sutton and placed them in see-through files. Sara had meticulously filed them in date order as if her efficiency might excuse her obsession.

She couldn't explain it to any of the group, let alone anyone in Chambers. They would think that she had lost it. Her obsession with Joanne Sutton. Sara couldn't logically explain why she was drawn to her. She was a pretty, immaculate housewife from a west Berkshire village near Reading. Middle class, middle of the road. Everything Sara despised and strove to avoid.

She breathed in deeply. The tang of the sour grass tickled her nose. This wilderness couldn't be more different to Joanne Sutton's Pangbourne cottage garden with its shining hot pink foxes, floppy poppies, sprinklings of lily of the valley and peonies. She wished she had never ever seen it. Of course, she shouldn't have seen Joanne Sutton at home alone.

What had possessed her?

Pete put through the call. Joanne Sutton sounded different. Her control was absent and her voice was shrill and unstable. 'I have to see you. Alone.'

Sara was silent. Desperate clients were her territory. Yet she was surprised that it was Joanne Sutton talking in this way.

'Can you hear me? Say something.'

Sara drew on her stock reply. 'Mrs Sutton, I am simply not permitted to meet with you without your solicitor, Mr Stephenson, being present. Or at the very least with my junior and Mr Stephenson fully aware of our meeting.'

'No.' Joanne Sutton sobbed, short of hysteria. 'I have to see you alone. You have to do this for me. Do you understand?'

Emotional outbursts only alienated Sara and drove her back to comfort of legal practice. 'It would be a breach of our Code of Practice. I am sorry, Mrs Sutton.'

Joanne Sutton wailed. Sara had only heard such a desperate and wounded cry once before. From her mother.

She walked rapidly to the door of her room to see if she could spot her junior, John, in the corridor. She put her hand over the receiver and yelled. 'John, get your sorry arse in here now, for God's sake.'

'Look, Mrs Sutton. When you're a little calmer, let's talk with Mr Stephenson.'

John appeared at her door. Sara mouthed Joanne Sutton and mimed slashing her throat.

'Why don't I put you through to John, my fantastic junior. He can help, and will outline the Code of Practice we need to adhere to at all times.'

She pointed to him and the phone. He gestured with his fingers to his mouth to remind her he was re-heating their takeaway curry. Joanne Sutton had either hung up, or she remained silent.

'He'll schedule a meeting for all of us together, okay?'

'Have you ever lost anyone close to you?' Her tone was cold and calm. It was as if she knew.

Sara was silent, too experienced to be drawn into a conversation about her life, but surprised by her knowing tone.

Joanne Sutton continued, 'A member of your family?'

Sara scratched vigorously at her eyelid, before remembering she had mascara on. It had already been a hellish day. Give her a five-minute listening to.

'What is it you want, Mrs Sutton?' Sara couldn't hide her sigh.

'I want you to come and see me. I need to talk to you in person about something. I deserve it. I have lost my daughter. Every day of my life is going to be overshadowed by this loss.'

John reappeared with her chicken tikka masala in a white plastic container with the rice and dhal in pots balanced on top. Sara waved him in and wrote on her pad. *A good bloody hearing I'm giving her. Your bloody job. Please note.*

She was hungry and keen to be distracted, afterwards she wondered if she had misheard her.

'You know exactly what that feels like, don't you? You can't escape your loss.'

'Excuse me?' Had she been looking into Sara's background? Surely not.

'My daughter, Jade, is dead. I am only asking for half an hour of your time.'

Joanne Sutton had lost her child. Despite herself, Sara was sorry for her.

She gave John a pained grimace. He slid further down her leather armchair and grinned in between his toppling forkfuls of rice.

'All right, Mrs Sutton. I will come and see you, but I will have to inform Mr Stephenson, okay? Let me put John on to sort it out.'

She spoke to Mark Stephenson. Like her, he moaned about best practice, especially with this case. Sara moaned back. If she's not telling you the whole story, what can I do? Anyway, it's probably nothing. She wants a good bloody hearing. They both laughed. Your bloody fault for not giving it to her Mark, my boy.

Sara worked on the train from Paddington, which, though direct, infuriatingly stopped in every outpost. Time-wasting made her fraught. Deep down she was worried, but tried to work herself out of it.

When she arrived and impatiently strode through the tunnel leading out of the station bang on to a bend in a high street, she didn't even notice her surroundings. Later that evening, she saw the red-brick village hall set back behind a car park, the Co-Op on the corner and The Elephant, a gastro pub and hotel, where she went afterwards.

Sara circled the shiny white Mini, luminous in front of the mock Tudor house. Joanne Sutton opened the door immediately. Was she hovering behind her white wooden shutters looking out for her?

She was wearing a bright red high-street dress that was too red and too short for a woman of her age – thirty-eight, Sara knew from the brief. She wore heavy foundation, which looked unnatural at eleven thirty on a Tuesday morning in the countryside. Her blond highlighted hair had that ironed look no longer fashionable in London. It made her appear immaculate and in control, protecting her from the loss her only child. She didn't smile or look particularly welcoming.

Sara tried to formalise the situation. 'Mrs Sutton, this is highly irregular. I hope it is a serious piece of evidence.'

'Sara, come in.' Clients didn't use her first name. Joanne Sutton hadn't to date.

It drew Sara further in, even though she knew she must retain a professional distance. She was bitterly regretting having taken this mad leap of sympathy. As she entered the hallway, old-fashioned with its gold wallpaper, mahogany hall table with a gilt mirror overhanging it, Sara couldn't immediately see any evidence of this lost family life.

There were three highly polished silver frames lined up on the hall table. Each one showed a white blond vision of a child in exquisite, immaculate boutique clothes. Their daughter Jade wasn't doing anything in any of the photos. She was close up, staring blankly into the lens. When Sara left a couple of hours later, she wondered whether the photos had been placed there on the hall table for her benefit.

Joanne Sutton was the most confident woman she had ever met. She wasn't remotely intimidated by Sara, her uber QC, swathed in a Joseph suit, swanning up from London into her small Home Counties home. She made direct, unfaltering eye contact, feeling no need to soften its gaze with the warmth of a smile.

Sara couldn't understand this kind of confidence when it wasn't attached to a career. How could a woman who did nothing for a living be this self-possessed?

Joanne Sutton led her out to a narrow strip of a garden around thirty feet long with low-slung fences, opening them out to the full view of the neighbours on either side. Joanne Sutton had already placed an off-white tray on an olive metal garden table to one side of the narrow decking. A cafetière of coffee, two spotty mugs, a matching jug and side plates, and a homemade chocolate cake were pristinely waiting.

Sara was horrified. The idea of settling down to a cosy cuppa in the garden had only reinforced their inappropriate intimacy. Yet she didn't refuse a second slice of the chocolate cake, more tasty than the organic one from Tom's Deli on Westbourne Grove. Joanne Sutton was determined to let Sara finish her coffee and cake before she spoke.

The time eating cake, which Joanne Sutton didn't fill with small talk, gave Sara an unexpected break. She gazed at the lush lawn, bordered by full, dense beds with an array of colour. Tall stocks waved in the wind with the odd purple allium adding to the colour and lightness. There were cream metal baskets hanging from both fences with white china pots, dense with pink petunias. An oak garden bench was decorated with two large brown knitted cushions, done up with oversized buttons. Every detail of Joanne Sutton's home was arranged, ultimately cared for, that Sara was stirred by her unresolved pain. She rationalized that it was absurd to envy Joanne Sutton. But she did. The feeling hadn't gone away.

Ben radioed to say he had had no luck. He was up a tree waiting for them. They all helped to pack up, before careering back into the bush to find him. Sara cheered up, spotting his capped head up above a Shepherd's Tree. They were off back to Gae, refuelled, re-energised and eager to spot animals.

'Secretary birds. Two flying.' Luke.

'Springbok a leaping.' Julian.

'Ostrich! Complete with orange bum feathers.' Lizzie.

'Over there, look, two beautiful impalas.' Dan.

'Zebra alert.' Matt.

'Twin zebra alert,' Luke.

'Christ. You're like a bunch of children with ADD.' Sara snapped.

They laughed together, hilariously happy. Unfettered laughter that left them aching and weeping with their jaws cramped. And Sara buried Joanne Sutton's evidence back into her subconscious.

Chapter 9

Verbesina encelioides. The Latin classification sounded more allur-
ing than 'wild sunflower', the species checklist translation. It
was commonly known as a South African daisy. Dan put down the
list and shifted up the terracotta lounger. His face was completely
sheltered by the beige umbrella. He half-shut his eyes. The daisies
merged into a bobbing block of yolky colour. The list was right:
it was an alien species. Native to United States and Mexico. Far
from home.

Dan was amazed by how easily he had adapted. He didn't like
animals. He was uncomfortable with domestic pets. He hated it
when Connie's cats, Rolo and Minstrel, unceremoniously pounced,
hairs rising. They smelled like a urinal. Lions up close and personal
had absolutely petrified him. Walking into black rhino, if they ever
found them, was going to be a potent test of his loyalty to Connie.

He had believed 'arid Savanna' to be exactly that. However,
there were four different but dominant grass species on the reserve.
This fascinated him. Dune Bushman's Grass (*Stipagrostis amabilis*)
was a hardy, tufted grass around two metres tall, which stretched
over the crests of sand dunes, preventing erosion. Then there was
the flowering Sour Grass (*Schmidtia kalahariensis*) held responsible for
Lizzie's hay fever, though he thought the Lehmann's lovegrass
(*Eragrostis lehmanniana*) was probably the culprit. It was an invasive
weed that produced large monotypic stands to crowd out other

species. Lastly, there was the bulky grass cover provided by the Silky bushman grass (*Stipagrostis uniplumis*).

He lay on the lounger thinking about grasses. He imagined telling his most fractious client, Rebecca Finkelman, that her new garden north of Orvieto was to be made up entirely of African grasses. The thought made him laugh inwardly. He could see the entire circular garden dense with two-metre high grasses.

Dan was drawn to the Kalahari in a way he had never imagined possible. It was the vastness of the land, the extremity of the sky, which appeared to fall on top of the earth. The Korannaberg Mountains were a cartoon image, towering over the flat veld. The veld was not some amorphous mass, but dense with fascinating species of flora and fauna. It struck him as he looked beyond the daisies to the horizon that if he had a strong desire for anything, it was a yearning for land. A place to physically grow his own roots after two arduous decades of doing it for clients.

'I don't want to go on about it, but it hardly compares with Ibiza, does it now?' Alan said, yet again.

Alan was flat on his stomach, tanning his back with his head tipped to Dan's side.

'It was luxurious in Ibiza. It was like, you know, five star. This is three star, I'm telling you, at a push.' He raised himself up on to his elbows.

Dan carefully rolled over on to his left side. He stretched his arm out for his suncream, which was in the shade on the wooden cube table beside the lounger. He had already applied suncream. The move bought him some time before he needed to respond.

Dan hated hurting anyone. He hated confrontation. It scared him. When he thought about why he loved the group, it was because they were utterly different to him: lively, funny, opinionated and emotional. Confrontational. He often discussed his inability to express his feelings with his therapist off Harley Street, not far from his holistic nutritionist, who had recommended his therapist. He always drew Dan back to his feelings about being gay. He was convinced it was at the root of Dan's fear of confrontation or, as he called it, his 'fear of controversy'.

Dan didn't want to be different. He never had.

He had an idyllic childhood in the countryside outside York, attending the local school where his parents worked as teachers. He was sandwiched between three siblings: two sisters and a brother. They were a close family. He kissed a girl, a friend of his younger sister, when he was fourteen. It was pleasurable, even though she had railway tracks on her teeth. He fully expected it to be the beginning of a journey, through losing his virginity to getting married young like his parents.

Bristol changed that. Away from what, he quickly discovered, was a pretty sheltered home, he looked at his sexuality afresh.

Late one night, they were in Matt's room at Wills, slumped on every available surface. Dan was sitting cross-legged at the foot of Matt's desk. Matt had the Rolling Stones loudly blaring from his cassette recorder; Connie and Luke were dancing, twisting round each other's legs. The door swung open. It was a third year, back in hall for his finals. 'Turn that bloody racket off! I've got to leave for a race at five tomorrow morning,' he bellowed.

Guy Francis, Dan later discovered. He was a rower, generously over six feet with a mass of strawberry blond hair, tanned skin and vast hands. He looked like a farmer or a Thomas Hardy character, Dan couldn't decide. Maybe they were the same person. As Guy leant forward to make his point known, his shirt flopped open. It wasn't his chest that caught Dan's attention, more the obviously generous bulge in his jeans. Dan's own slimline version, tucked neatly into narrow jeans, stirred.

Dan didn't tell anyone. He was ashamed of his feelings, determined to bury it as a horny coincidence rather than... what? He didn't want to know. He wasn't wild or complicated. He didn't want to be lumbered with any label, let alone gay.

He went out with a friend of Connie's for nearly a year. She was pretty, almost beautiful. A solemn, dark-haired Italian girl called Elisabetta, who was eager to please. They had sex every time they stayed the night with each other, two or three times a week. Only he didn't think about Elisabetta at night. He fantasised about Guy. Still, he never confided in his friends. He assumed they were unaware.

The first weekend of their second year, they moved in to Harley Place. Finally, a house of their own together. They barely unpacked before Matt and Luke went to the supermarket, returning with armfuls of crisps, peanuts and cakes. They had six-packs of beer under each arm. Music blaring, they ate, drank and basked like lizards on the roof terrace in Indian summer sunshine. The sun sank coolly out of sight. They were profoundly drunk and turned to 'Truth or Dare'.

Luke went first. He chose 'Dare'. Sara instantly dared him to walk along the stone parapet of the roof terrace. Lizzie put her hand to her mouth; Connie smiled because she knew Luke wouldn't falter. Dan was happy and secure with his close friends.

It was his turn next. He had no desire to do desperate antics, especially as he was sickly drunk.

'Truth', he said without thinking.

It was Connie's turn. They smiled at each other. 'Are you gay, Dan?'

Dan's embarrassment was fast followed by acute pain.

'You are drunk, Connie. Or crazy,' he tried to say lightly. 'I was with Elisabetta until the summer.'

The others seemed to sober up. They were eyeing each other. It dawned on Dan that they had already talked about this subject, about him. He was mortified. As he tentatively looked up, he caught Sara's eye. All he saw was concern and sympathy. He realised he couldn't deceive the group.

'Yes, I think I am.'

They cheered. It was overwhelming. The love and support of his friends. They forced Dan to be brave and honest.

Back with the group again, Dan's concern about his relationship with Alan was increasing. The real problem with Alan was there wasn't a problem with Alan. Dan loved him – they never argued, had sex regularly and had created a home together. Yet something was missing. Something intangible, but real. A growing certainty that they couldn't move forward together. They didn't share a future. What that future was exactly, Dan was less clear.

'I'm burning.' Alan catapulted off the sun lounger. He stood barefoot on the decking. 'Christ, the decking's burning hot and all.' He hopped his feet into his black flip-flops. 'It's too hot to lie in it.

Ibiza is perfect for sunbathing.' He pulled his silver Ray-Ban Aviators down his nose to inspect his body. 'Crazy or what – I'm burnt on my elbows and knees.'

He waited for Dan's reaction.

'Poor you. Maybe you missed those spots.' Dan was genuinely sympathetic. 'You need to put block on your elbows and knees.'

Alan wasn't listening. 'It's the bloody bed burning me. We need towels. In Ibiza, they brought them out automatically.'

Without another word, Alan strode towards the lodge. Dan closed his eyes. He wished they didn't have such a long break between brunch, which they had eaten quickly at nine thirty, and their drive out at five thirty this afternoon. It was too much time to think.

'Daniel, hi there.' Katherine sat easily down on his sun lounger. Her tiny behind close to his elbow. Her red hair swung evenly out under a vast white straw sun hat, luminous above her pale yellow sundress. 'A penny for them.'

Her enthusiasm for English idioms amused Dan. He was fond of Katherine because she had made Matt happy. Katherine was warm and kind. Qualities that Lizzie and Sara purposefully failed to spot.

'How are you feeling?' Dan asked, touching her white arm, narrower than a child's.

'Do you know, it's all in my head. It's the worry about Dawn, the surrogacy. The stress of the whole issue really.'

'I can imagine.'

'Matt has been brilliant. There isn't a man on earth who would be as supportive as he has been to me. I rely totally on him.'

'He is wonderful, but you deserve each other.'

She eyed him penetratingly. He felt uncomfortable and sat up, reaching for his white T-shirt.

'Back to what's on your mind. What's going on with Alan?'

He was nervous of Katherine's directness, but he couldn't help looking to see if Connie and Lizzie, who were sunbathing on the other side of the pool, had heard her.

'Nothing,' he said automatically. He didn't want to confide in Katherine, much as he liked her. If he was going to share his thoughts with anyone, it would be Connie or Matt. 'It's all good.'

'Good? You don't look it,' she stared at him.

'Every relationship has its ups and downs.' Does it? He wondered.

'Have you talked about it?'

He was silent.

'You must express what you feel, Daniel. Open up.'

He looked up at Katherine, hoping to evade her questions by being vague with his answers. 'It's an issue of moving forward.'

To what? He wondered.

'Don't get me started on that, Daniel,' she wagged an index finger vigorously. 'It's an issue for man or woman. Gay or straight. For me, it was about moving on to a family. It was non-negotiable. Matt totally got the deal. Hey, I was up front with him.'

Dan had a disquieting sense that he didn't know what he thought, unlike Katherine and indeed all the group.

'You need to explore it. Life is not a dress rehearsal. Tell him he needs to grow up.' Her pointed finger wagged at him. 'Tell him what's important to you.'

What was important to him? Maybe that was the crux of the matter, but he wasn't about to explore it with Katherine. He looked hopefully for a waitress. 'I had a wonderful fresh lime juice and water. Would you like one?'

Katherine was not in the mood to be diverted. She gripped his arm. Her hand was surprisingly cool, unaffected by the heat.

'You know, Daniel,' she held his gaze to make it clear this was a big deal. 'There is nothing that I wouldn't say to Matt, or Matt to me.'

Alan returned with a white-towel tower as high as his forehead. Matt watched him gingerly feel for the decked step with the toe of his left flip-flop. He eased down the first step and then the second. Dan watched him distributing the towels to Lizzie, Connie and Sara on the other side of the pool with an elaborate explanation of why they were vital to protect them from burning. Dan smiled at his childish eagerness. Alan sat on Lizzie's sun lounger for a while. Dan had noticed they were getting on well. He knew the rest of the group didn't particularly like Alan, maybe that was the reason Dan was feeling uneasy with him.

Alan started back in their direction. 'Now's your chance,' Katherine hissed, swaying nonchalantly inside with a casual wave of her hand at Alan.

'Is she all right?' Alan asked, as he handed Dan two towels. Alan was such a kind man, such a good man. Surely that was a more important daily consideration than some vague long-term view of his life?

'Yes. I think that she's anxious about the baby.' It probably did explain why Katherine was eager for him to confront Alan. She was passing her own anxiety on to someone else. 'It makes you question your life, I suppose. Wonder what it's all about.'

Subtlety never worked with Alan. The group was different. They read into Dan's silence, his pauses and his subtle asides. They understood him. After all this time, Alan should too, surely?

Alan was bending over, rubbing more suncream around his knees. Dan watched the cream get trapped in the dense brown hairs on his lower thighs until it disappeared. Alan stood up. 'Can you do my back?'

Dan got up, took the tube and squeezed a dessertspoon on to his hand. He carefully spread it across Alan's shoulders and upper back, before rubbing it meticulously in. The conversation they needed to have wasn't one you could rush in between applications of suncream.

Alan lay back down on his back. A blank canvas mirrored in his shades. After a second's hesitation, Dan sat with his bottom wedged beside Alan's elbow. It was easier to talk to Alan while his eyes were closed and behind sunglasses. Alan didn't move.

'Matt and Katherine, you know, their whole thing with this surrogate, Dawn.'

Alan didn't react. Dan was angry, he couldn't pinpoint why – it was something to do with his general lack of responsiveness.

'Alan, are you listening?' He heard his own impatience and tried to breathe slowly in and out.

'Yeah. Their surrogate, Dawn.'

'Well, it makes you realise. We're no longer young. We have to see the big picture of our lives. Do the things that are important to us.' Dan wished he could properly articulate this feeling he had. He wasn't on the right page of his life. He wanted something more grown up. What did that mean?

Alan didn't move. Dan wondered what Alan was thinking. Or whether he was thinking at all.

'Are you wishing we were old?' Alan finally said. 'I mean, who the hell wants to be middle-aged? Peter Pan, that's me.'

Of course Alan would bounce back with something superficial. Perhaps it was a victory, of sorts. He had made Alan state his fear of growing up, which exactly mirrored Dan's desire for it. He wanted the conservatism of middle age and his parents' middle-aged contentment. He had been craving it since he came out.

He didn't say anything. What could he say? He couldn't – wouldn't – argue Alan out of his viewpoint. Alan was what he was. Dan didn't feel disappointed, on the contrary, reassured.

Conscious Katherine might return to haunt him, he decided to escape. He mumbled excuses: emails to do, the heat. Dan slipped his feet into his leather sandals and walked slowly back to their room. They had no wireless signal there. He carried his laptop back to the lodge where the WiFi was strongest. He retreated up the spiral stairs to the library and picked the soft beige leather sofa closest to a cabinet displaying warthog horns. He opened up his emails. There were four from Rebecca Finkelman. She would have some complaint and he couldn't face it. He opened a note from their friends Marco and Pierre – a couple in fashion – who were suggesting a long weekend together in New York for Easter. The rest was a screenful of work emails. Was this his life? Then he spotted one from his old schoolfriend, Josephine, an artist who lived in a beamed attic in a tiny medieval hilltop town, fifteen minutes outside Florence. They had visited her once. They had slept on a futon in her art studio. Alan hated it. No beach, no luxury.

Dan clicked on her email.

Dearest Dan

I spied this house for sale on my walk yesterday.

You would appreciate the beauty of the setting. Olive groves encircle the house and lake, set in three acres right at the crown of a hill. The sunsets are spectacular.

It is derelict, but it has its original floors and beams.

Needs love, lashings of attention and taste. Which you have, of course.

A gardener's paradise for seven hundred thousand pounds!

Hope Africa is amazing?

Love, Jo xxx

The sun shone visible rays over ancient, squat olive trees. They appeared darker under its glare. The photo was filled with trees. Far behind them, a towered Tuscan farmhouse stood dilapidated, worn and faded. A symbol of endurance.

Dan brightened the laptop screen. He re-angled it until it was nearly vertical. Then he leaned forward and stared hard at the photo. He was searching for some missing detail. Something he couldn't see, but he was sure it was there.

Chapter 10

Matt intended to race out in search of Katherine. He replaced the guest phone into its cream holder, heaved himself up from the low studded stool and strode across the library. His sense of foreboding was echoed by the sound of his feet heavy on the worn wooden floorboards. Before he reached the spiral staircase, there was Dan uncharacteristically slouched on a low leather sofa. He was staring hypnotically at his laptop. His mood appeared to mirror Matt's, and he hesitated. Dan looked up, definitely distracted. Matt realised too late that he had projected his emotions on to Dan. Projected his emotions. What was he thinking? Katherine was getting to him. He was resentful. Why did he have to be the one who took the call?

Dan spoke, glancing up at him. 'Mattie, you okay?'

It was the same warm, generous tone he had used when Katherine had told the group about Dawn and their baby. The same warm, generous tone he always used. Matt was choked. What would he do without his friends? He knew what he ought to do – tell Katherine first. Perhaps if Dan hadn't spoken, he might have moved on, straight down the stairs, his arms reaching out for Katherine. But it was Dan. And Dan's kindness arrested him. He didn't want to move past him to deal with Katherine. He hadn't the strength. He bent down to sit beside his dear friend. Dan would be concerned, but loyal to Matt first and foremost. Perhaps it was the fundamental difference between friendship and marriage. The latter was a more complex cross-current of passions, needs and hopes that were beyond Matt.

'Oh Christ, Dan, it's over. I'm finished.' Matt gave a start after the words left his mouth. He had meant to say, I've had some bad news. Already, he was fast-forwarding to the end as he believed Katherine would do.

'Is it the baby?' Dan immediately asked. The emotional shorthand he had with Dan, Connie and Luke was wonderful. Matt had really missed them.

'Dawn's got pre-eclampsia.'

Dan's lack of reaction reminded Matt of his own as the nurse had spoken. It had sounded serious, but it had meant nothing to him.

'Which translated means Dawn's got high blood pressure and high amounts of protein in her urine. I don't know exactly what that means. The hospital says it's serious for Dawn and the baby. They might have to induce her.'

'Oh no,' Dan reached easily for his shoulder. 'Horrible. What an awful shock. You poor thing.'

Matt slumped forward, his wide hands spread over his knees. He was sweating round the back of his hairline and down his neck. It was hot up here. He looked up at the thatched roof. From inside, you couldn't see the damage the baboons inflicted from the outside. For a moment, he madly thought of escaping on to the roof. It made him think nostalgically of the roof terrace in Harley Place. If only life was that simple. He wanted to go back to their room, have a freezing shower, lie down and try and think straight. But he was bound to bump into Katherine.

Dan continued brightly. 'Listen, don't worry, Mattie. You read about women giving birth eight weeks early all the time. The baby will go into special care for a while. It will be okay.'

Matt didn't know whether it would or wouldn't be. He was logical enough to know that. He had a sickening yet certain knowledge that followed a third port. A hangover to end all hangovers would follow. He suddenly realised that he wasn't even thinking about Dawn, this generous woman, who had put herself through

80

this physical hell for them. He was more concerned about Katherine's reaction to the news. And their future. And that revelation appalled him.

'I need a drink,' he moaned, resisting the intense urge to curl up in a tight ball on the sofa. He imagined Katherine's displeasure. How can you consume alcohol at a time like this?

Dan was up. 'Red, white or rosé? It's really hot up here. I advise white or rosé.'

He smiled. Dan would never offer him anything stronger. 'A pint of white please.'

As he sat blankly looking at his clipped nails, he heard Katherine's voice downstairs: sharp and refined as crystal. How could he tell her there was a problem? After she had spent months imagining issue after issue: worrying for Dawn, worrying for the baby, worrying for them.

Dan nudged a glass into his hand.

'Mattie, you should tell her.' The way Dan suggested it was gentle. 'She said to me that you can tell her anything and vice versa.'

'I am her rock. I know that.' He was upset by his voice, which melted away from him. 'She tells me every emotion as she experiences it, but I couldn't possibly do the same.'

Katherine was a beautiful, intelligent, successful, sexy woman; he was an overweight, divorced solicitor, whose ex-wife ran off with a partner in his law firm. The power was obviously in her favour. She had married him, undoubtedly loved him, but she could easily change her mind, move on, go back to New York. In any negotiation, there was a price. No baby, no deal. He stood up, appalled by his self-reflection, when his own flesh and blood might be at risk.

'What matters is the baby,' he said with a certainty he didn't feel. 'It's the baby that matters,' he repeated, before adding rapidly, 'And Dawn's health, of course.'

Dan nodded, before he said firmly, 'Exactly, Mattie. Why don't I google pre-eclampsia? It's good to know exactly what we're dealing with.'

'No, no. Please don't,' said Matt hastily, shuddering. 'I don't want to know.'

Dan nodded supportively.

Matt drew strength from him. 'This whole surrogacy issue is so complicated, Dan. It is counter-intuitive. To get a woman you don't know to carry a child for your wife. To pay her, ultimately, to have a baby for you. To me, it's modern life gone mad. I'm conservative, middle-aged and middle-brow. I read the *Telegraph*, for God's sake. I grew up in Hampshire. How have I ended up in this place, Dan?'

'Firstly, you want a baby and unfortunately you can't have one in a more straightforward way.' Dan always was able to put things into perspective. 'Secondly, you are in love with Katherine and she desperately needs a baby.'

Matt sighed. 'Yes, she does and it is far worse for her. But our marriage is so new and tender. Can it survive this? I don't know, Dan.' He had a clear head that came to him uniquely from a drink. It gave him resolve. 'I'm not going to tell Katherine about the preeclampsia issue. When the baby's born, even if she is premature, Katherine will be happy. All Dawn probably needs is a few days' bed rest. She's in good hands.'

Dan nodded. 'Of course, she is.'

'I'll only worry Katherine to a near breakdown. She'll insist on flying back, ruining the holiday for everyone. I can't do that to Connie.'

Matt was conscious that the whole conversation had been about him. Yet again. His marital problems. It happened easily with Dan because he was such a good listener. Matt was acutely aware of the imbalance. He corrected it now.

'Dan, mate, my decision's made. Now, I want to know how you are.'

Dan eyed him cautiously. 'I don't know, Mattie. Compared with the situation you are in right now, or poor Luke, there is absolutely nothing wrong with my life.'

'But...' Matt shifted his weight towards Dan, causing the sofa to visibly sink.

Dan sighed.

'You're not happy,' Matt said helpfully.

Dan relented, 'I suppose I'm not. Though even saying that I feel grossly self-indulgent. What is wrong? Absolutely nothing: I love my work, I'm doing well, I have a lovely home and I'm healthy.'

'So?'

'I'm not happy with Alan.' Dan blushed, as if what he said was a revelation. Dan had always been funny like that. Back at university, he believed that none of them realised he was gay. Now he thought his floundering relationship with Alan was equally invisible.

'It's a tiny thing that I cannot shake off,' Dan hesitated. 'I want to move forward, grow up somehow. I want the happy, conservative life my parents have got. Pretty difficult as a gay man living in London.'

Matt smiled. 'I never thought that I would be a divorcee living in a flat having a surrogate child. I thought I'd be living in Hampshire with three children and a nice homely wife.'

'So, Mattie, what to do about it all?'

'You need to get blindingly drunk and then spill the beans to that Ibizan beach bum of a boyfriend of yours.'

Dan laughed. 'Matthew, you are outrageous.'

'Oh God, I wish.'

Chapter 11

Jules walked unannounced into the bedroom. He didn't need to say anything. Not with her. He was an Alpha male. A man with broad shoulders and a broad mind. He was exactly her type. Fine hands. She fancied men with well-manicured nails. He closed the door behind him, locking it. His dark glint and charming smile was focused on her alone. She saw shyness, a slight sexual insecurity in it. She was the only one who did. She saw him when his guard was fully down. She smiled back. A come on with a certain sexy charm, but not too eager or brash. He had caught her standing there in her knickers about to have her siesta, tiny pink lace knickers that she had bought at La Senza. They were a little tight. But he would get more turned on getting them off her. He pushed her back towards the mosquito netting, firmly but gently. He parted it with one hand, moving her swiftly back on to the bed. 'I want you, Lizzie.' He was aggressive yet tender as he bit into her ear. His hands rubbed both her breasts. 'God, they turn me on. You turn me on.' One hand moved insistently down her stomach, which he caressed on the way down to the gap between her legs. She started to moan. 'Jules, Jules.' She was already wet. He climbed inside her. The force, the thrill. She was coming. She tried to stop it from happening. She wanted this fantasy to last. Jules. Her Jules. As he was meant to be. But he was so intensely in her recent memory that she came far too fast with an inward moan.

Lizzie used her top sheet to wipe between her legs. She turned towards the wall and fell into an exhausted asleep. The heat rash, which had driven her out of the sun, was completely forgotten.

Julian marched purposefully into their sitting room. 'The ex-Head of the British Army, General Charles Green, is staying here.'

Connie nodded and smiled, pointing to the phone, 'Lou.'

'That fantastic white-haired gentleman with a long lens camera that could belong to a wild-life photographer. He led our troops in Afghanistan,' Julian continued.

She smiled at his enthusiasm. 'As you can probably hear, Dad's thrilled because some old army chief is here, which means the Kalahari is the new place to network. Forget Davos.'

Julian smiled. 'Mum is being harsh, Lou,' he raised his voice.

Lou, their eldest daughter, was relentlessly sarcastic about Julian and his political life. Leo and Lou were the two who took after Julian – clever, outspoken and uncompromising. 'Charles Green. Oh that big knob. My God, Mum, he's going to bore you rigid trying to defend the wrongs of trampling nineteen-year-olds' boots over other people's countries. Then you'll have to have him for dinner. I bet you twenty quid Dad's already invited him. Go on, ask him.'

'Lou wanted to know if you have invited him to dinner yet?' repeated Connie smiling.

'I've got his card,' Julian flashed it triumphantly. 'We must invite them as soon as we are back in London.'

'Jesus, he is such a political pick-up merchant. Put him on, Mum.'

Connie handed the phone to him.

'Lou darling, don't tell me that scruffy, slouchy excuse for a boy-friend is in our kitchen, wolfing Sally's finest chocolate cake? Rolo should be content with Whiskas from his own bowl at home, while you take your brilliance upstairs to your desk to guarantee that string of A*s that you are more than capable of, if you ever pull your little toe out of Rolo's ear.'

She couldn't hear Lou's reply. Rolo was in their kitchen because that was where he was after school. The fact that his name was the same as their cat had led Julian into a cul-de-sac of jokes that heartily amused him. Even Lou, with her endless capacity for being the butt of Julian's humour, was annoyed, not least because he greeted Rolo with, 'Hello. Whiskas or Kitty Cat?' When Lou complained that he was humiliating the love of her life, that normal dads didn't behave this excruciating way, he pointed out that it wasn't his fault that her boyfriend's namesake was feline. Julian was happy to call him something else, but until he was re-named – the boy, not the cat – he couldn't take him seriously.

Connie left them to chat and went to lie diagonally across the wicker sofa on their raised, decked terrace, the outer edge of which marked the start of the reserve. The view was one hundred and eighty degrees wide and hundreds of kilometres deep. A kudu wandered past and then a trio of impala. A small part of her wished that the children were here to share it with her, though she delighted in being here without them. It allowed time for her life to breathe. She had thought more in the last twenty-four hours than she had in the last ten years at home. Of course, she was far away, she had physical and mental space to think. But it was also because her old friends were here, particularly Luke, which restored her past and gave her present some context for the first time in ages.

His watchful presence made her feel guilty with the benefit of hindsight. She had dumped him unceremoniously. She blushed thinking about it now. Connie was less certain and more dreamy, like Luke in many ways. But Julian had been sure, he had made her sure.

Connie knew that Julian would call her the next day. She hovered around Harley Place, uncertain whether to go out and avoid him or face the inevitable call. Lizzie also hung around. She watched Connie warily as they made lunch together in kitchen. Neither of them wanted to face what was going to happen. Connie didn't ask about Lizzie's date – an obvious omission. Back then, Lizzie didn't miss those kinds of signs. Luke was off playing rugby for the Wills Hall team. Connie was relieved. She felt she had already crossed a line.

Julian rang in the middle of the afternoon, by which time Connie was relaxed and had gone back to their room. Lizzie answered the phone. Connie remembered seeing her standing in their open doorway. She didn't say anything. She stared at her. Connie blushed furiously.

'Unbelievable. Why would you do this to me? To Luke?' Lizzie turned abruptly away.

Connie was too nervous to go take the call. She grabbed her jacket and cycled furiously to watch the rugby match.

As Luke spotted her, he radiated that golden smile and gave her his signature half-hand wave. She wanted to run on the pitch and hold on to him. When he came off at the end of the match, she kissed him passionately. He kissed her back, but as he pulled away, he noticed her expression and frowned.

They had stayed in the pub until late. By the time they got back to Harley Place, Julian had rung countless times. The group was stationed in the sitting room. They stared at Connie. She wanted to scream 'I haven't done anything'. Only she knew it wasn't true. She knew she was about to walk away from Luke and her life as part of the group. She was about to move on. Luke looked at the others and then back at Connie. There was nowhere to hide. They knew each other inside out.

The phone rang into the silence. No one moved.

Lizzie said, 'Connie, are you going to get it?' It hadn't been a question.

Connie looked at Luke, begging him with her eyes not to let her go this easily. If he grabbed and held her, if he declared his love for her, if he insisted he was never, ever going to let her go, she wouldn't have taken the call. He didn't. She could see he had already withdrawn from her. He had let her go.

'Hello, Constance?' Julian was enthusiastic.

'Yes.' Connie was numb, yet certain.

'It's Julian Emmerson. We met last night.'

'I know,' she replied.

He coughed slightly. 'I really would love to take you out for dinner, if I may?'

Connie breathed in with a new nervous energy that had always been alien to her. She was certain her life was about to change forever. 'Yes. Yes please.'

Julian waved the phone. 'Darling, are you okay?' He looked concerned.

Connie nodded furiously. 'Do you want to speak to Sally?'

Connie didn't. She should, if only to check she was okay, but she wasn't in the right frame of mind to dig back down into her domestic life.

Julian looked questioningly at her. 'Sally, all good at your end? No overnight guests? Thank you for safeguarding our castle against the great teen invasion.'

Julian was always good with people, Connie thought, not for the first time. Sometimes, she couldn't be bothered to speak. She was in her own head and had no desire to be forced to face reality. It was the reason Luke and Connie split up. They were both locked inside, neither had been prepared to face the other and discuss their future. Julian had forcefully presented Connie with an alternative way forward. A great and powerful alternative. She had taken it.

'Fabulous, good. Thank you, Sally. Speak soon.'

Connie relented and waved her arm at Julian, took the phone and stretched her neck to energise herself.

'Sally, hello. How are you?'

'Good, thanks, Connie.' Sally was always surreally calm. 'How is it?'

'Amazing. A real trip of a lifetime. I can't wait to show you the photos.' Connie felt guilty again. It was unfair, leaving Sally, seven and a half months pregnant, with four children, however teenage. 'Are you okay?'

'I'm great, thanks Connie.'

'Don't forget, my mother's on standby. If it starts to feel too much.'

Sally had the easiest pregnancy, as if she wasn't pregnant except for the stability ball sucking on to her belly. She never referred to her growing baby. Connie thought that meant the father had to be a sperm donor. Whenever Connie brought it up with Julian, he insisted she had no right to pry.

'Have a good week, Connie,' Sally said.

'Thank you, I'll call you tomorrow,' Connie heard her own neediness, which wasn't reflected in Sally's goodbye.

Connie forced herself not to be disappointed. Sally was

detaching herself because she was leaving. It was a wrench for her too. She was losing their whole family who had been her life for over ten years. She was planning to take six months maternity leave, which Julian rightly suggested they owed Sally, to bond with her new baby in her new home, a cottage in North Oxfordshire. Then she would get a job locally. Connie and Julian had helped her find an endearing two-bedroomed house outside the village of King's Sutton. It was a ten-minute drive to their constituency home. They could see her most weekends.

Julian was slumped down at the other end of the sofa with his phone. He sighed. He was doing that a lot lately. He seemed permanently distracted. She looked out across the reserve. Breathe and enjoy the view, she told herself. Only she couldn't. She didn't ask him what he was thinking about and he didn't ask her. He got up and dramatically swung back into the sitting room. 'Well, where is the phone now?'

'Back on the table over there,' She nodded towards the black receiver on the corner table.

He headed for the privacy of their bedroom. His voice could be faintly heard through the dividing wall. She released a tense sigh. She lay flat on the sofa and closed her eyes.

Focus on your breath. Don't let the thoughts get in the way. You need to breathe, stay calm and detach yourself from everything going on around you.

Her yoga teacher hadn't met Julian.

She heard his footsteps, less decisive now, walking back out on to the terrace towards her. He crouched down, leaning his shoulder against her arm. He stroked it like she was a child. 'Darling, can I get you anything?' He murmured. 'Iced water? You must be hot out here, poor thing.'

Afterwards came the concern, the tenderness. The predictability was reassuring. She knew that the phone call wouldn't change anything, wouldn't erase their life together. Just jolt it. She closed her eyes.

'You're getting a lovely tan.' His words were designed to soothe her, but actually they soothed him.

She opened her eyes and surveyed his face. She saw remorse scratched into his features. She pushed it away. She wouldn't deal with it.

'Fancy a sleep?' Forgive me, for I have sinned.

They moved independently to the bedroom. The elegant white room had a dark four-poster bed with the mosquito net hanging over the tall frame. It was in the centre of the room with an unadulterated view from it, through the glass door out to the reserve. Julian unwound her sarong with a mystified expression that he reserved for things utterly bizarre. He dropped it uncoiled to the floor. She stood in front of him in her white bikini, a bold choice, she had thought, for the first day by the pool. He looked her over appreciatively.

'You're in such great shape, Constance,' he stated, resting his hands on her hips gently jutting out above the line of her bikini.

As she sat on the edge of the bed and stretched her arms up to start unbuttoning his shirt, he re-played his conversation with Lou.

'I'm not convinced that bloody boyfriend hasn't moved in, in our absence,' he grumbled. 'Sally sounded deliberately vague.'

'Probably,' she said cheerfully. From this distance she didn't care.

She wondered whether there were couples out there who smoothly choreographed sex featured in films; who moved from under to over, up and down without awkwardness. Even after twenty years, Connie and Julian both tended to struggle to get Julian's boxers off while they were under the duvet. Trying to pull down his rather voluminous long board shorts, while he was on top of her now, proved next to impossible. They both laughed.

'I'm getting fat,' he moaned.

'Yes, you are.' Her only revenge.

'Bitch!' He mock-slapped the side of her bottom. 'You owe me big time.'

They were there. He kissed her. Every kiss made up for it somehow. Everything else was forgotten.

Afterwards, he was the first one to speak. 'I do love you, Constance.'

Whether he was begging her for understanding, or for her forgiveness was never clear. Ultimately, it didn't matter. She didn't say she loved him back. How could she? Her reserve was all she had. And their shared love of their family. The living proof of the strength of their history together. Only they had the same reference points. Connie rolled over and smiled.

The Emmerson clan always watched television in Connie and Julian's bed. The tradition started when Leo and Lou were little and continued despite the size of their family. Their bed got bigger, but it wasn't large enough for all six of them, which was exactly the point. They would loll over each other, fight for space, even resort to bringing their own duvets and pillows down two flights of stairs to Connie and Julian's first-floor bedroom. Yet they all loved it. It was a weekend night retreat from their busy teenage lives back into the heart of their family.

'Let's watch *Downton*,' suggested Connie, one night when they couldn't resolve their choice.

'Mum, nothing happens in *Downton Abbey*,' moaned Hector.

'It does,' pursued Flora. 'There has been a murder, off set without guns.'

'I think we should watch a James Franco movie,' murmured Leo.

'What about Monty Python?' Julian was always happy to suggest something he knew would never get past the teen police.

'Lame.' Lou rolled her eyes.

'*Life of Brian* is a classic. Facebook someone, they will tell you,' Julian insisted with a flourish. 'Your education is far from complete without it.'

'Not tonight, Dad…' Leo rolled his eyes.

'What kinda night is it, Leo?' Julian staged in a deep, lethargic voice.

'*We're the Millers*,' Lou sounded triumphant. 'It's out on DVD. It's funny in a wacky kinda way.'

'What?' Julian snorted.

'You know what I mean, Dad.'

'If only I did, Lou. I'm lost in oblivion.'

'It's supposed to be good, Dad.'

Julian grinned. 'Okay. Let's do it.' He bounced into the middle of Lou and Leo.

'Daaaad, move over. You lump.'

'Teen trash, can't wait,' Julian curled up beside Connie, resting his head on her shoulder and grabbing a handful of salty and sweet popcorn from the bowl, politically placed on Connie's lap to be equidistance from all the under age.

'Shush, Dad, quit the commentary: we're trying to watch the trailer,' Lou snapped.

Julian smiled, amused and happy. Connie smiled back.

Chapter 12

The grass scratched at Luke's legs. It was thigh high and dense. They were treading through it in pairs. Their steps created a path. He was glad he had bought a new pair of desert boots, which were perfect for safari on foot. He was with Julian, immediately behind Sara and Gus, whose gun was slung confidently across his lower back. Luke was wearing his new grey Gae T-shirt. An expensive 520 rand (which he automatically translated to around forty pounds), doubtless due to the San markings circling the chest, created by some South African designer.

Far away but as visible as a Barbara Hepworth sculpture in a field, three giraffes stood behind a clump of thorn bushes. Their preposterous necks towered into the blue. They looked outsized even out here. While every living creature was on the move and on the make, they were still and silent. The one furthest to the right was delicately leaning over the top most leaves of an acacia tree; while the other two held their fine heads high and looked unblinkingly at them.

'These three are girls,' stated Gus, 'Can you see their bellies are rounded?'

Luke thought their faces marked them out as female: fine cheekbones, mysterious eyes with elaborate mascaraed eyelashes and a gentle expression. Knowing yet unknowable.

After they had returned from their morning safari he went

straight to the massage hut in plenty of time for his ten-thirty slot. Kimberley was free and offered to start right away. Her hands were stronger than he had expected. He wore his T-shirt and didn't let her do his back, insisting that she concentrate on his legs and feet. She was a good masseuse and he let his mind wander. If only Julian knew.

'What do the blokes have?' Sara had to ask. 'Penises?'

Luke shook his head, as he did he caught Connie's eye. She was obviously thinking how crude Sara was.

'You could say that,' Gus seemed unbothered about Sara's behaviour. 'They have a penile bump in the middle of their bellies, eh.'

'They are calm,' Luke murmured. He was watching the giraffes, but he was thinking about Connie. She was so self-contained. Like his mother, come to think of it. Her easy silence was a welcome relief.

'They aren't silent, eh. They do have a voice box. Under extreme stress, they snort, even bellow.'

Under extreme stress, Luke had never bellowed. He had held his scream inside, never breaking his vow of silence. When Emma shouted, his heart would thud violently and his left eye would twitch. Even the thought of her would sometimes make it do that.

When Connie had left him for Julian, he had said nothing. They never had the post-mortem that any other couple would have after a three-year relationship. Matt and Dan had insisted they must talk. Luke had been sure that they had nothing to talk about. If she was leaving him for Julian, he didn't want to know why.

Gus continued, though he seemed to be talking more to Sara than anyone else. 'Most of the time, they use visual signals instead.'

Luke wished that he could communicate like that. Stay speechless and signal his needs. In one generational leap, his father had become an antiquated chauvinist. Dad religiously ate his dinner in silence, before adjusting his worn cushion – the one his mother had embroidered for him when they got married – and settling into his armchair for the night. When his mother had cleared up the kitchen, she would pour him a small whisky on ice. He would then light a cigar from the box on the side table beside him. He would watch one TV programme and then the news, while his mother knitted endless warm jumpers and scarves for Luke and the farm help. Nothing was expected of his father. Not that Luke minded cooking and clearing up. He was rather obsessive about domestic chores. It was relaxing to create order. Yet he envied his father's freedom from emotional demands.

'Those giraffes are as silent and self-contained as you, Luke,' Julian nudged him, 'You've finally met your match.'

Luke tried to smile. He avoided eye contact with Julian. He was surprised at how much animosity he still felt towards him. When Connie had taken the train up to London for her first date with Julian, he had spent the day clearing his things out of their room and moving them into the tiny box space at the back of the sitting room. He dealt with his feelings by boxing up anything he had that reminded him of Connie and putting it in the Harley Place loft.

Fifteen feet away from this graceful trio, Gus stopped and turned. 'Giraffes aren't aggressive. Though they do have a ferocious kick, so we won't get too close. I don't want to disturb them, eh?'

'Definitely not,' Connie said eagerly.

Luke smiled at her enthusiasm. Luke had been keen to see rhino, lion and buffalo. He had surprised himself with his fascination for these giraffes. They watched their safari guests with mild interest. They were poised with their legs slightly apart, like a catwalk model with an unreadable expression. Luke could imagine them being brought down by a lion and maintaining this dignity. He stood transfixed. He could only vaguely hear Matt and Katherine talking softly at the back.

Gus coughed to keep them on track before speaking more loudly than usual. 'Giraffes are the tallest and largest ruminants. They're even-toed ungulates.'

'Watch it, Gus,' Sara said. 'You are a bit free and easy with ungulates. Translate.'

'Even toed-hoofed mammals,' he said smiling. 'Lizzie will be delighted to know that their full name is *Giraffa camelopardalis* because their faces superficially resemble camels. But they are not in the same family, eh. They have more delicate features.'

95

Gus signalled for them to move forward. Luke shifted to walk with Gus. 'They are dark, aren't they? I imagined that they would be a lighter shade of brown.'

'Their markings get darker as they get older. These three are probably about fifteen.'

Before she had started the massage, Luke had vaguely imagined that he might have his first ever fling with Kimberley. She was lean, smooth and toned. Not an ounce of fat. She was an attractive girl for a one-night stand. Not that he had any experience whatsoever of having a fling. He had only slept with three women in his life. After the violence inflicted by Emma, he couldn't imagine exposing his body to anyone. Anyway, Luke couldn't make himself into the kind of man who could have casual sex with anyone. As her hands worked effectively up his thighs, Luke hadn't thought about sex with Kimberley. He had imagined making love to Connie.

Luke moved to one side ostensibly to take a photo of them together, along with Gus and his gun. Through his lenses, he watched Connie. She was wearing tight pale beige jeans and a flimsy white shirt, which reminded him of that nightie she used to wear. Her features were fine: her button nose, high, thin cheekbones, bright blue eyes and her brown-blond hair, which swept back to the nape of her long neck. He started snapping. He zoomed in, until he framed her from the arch of her neck to the tip of her forehead. He ran the risk of Sara noticing, or worse, Julian. He didn't care.

He quickly took a group photo. It was a great one. He had rarely seen his friends during his marriage to Emma, yet he felt even closer to them now, as if his suffering made his friendships more potent. He wished he could pour his heart out to Matt. Tell him everything about his relationship with Emma.

'Which particular species of giraffe are they?' Sara said peering out from under her khaki bucket hat. Luke gave her an affectionate tap. She looked like some mad zoologist from an era when women didn't travel independently. She was wearing a safari dress that was expensive and trendy enough to have an unflattering A-line that settled somewhere between her knees and mid calves.

Luke caught Gus looking at Sara intently. Luke wasn't socially astute, but he knew that look. Not that Sara or the others seemed to notice. Sara should come with a warning: approach with extreme care, will bite any stray male.

'There is only one species of giraffe,' Gus said.

He had taken long enough to answer to give Sara the opportunity Luke knew she loved to question him. 'Are you positive? I am sure that they said there were nine species on *Inside Nature's Giants*.'

Julian waded in. 'Apologies for my friend. One minute she's quoting Disney, now it's Channel 4. Please ignore her.'

Luke reluctantly noticed Julian's sensitivity to Gus.

Gus didn't back down. 'Sara, you are partially right. There's one species but nine subspecies defined by geographical areas. The one here is the South African subspecies. And there are about twelve thousand giraffes left.'

Luke gave Gus a slight wink. 'You got her there.'

Gus smiled appreciatively, even his smile made Luke think about love.

It was the first Friday night formal dinner at Wills Hall at the end of Freshers' Week. Luke was gawky in black tie with his second-hand academic gown hanging down over it. The first few boys he spotted in the corridor were in suits and ties. He must have misread the brochure. He stood nervously by the door, holding a half-empty beer glass for support. He rarely knew who to approach or what to say, but dressed as he was, he was incapacitated. He moved to stand by the high window and stared glumly into the room. He rallied a little and made a concerted effort to look out for the two boys he had met on his corridor: Daniel and Matthew. They were nowhere to be seen. He felt her first. She touched his hand with hers as she took his glass with her thin, cool fingers. He looked up nervously. He saw his own social anxiety mirrored in her face. It made him smile. She smiled straight back. She was almost as tall as him with impossibly long thin legs. A bright pink sequinned flapper dress hung off one shoulder blade as if she had carelessly thrown it on. She wasn't exactly wearing her gown. She had pulled it on as far as her elbows as if she couldn't be bothered to get it as far as her shoulders. The material bunched and ruffled along her forearms like a gigantic kimono. 'I'm Connie,' she took his hand with her free one, which she could just about release from the gown. 'I don't know anyone except that blond girl. She's called Lizzie.'

She waved at Lizzie's back. He hadn't been able to think of anything to say back. He murmured, 'Luke.'

'Luke, mate,' Matthew called loudly across the hall, giving him a vast wave. 'Hello.'

Luke reluctantly let go of her hand and turned to give him a half-wave back. He fully expected Connie to be gone by the time he turned back round. She wasn't. Connie slipped her hand into his. She stood beside him, waiting for Matthew with Daniel close behind. She didn't say anything. For a moment, Luke worried that she was expecting him to make conversation. He glanced over at her. She stood beside him in silence. He was relieved. He was happy looking at her. She had a delicate face and startling blue eyes that looked out at the hall with the same wonderment he felt.

'You look smart, Luke.' Matthew reached them in a suit and tie. He eyed Connie. 'Well, hello. Are you going to introduce me to this babe on your arm?'

Luke blushed. 'Connie, Matthew.'

Daniel was with them. 'And Daniel.'

She smiled at them. 'Hello.'

'Hello, lovely Luke. I hope we're not interrupting?' Matthew asked.

'No. Not at all,' Luke said quickly. He was sure his feelings were best kept in his head.

He sensed his mistake. She let go of his hand. He watched silently in horror as she made her excuses to Matthew and Daniel and pushed through the thick crowd away from him.

'Oh God, mate I'm sorry. We've botched that up for you,' Matthew moaned.

Luke tried to wave away his concerns. He couldn't speak.

'She looked keen,' Daniel insisted. 'She is beautiful.'

'Sexy too,' Matthew added.

Luke mumbled back, 'I don't think so.'

'What? You don't think she's attractive?' Matthew looked amazed.

'No, I mean…' What did he mean? 'Not my type.' What was he

talking about? He hadn't had a girlfriend. How could he have a type? If he did, she would be exactly like Connie, down to the height of her collarbones.

He looked to see where she was in the room. It wasn't hard to spot her. She was taller than most of the girls in the room, a beacon of vibrant pink.

'I can't believe it. The pair of you,' Matthew was exclaiming enviously, 'Daniel here has already been asked out. Can you believe it?' He gesticulated at a small girl with long dark hair.

'Lucky you,' Luke said, nudging Daniel warmly. He risked looking up again. She had her back to him. He reached for his drink, but realised that he had given it to Connie, or rather she had taken it.

'What about you, Matthew? Any girl caught your eye?' Luke diverted the attention away from himself.

'Oh, there are so many pretty girls here... I have to say I'm rather overwhelmed. Too much choice.' Matthew murmured. He was starting to sweat around the collar of his shirt.

'Exactly. Too early to choose.' He took another slug and passed it to Matthew.

People started to sit down at the long tables, which didn't have a table plan, unlike the High Table.

Matthew and Daniel led the way. Luke followed. They settled down into the L-shape of one corner with Daniel in the middle.

'Are these seats taken?' Lizzie asked. Connie stood behind her with another girl.

'No, no. We would be delighted,' Matthew urged. 'I'm Matthew.'

'Lizzie,' she smiled running her hand through her hair. 'Oh, and Sara and Connie.'

'We've met Connie,' Matthew insisted. 'Sara, hello. Haven't I seen you somewhere? Are you reading law?'

'Smart, you are,' Sara had smiled. 'How are you finding it?' She sat down next to Matt.

Luke looked down as Daniel got up. 'Why don't one of you sit between Matthew and Luke? I'll come round the other side.'

Lizzie moved round and Connie sat down next to Daniel, across the table from Luke.

He tried hard to think of something to say to Lizzie. 'What are you reading?'

'English. I absolutely love it. It's fantastic.' Lizzie smiled encouragingly. 'What about you, Luke?'

'History.' He tried to think of something witty to say about it, but he couldn't.

'Connie's reading history.'

His stomach lurched.

'Connie,' Lizzie called across the table. Connie looked up at her. 'Luke's reading history.'

'Really.' She didn't look at him, but added calmly. 'Daniel is reading English.'

'Goodness, really? Let's swop places, can we? No offence.'

Neither Luke or Connie moved or spoke, but Lizzie had enough momentum for all four of them. She squeezed one leg and then the other out and off the bench and moved round to Connie's place next to Daniel. Luke fully expected Connie to object. She looked at Lizzie for a moment and then silently got up.

She glided round to the space between Matt and Luke. He tried to make as much room for her as possible, pressing against the person on his other side. She didn't need it, even with Matt on her other side. She slid gracefully on to the bench. Neither of them spoke.

Connie moved his glass back in front of him. 'Sorry, I took it.'

There were fresh ones on the table in front of them. Luke had no idea what to say. 'No problem. I've got more upstairs.'

She paused, 'Well, then. I'll keep it.'

He risked glancing at her. She wasn't smiling.

'Please do.'

He couldn't keep the concern out of his voice. He was doing this all wrong. Connie's blue eyes rested on him for too long. She didn't appear to be uncomfortable. He looked straight back at her. He didn't know what to say. He simply reached for the hand nearest his on the bench. He slid his hand on top of hers. Her hand moved out from underneath. She lightly brushed her fingers against his. Luke captured her whole hand, trying to hold it without squeezing it. The feeling of her fingers gave him the most intense sense of belonging.

He wasn't wrong. She stayed holding his hand for three years.

Chapter 13

Gus's commentary was a loud TV in the corner of the room. Matt didn't want to listen, but a few facts struck him, however reluctantly. African buffalo killed around two hundred people a year. Hence their nickname: 'Black Death'. They were highly unpredictable, prone to charging. How great to get away with being that high maintenance. There was no political correctness in the Kalahari. It was okay to be a sexually dominant male throwing your weight around, and then roaming off in a petulant sulk behind an acacia tree. The African equivalent of hiding in your 'cave'.

The lone male buffalo's sullen brown flesh partially camouflaged him. Blessed with a body crushing any Seca scales at a gravity-defying nine hundred kilos, he couldn't exactly hide behind an acacia tree. Like a Welsh rugby player from the seventies, this beast was all body with no neck and drooping cauliflower ears. He might be mistaken for a farm bull, if it weren't for his horns. He was a mature bloke, according to Gus, hence one metre and sixty centimetres of horn, meeting above its eyes in a barnacled cliff of bone called the 'boss'. It used this ugly eyesore to head butt sexual opponents, sometimes inflicting critical carnage.

Matt was large, but not living out in arid Savanna. Sophisticated urban women deleted any reference to his naturally male genes. First Annabel. Now Katherine. He shifted his knees, which were pressed uncomfortably into the seat in front. He looked at

Katherine: beautiful, bewitching, yet reducing. He was a blokes' bloke, really. He enjoyed nothing more than watching a rugby game with a few friends and a few more beers. Get drunk, have a laugh.

He was so desperate to be accommodating to Katherine that he was masquerading as a Zeta male. Katherine had coined the phrase first, writing a feature in her magazine about the new trend for 'Zeta males': aka Matt, whom she described in detail, concluding he was 'perfect husband material'. An Alpha or Beta male was a neanderthal man hiding behind romanticised, socially acceptable labels, Katherine insisted. Not the Zeta male. He never did anything because he was a man. Oh no. The Zeta didn't think like a male; he didn't act like a male.

Matt was submerged by a wave of hopelessness. To rub it in, the buffalo emerged from behind the trunk. He was looking directly at Matt, challenging him. Are you a man or an urban wimp? Come on, prove it to me. What came next surprised everyone except Matt. He knew what was going to happen, what should happen. Natural law out in the Savanna, where Darwinism ruled over Twitter.

The buffalo charged. He moved with such speed for a hefty, old man that Matt was utterly transfixed. Matt wasn't scared at all. He was relieved. Things were as they should be.

The rest of the vehicle erupted. Katherine's voice was the highest-pitched. Dan's voice staccato: 'No, no, no.' Julian's predictably tense: 'I would love to make it back to London, alive, please.' 'What's going on? Gus, please talk to us,' Connie struggled to keep calm. Julian's firm retort: 'Keep calm, troops. Gus and Ben have got it under control.'

Unemotional, Ben murmured to Gus, who jerked through his gears, lurching them diagonally forward into deep grasses to the left of the track.

Gus shouted: 'You guys okay? As I have said, I would never take any risks eh?' He kept cracking on through the sand, whipping them away.

Who can outdrive a buffalo? Matt wondered, feeling calmer than he had all afternoon. The buffalo was charging, helmet down, feet pounding, though he was no longer moving in their direction.

He veered off, thirty degrees away from them. He slowed to a gentle trot. He decided that they weren't worth the effort. Nine urbanites? No contest. Matt smiled to himself.

He had called for an update before they left for their evening drive. His call came minutes after Dawn had been rushed through for an emergency Caesarean. Fleeing an aggressive buffalo enhanced his powers of sober observation. It was too late. They could never have got to the hospital in time, even if he had had the guts to talk to Katherine at lunchtime. They were far too far away to change the course of events in Manchester. All they could do was to wait, drive it out in the Kalahari.

There was no point in Katherine doing the waiting and worrying. He had made the decision not to tell her. He had to be man enough to live with it. Dawn, their baby's survival and their future were out of his hands. He was free for the first time since they had decided to backpack solo along this bandit route of surrogacy. Whatever the outcome, he regained a sense of his own freedom.

Katherine was keen to wait until they were married before trying for a baby. She had a strong sense of what was appropriate. On their wedding night they weaved back to their hotel, a kilometre from Katherine's parent's white clapboard house in Vermont. Two days before, Katherine had playfully thrown her last pill packet away out of the train window on the journey from New York.

As he fumbled to unhook her elaborate bodice, he said, 'Let's make a baby.' God knows if he actually meant it.

They didn't talk about babies again for four months. Matt didn't even think about them. Or the obvious fact that Katherine wasn't pregnant. Matt was simply excited to be living with Katherine. He was focused on helping her settle into London and her new job.

One night, he was opening a bottle of red wine when Katherine came up and took it decisively out of his hands and placed it firmly on the coffee table. Her expression was stern.

'I don't want you doing that right now.'

'What's wrong, Katherine?'

She folded herself down on to their sofa. 'It's four months. And I am not pregnant.'

Matt relaxed. 'It's early days yet, darling. Don't worry. You will be soon.'

Katherine pursed her lips. 'I'm not leaving this to fate, Matt.'

Matt nervously eyed the unopened bottle on the coffee table. 'Of course,' he said though he was not sure what she meant.

'We need to address our diets and our lifestyle.'

'Sure.' Matt was eager to meet her halfway. She was anxious, which was understandable. She desperately wanted to have a baby with him.

'No caffeine, no alcohol, no artificial sugar, no red meat,' she said. 'Lots of oily fish and vegetables and omega-3 oil.'

'I thought you were taking folic acid,' he countered.

'Omega-3 oil as well as folic acid,' she insisted.

Matt sat down beside her, holding both her hands in his and kissing her gently on the lips. 'Katherine, I know you're worried, but I don't think this is necessary. It's waffle generated by the magazines.'

'It is vital, Matt,' she insisted. 'Don't you see?'

Matt sensed this talk was premeditated and planned, which he felt put him at an unfair disadvantage.

She bent down to her handbag on the floor and brought out a card that looked like a cheap room temperature gauge. He waited. He already knew that if Katherine had her mind set on something, he was better letting her talk her way through it.

'An ovulation calculator,' she solemnly pronounced.

Matt tried to regain his calm. He had to talk her down.

He gave, he hoped, a winning smile. 'Sorry, Katherine, darling. We need to keep perspective on all this, don't we? It's only been four months.'

They made love, though Matt couldn't help wondering whether it was because Katherine had the desire or that the ovulation calculator determined it was the optimum night.

In the morning, she offered him a hot water with freshly squeezed lemon juice, instead of his habitual coffee. As he accepted it, he noted her hold over him.

He thought about the hot lemon, which had been the start of it, when he was waiting on one of the smart brown leather sofas at the London Women's Clinic in Harley Street. The reception reminded him of a successful businessman's hotel, where the decor signals stylish professionalism. The tiled flooring was only disturbed by tall potted plants, the right-angled sofas, neat cushions and unbroken lines of magazines upon a vast coffee table. The manicured interior didn't make Matt calm. Quite the opposite. He felt as if it were a disguise: making right the wrong of this highly interventionist, clinical way of making babies.

He stared at a pamphlet, entitled 'Getting Started', which Katherine had silently passed to him. He couldn't process what he was reading:

IVF
ICSI
Intrauterine insertion (IUI)
Egg donation and egg sharing
Surgical sperm retrieval
Surrogacy in the UK
Frozen embryo transfer (FET)
Time lapse imaging
Low cost packages
Egg Freezing
Other treatments

He looked anxiously at his shoes, hoping Katherine could sense his alienation. But she was focused. She wanted them to do the 'Three Cycle Package', she informed him on the Underground. Three IVF treatments for the price of two. She had already read everything about this clinic. It gave them the best possible chance of success against the lowering odds as she was over thirty-five. Having done extensive research, she was convinced by this service, unquestioning of the rights and wrongs of it.

Matt glanced at her. She was staring straight ahead, keen not to be diverted by his doubt. He wondered whether it was easier for her because she was American, used to paying for what she wanted. Matt was profoundly uncomfortable with it. He wanted a baby as desperately as Katherine did, but he couldn't reconcile it with the intensely uncomfortable feeling he had even being in this Harley Street waiting area.

'Mr and Mrs Carlton?'

Katherine sprung up. She didn't turn round to check he was behind her.

Matt struggled off the sofa and stood midway between the seating and the doorway. He was holding the leaflet. He debated whether to take it with him. He flung in back on the pile on the coffee table and walked slowly up the corridor after Katherine.

Chapter 14

Gus slowed down for a rare herd of impala, which gleefully danced in front of the vehicle. They were the most delicate of antelope. Spotless Bambis with skinny legs and catwalk faces. Lizzie was annoyed she had forgotten her species checklist. She must remember to tick them off.

'You have seen a lot,' Gus enthused to Lizzie, as she leant over the seat behind him. 'You should buy a lottery ticket.'

Lizzie grinned. 'We have, haven't we?' Gus was rather attractive in a boyish kind of way. He wasn't her type, of course. She was attracted to men, not boys.

'Do you use that line on every one of your guests?' Sara quipped from the back row without turning away from the impala.

If Sara was less fierce and more open-minded, she could probably have a fling with Gus, Lizzie thought.

'Sara,' Gus sounded annoyed. 'Honestly, you have seen a great deal in two days. Believe me.'

'We have. We really have Gus,' Lizzie said in sympathy. Sara could be harsh, especially with men. 'Now, what about your pet meerkats...'

'Habituated meerkats,' Gus insisted, 'They are not tame, eh.'

'Too tame for us, Gus,' quipped Jules. He was looking straight at her. A little tame for you and me, he meant. 'You see, Gus, Lizzie here would far rather be walking on the wild side with black rhino. Wouldn't you, Lizzie?'

'It is too tame, isn't it,' she echoed, 'Hardly compares with charging rhino, Jules,' she echoed.

When Lizzie first met Jules, he might as well have been a black rhino. She thought he was wildly sexy. He was a friend of her cousin's, who was two years ahead of her, and already had his own flat, off the far north end of Ladbroke Grove. His flatmate was Jules. They had been at university together, both reading PPE and determined to enter politics.

Her cousin made an overcooked pasta lunch. The two of them were both wading through a deep colourful bowl when Jules emerged in the doorway. It was the only way Lizzie could describe it. He filled the room. He was tall, broad, wearing a navy suit that made him look more imposing, even at twenty-two. He had a neat pile of rolled newspapers under one arm and a briefcase in the other hand. Lizzie didn't know any men who owned a briefcase. He had been interviewed by the Conservative constituency selection panel for a marginal seat in Yorkshire.

Despite being obviously grown up, he peeled off his jacket and tie, rolled up his sleeves and sat down beside Lizzie, equally determined to make her laugh, to charm her. She flirted back. When she reluctantly left late that evening to get the last train back to Bristol, he asked for her phone number. He rang Harley Place before she was awake the next morning. Luke stumbled out of the room that he shared with Connie.

'Lizzie. Julian someone or other on the phone.'

At the time, Lizzie loved Jules's decisiveness: he knew what he wanted and he went out to get it. Lizzie responded in kind, inviting him down for the night the following weekend.

Jules was right. Safari wasn't about turning up to a pre-designated site for a guaranteed close up of meerkats. There were two other vehicles already there. Apparently, a film crew from Wildlife TV had been filming them over several weeks. A student ranger had spent the last six weeks making them comfortable with human beings.

They walked up a track to an open stretch of land, lightly whispering with leggy grasses. There was no sign of any animal life.

A sweaty student, hot enough to have lank hair, stumbled over to them. She wiped her forehead on the sleeve of her khaki rolled-up shirt.

'Hi, Jane. How're you doing?'

'Hello, Gus.' Jane's vowels were pure Home Counties.

'Are you out here on your gap year, Jane?' Jules was obviously curious.

'Not exactly. I am training to be a ranger.'

'Really? An English female ranger. How fantastic. My daughter Lou would love to do that.'

'She would, wouldn't she?' repeated Lizzie to reinforce their connection. It was one of her great strengths that his children loved her and she was good with them. It would make everything easier.

Lizzie was beyond wanting her own children. She had had a crisis in her mid-thirties, about the time when she was turned down for the commissioning editor job, when tiny feet were all that mattered. Her body craved babies. The heat of biological urgency was directly related to the probability of pregnancy, which had dwindled to nothing in her mind. White coals were warm, but not glowing. There was no real chance of relighting the fire. Best to kick away the remaining charcoal, let it blow away on the breeze.

'So, where are these little pets?' Jules asked Jane.

Someone had to keep an eye on Jules. She knew he strayed. Not that it was his fault. She blamed it firmly on Connie. She had this amazing lifestyle: a gorgeous house in London, one in Oxfordshire, holidays and lovely clothes. But she didn't give Jules what he needed. Thankfully, Jane wasn't pretty. She was wearing a pair of wonky black classic Ray-Bans, which stood out on her blanched and spotty face. She had an unwieldy teenage body, which she held uncomfortably, hugging her arms under her breasts.

Jane was sufficiently intimidated by Jules into saying nothing. She walked away from them across an unprepossessing stretch of sand and grass strewn land. They followed her in single file. Luckily, otherwise they might have walked over him. One solitary meerkat stood high on his hind legs. He looked at Jane and then at Jules. They shushed each other.

Gus spoke. 'It's fine to talk, eh? Jane, will you tell the guests about the meerkats?'

The sweat pooled around the base of her neck, as she struggled to get started.

Jules wasn't the most patient person. Why should he be? 'Jane, where are the rest of them?'

Matt normally chided Jules when he was a little abrupt. He said nothing. He was unusually quiet. He looked absorbed by some private joke known only to himself. Katherine looked concerned. Lizzie wickedly wished that they had had some sort of row. She was ashamed.

Jane stuttered. 'You see, the one here. He's the one left.'

'And then there was one,' Sara intoned.

'Mmm…' murmured Jules.

Gus jumped in. 'Okay, Jane what you should explain is that it is an extraordinary achievement for us to be a few feet away from this meerkat. And it is the result of weeks of you sitting here, talking to them, even singing, I believe.'

They laughed.

Jane scratched at the acne on her neck. 'They seem to enjoy it.'

Gus laughed. 'Well, she is from England…' He waited for the protests to die down. 'This meerkat has been left here on purpose. He is a "sentinel". He is looking out for danger, while the others search for food, particularly scorpions, which they love. He will sacrifice his life for the group, eh?'

'We love a little self-sacrifice, don't we campers?' Jules smiled.

Lizzie spoke without thinking. 'Well, that's Connie's department.'

There was silence. She panicked. She hadn't meant to say that. She often thought Connie was a martyr, obsessed by her domestic life and children, but never said it aloud. Her own words shocked her. Connie was such a generous friend to her. She reached over for Connie's arm. 'Oh Connie, I was joking. God, with kids you have sacrificed a lot.'

Connie gave that infuriating unreadable smile. What did it mean? Her self-possession unnerved Lizzie. Why couldn't she say what was on her mind?

'Too right.' It was Luke, which made Lizzie feel uneasy. She had no wish to revisit that day in Harley Place. She wanted to remember the good times.

Matt sighed. 'What do any of us know about sacrifice? We lead such safe, little lives.'

Connie moved beside him and gave his arm a squeeze. Luke moved round to his other side.

Lizzie had had enough. They were getting too intense. She was left out of whatever drama was unfolding around her. She had an idea. One that she knew Jules would love.

'This meerkat moment calls for a tune.'

Lizzie had a great voice. She didn't have her own flat or a good job or a man, but when she sang in a bar or on a train people stopped what they were doing and listened. She had once sung for the group on the way to Connie's house in Oxfordshire and a man had moved from the next carriage to listen to her. She had sung for Jules late after that first lunch in her cousin's flat.

She gave a quick cough, raised herself up and swung out her arms. Her throat roared low, long. '*Summertime.*'

'Lizzie, you could make it big as a singer,' Alan called out.

She sang deliberately slowly.

'Yes,' said Jules. 'Go for it Lizzie,' he turned to Gus. 'She has a superb voice.'

She was excited. Vindication, recognition. She raised the volume. Singing out across thousands of kilometres of desert. Singing across a continent. Singing to Jules. She wanted to remember every breath.

'Oh, Christ almighty. They are coming out,' said Sara. 'Don't stop, Lizzie. You are the Pied Piper of the Kalahari.'

Lizzie glanced sideways. Four meerkats had popped out of several previously invisible holes. They stood, looking alert, looking at her. She lowered her voice slightly. Two more appeared. The group was more transfixed by the meerkats than her. She couldn't help sucking in a huge gulp of air and belting the next two lines. She was singing to Jules, to her best friends, to the meerkats, to the horizon. She was invincible. Nothing could stop her now.

When it happened, it was unpredictably violent. Like a quiet couple nobody noticed in the corner of a bar until the man calmly stood up and shot the woman in the head with a silenced gun. Then everyone retold the crime from their own standpoint, some having predicted it, others not.

The Black-chested Snake Eagle dived for the smallest meerkat. Its chocolate head and chest covering its white belly as it descended with chilling accuracy and swooped up its supper in one clean, faultless move. Down, down, up, up and seamlessly gone from sight. The eagle didn't falter, it didn't stop, it didn't make a sound. Nor did the meerkat. It hung from the eagle's mouth, limp, possibly already dead. Its lack of protest added to the horror.

No one said a word. Lizzie stopped singing. It was the first time she had ever been silenced mid 'Summertime'.

Chapter 15

Traditionally, a boma was a circular enclosure for livestock, created out of tall reed stakes. The same encircled space had provided British colonial officers with makeshift offices, and more recently sheltered tribesmen from the wind. Gae had converted this boma into a private outdoor dining area, where the roof was a navy sky sprinkled with stars. An open fire pit flamed with uninhibited craziness in the centre of the fiery red sand. Tall torch lanterns danced shadows round the reed stakes.

Their table was majestically alone in this seductive space. Sara sighed, a peaceful exhalation. This was the most beautiful dinner. The reserve's own springbok charred over the fire, the pumpkin delicately infused with rosemary, the lamb skewered with the same herb and the traditional pap – a light baked couscous – alongside the Thelema Cabernet Sauvignon was deeply satisfying. As she reached once more for the black earthenware pot of springbok, she was suddenly aware she was happy. Was she ever this happy in London?

She couldn't answer that question. Of course, she was stressed and unhappy after what had happened. Everything she had worked for her whole life was threatened. The question was when would it ever end? She hadn't thought about Joanne Sutton since this morning. She was physically far away. She had to move the same mental distance. It was the joy of a holiday that was alien. You could forget everything else, peel away the layers of your daily life. Only in her case, Sara wasn't sure what would be left.

Connie rose to her feet. Julian tapped his glass with his spoon in that annoying, pompous way of his. The group stopped talking, clattering.

'Pray be silent for my beautiful wife.'

'I'm not going to give a speech,' Connie was beaming, which made Sara even happier. 'I wanted to say that I will never ever forget being here with you, my dearest friends. Thank you for coming. From the bottom of my heart.'

They were moved to shout, even Dan.

'You know I'm no good at this public-speaking business,' Connie held one hand to the side of her face. It reminded Sara of Luke's gesture when he was shy. 'I've asked Gus to share the plans for the rest of the week.' Connie grinned.

Gus stood up. He was blushing. Sara smiled, imagining him cross-examining in court.

'Well, Connie should be filling you in, but here goes. Unfortunately, there's a storm coming in later tomorrow. But we should get you out riding in the morning.'

Matt shouted, 'I'll pay good money to see Julian on a horse.'

'What do you mean?' Julian snapped in mock umbrage. 'I was born in the saddle.'

Dan interjected. 'Julian, please. Gus, do continue.'

'Connie has booked the sleep-out deck in the middle of the dunes. It's incredible. Newly built. It's for a maximum of three people and she was hoping to tempt Sara and Lizzie out there.'

'A girls' night out,' Sara laughed, surprised by her excitement.

Gus immediately turned to her. 'Yes, it is incredibly beautiful sleeping out on the dunes. And extremely luxurious, eh?'

'I should hope so, Gus,' she teased gently.

He blushed again, which amused her. 'Well, then we are going to track that black rhino.' There was a cheer from Julian. 'Hopefully find you some cheetah and wildebeest along the way.'

He paused and fumbled in his pocket for a piece of paper folded into repeated, neat squares. He took his time, laboriously unfolding the paper. He was surprisingly secure and confident.

'Oh yes and then dinner out on the dunes,' he looked at Connie. 'And the finale… Do you want to say?'

Connie shook her head.

'Hopefully, if the wind's right, you will end the week on a balloon ride over Gae with John. He is a great balloonist from Jo'Burg.'

'Connie, that is amazing,' Luke said.

Sara stood up. 'To Connie. Without you we would never have been dragged kicking and screaming to the Kalahari.' She was overwhelmed by her feelings for each one of them. 'You are such important friends to me. I don't know why it's taken so bloody long for us to be together again.'

She sank back down. She felt the glow of friendship and, yes, even contentment. Julian got up abruptly and moved round the table in her direction. She tried to catch Luke's attention to avoid Julian's eye. She didn't want to engage with his snappy sarcasm. Luke tried to move his chair back in the sand, but ended up tipping it over. He struggled to right it. Connie moved to help him. They both stood up awkwardly and wandered towards the bar.

Sara sighed. Julian took Luke's place to her right, leaning in to her, smiling. 'Sara, you need a good shag.'

She rolled her eyes at him to show she could take the joke. 'What? Are you volunteering?'

Normally, Julian would have batted it back, but he frowned. 'On a serious note, Sara, I am worried for you.' He gently prodded the tablecloth to make his point. 'That crime reporter Alistair Bent has waded in. It sounds serious to me. You are following it, aren't you?'

She yawned elaborately, but her heart was accelerating. 'Alistair's a prat. He's only tweeting because *The Times* will never print his rubbish.'

'I'm not sure. He insists that new evidence is going to come to light.'

It needs to be a serious piece of evidence, Mrs Sutton.

'Has he got any ideas?' She feebly batted back.

Sara could see Joanne Sutton's cool eyes when she first took her through the sequence of events that early morning when Jade disappeared. By then Sara had been briefed, the Suttons were charged, Joanne Sutton was on bail and her story sounded highly rehearsed, even scripted.

Only Sara didn't see it. Her gut told her the exhibits were weak: her DNA on the teddy bear in the Range Rover boot and a signed witness statement from a neighbour who saw the Suttons leaving in Nigel Sutton's Range Rover the previous evening without Jade. The neighbour would buckle under cross-examination. It was a dark night, there was no street lighting on their lane; and there were tall poplar trees between the two houses.

How can you be sure of what you saw?

Of course, there was the risk the jury would believe her, but it was tiny. They had the best Scenes of Crime Officer, Lee Pattinson. He had scrutinised the Suttons' house, her Mini, his Range Rover. After twenty-five years, nothing escaped him. He only came up with a minute blood clot on the side of the Suttons' bathroom. It was Jade's blood. What did that prove? Pattinson's inadmissible opinion was Jade hadn't slept in her bed for several days, before the morning when the Suttons reported her missing. Of course, the large quantity of sleeping pills in Joanne Sutton's bathroom cabinet was noteworthy. But there was no proof that they gave them to Jade.

The jury would be in line with Sara's junior, John. How likely was it that a middle-class couple living a comfortable, happy life in shiny Pangbourne would murder their only daughter? If they had, where was the body? The police had done an extensive, repeated search, the most intense ever carried out in the UK. They had combed West Berkshire and all the surrounding counties, followed up on every lead that Jade's beautiful face had prompted.

Julian cut across her thoughts, persisting: 'He predicts a high-profile retrial.'

'Does he?' she said automatically. 'He's wrong about the Jade Sutton case,' Sara continued. Arguing always gave her confidence. 'What new evidence could come to light? Look, you would need the bloody body in their garden.'

Sara was unavoidably pulled back to that day in their garden. Joanne Sutton didn't eat any cake. Sara could have told that from her figure. She waited for Sara to finish her second slice to the point of pressing down the last crumb with a forefinger and licking it bare. When she had finished, Sara was forced to return to the seriousness of the situation. She ate desperately to buy time to figure out Joanne Sutton.

Had she lured Sara to Pangbourne under false pretences?

After his massage, Luke had made a conscious decision to avoid being alone with Connie. It was the best solution. When his chair slipped, she suggested they went to the bar. He hesitated, but she touched his arm and pointed to Matt, who was already there on his own. Luke relaxed and followed Connie through to the bar. Matt was balanced on the nearest barstool.

'Luke, Connie.' His face brightened.

'Where's Katherine?' Luke asked instinctively.

'Hit the sack. It's stressful.' Matt groaned. 'For her and for me.'

'It will be worth it, Mattie,' Luke insisted.

'Luke's right,' Connie added.

Luke glanced at her quickly.

Matt didn't seem to notice. 'Can we collapse on those sofas over here?'

They slumped down. Luke consciously took the end of Matt's sofa, leaving Connie alone on the beige one. Connie said nothing. She had that dreamy, faraway look.

Matt lurched up from the sofa and touched her lightly on one knee. 'Penny for them?'

She shrugged. 'Nothing. A little drunk, a little tired. But Matt, I am worried about you and Katherine. It's hard on both of you.'

Matt sighed. 'Yes, it is Connie. It's a madness. Can you believe it's me having a surrogate child? How did I end up here?'

He ruffled his hair, which made Luke smile. It was such a familiar gesture.

'Via Manhattan.'

They both laughed.

'And the bloody IVF clinic.' He groaned. 'I haven't told you, but we tried IVF three times.'

Luke squeezed his shoulder. 'Tough.'

'Well, we are too old to adopt. So here we are.' He bowed his head. 'The question is: what if it doesn't work out?'

'It will, Matt,' Luke said, he hoped reassuringly.

He sighed, 'Actually, things aren't great. First, I got a call from the hospital – Dawn has pre-eclampsia and she's gone in for an emergency C-section.'

'Oh my God, Matt,' Luke said. 'Why didn't you tell us sooner?'

'I told Dan.'

They both looked at Matt and then glanced at each other.

'I haven't told Katherine. I know, Connie, please don't start.' He held up his hands. 'It's in the hands of the gods. What good would telling her do? Can you imagine her worry and stress?'

Luke spoke first. 'I understand, Matt.'

'There is no right or wrong about these things,' Connie said calmly.

'There certainly isn't,' Matt agreed. 'It's a roller coaster. You can't imagine what it's like having Katherine pumped with hormones, making her crazy and exhausted. Not to mention the joy of squirting your load into a sample pot.'

'Horrible.' Luke wanted to say something more supportive. He gave him a hug.

'She was pregnant each time but never ended up keeping a baby.'

Connie took his hand. 'But you are still so strong together. You must share what's going on with her.'

Luke was jealous of Julian all over again. Did Connie and Julian really talk? They must do. What else held them together? He had always believed that they had better sex than she had with Julian. It wasn't vanity. He knew it in his gut. She married Julian for a long list of his dynamic qualities. Sex wasn't on it.

'You know, Connie,' Matt sighed. 'You are right, objectively. I'm the lawyer, but subjectively all I want is to keep Katherine. I love her.'

'I'm not sure that you keep her by lying to her,' Connie pursued.

Luke blushed. He lied to Emma. He said he loved her when he didn't. He had never told Connie he loved her. He took it for granted that they had a deep-rooted understanding. Only they didn't. He never stopped thinking about how much his silence had cost him. Early on in his relationship with Emma, he made a conscious decision to say he loved her. He couldn't express himself the way he had with Connie. He was instinctively distant from Emma. She knew his declaration was far from the truth.

Matt shrugged his shoulders with a certain resignation. 'Anyway, let's change the subject. Luke, what's it like being a full-time dad? Enlighten me.'

He eyed Connie before answering. 'Wonderful and challenging.'

Matt laughed. 'Only you could sum up something momentous into three words. Hah. I've missed you, Luke.'

Connie stared at him. 'You don't feel awful taking them away from Emma? I know you can be flexible with your work, but she was at home with them. She is their mother. You have made all three of them suffer.'

Luke wanted to shout at her. You have no idea what you are talking about. Right now, he wished she was Sara, or even Lizzie.

Instead he said, 'Connie, it's complicated.'

'Well, explain it to us.'

Matt looked away. He had never been very comfortable with the two of them together, Luke recalled. They had had a sparse shorthand that left Matt lost.

'Julian, do come and join us,' Matt said loudly.

Luke followed Matt's gaze to Julian looming in the doorway. He looked down. Julian wandered over. Connie gave that irritatingly over-bright smile she reserved for Julian.

'I'm ready to hit the sack. Constance?'

'Oh, I thought I'd stay up for a bit. We're catching up, aren't we? If you are okay with that? We can't call the children again until the morning, though Lou and Rolo are bound to be up...'

Luke watched her doing that charade she did with Julian. Julian made Connie talk too much. Luke was convinced it was because he made her nervous and insecure.

'Sure, why not?' Julian said. 'Good night, diehards,' he added with an exaggerated wave.

Connie waited until Julian was no longer visible through the window to get up from her sofa. 'I don't want to miss anything – I need to be nearer to you both.'

'Hang on, lovely, you sit here,' Matt insisted. 'In between us: a rose between two thorns. I'll take your seat.'

Luke shifted slightly up the sofa away from Connie, but she moved towards him. 'I would love to see Ella and Finn again soon. What are they like now?'

Luke smiled. 'Ella is tall and elegant – she always wears dresses. She is strong with a great sense of humour. She's really wonderful,' Luke paused savouring the thought of her. 'Finnie is quiet and self-contained. He loves building anything but particularly Lego.'

'Like you,' Connie gave her half-smile. 'Has he got your old Lego set?'

Luke nodded and smiled back. Finnie was like him. After a particularly gruesome night with Emma, Luke was in the bathroom trying to aim antiseptic spray down on to his lower back when Finnie had walked in. Luke had rushed to cover himself with a towel. Without saying anything, Finnie had picked up the spray, moved the towel Luke was using as a shield and sprayed his back for him. It had been such a tender but terrible moment. He had realised his children were fully aware of what was going on. He wasn't saving them pain by staying with Emma.

He finally spoke. 'It's tough, but we are pulling through together. They are with my parents this week, having a great time on the farm.'

Connie slid her hand over his. He had to look up at her. Those blue eyes had been part of him for three years.

'It must have been awful. Divorce, I couldn't do it.' Connie quickly turned to Matt. 'And for you too, poor Matt. Of course.'

At the mention of his name, Matt lurched up. 'Luke, mate, I love you, but I desperately need to get some sleep. I've got a big day tomorrow.' He leaned over to squeeze his shoulder. 'Emma didn't deserve you. And we all love you. I do want to talk to you about it properly. We will, okay, mate?'

Luke gave him a half-wave. 'Don't worry.' He got up.

Matt pushed him back down. 'Hey, I don't want to break up the party. I'll see you tomorrow. Come what may.'

Matt had been his foil at university with his blustery good humour and down-to-earth chat. He had filled the gaps. Now Matt was gone, Luke sat in silence. He knew Connie would feel less obliged to talk. She too could sink into silence. He thought of her wedding present, which had saved him. He believed in the inevitability of his fate, particularly at that moment.

She gave them a vast canvas of grey waves painted as if the artist, Andrew Pollock, was himself in the water. Luke never lived by the sea, but he was drawn to it. Connie and Luke spotted some of Pollock's first paintings in a gift shop in Clifton. Luke fell in love with Pollock's art. They had no money, even though the artist's work was relatively cheap at the time. By the time he was engaged to Emma, Luke was already extremely wealthy. He could have commissioned a series of Pollock's paintings, but he forgot about his work and how happy it made him.

Connie dropped the painting wrapped in a brown paper and a huge purple velvet bow into his office. She didn't leave a card with it. Luke wanted to keep it in his office but he brought it home with him. It had been a stupid move.

Emma lifted the canvas off their open plan kitchen wall, propped it against the lower kitchen cupboards and took a knife from the block and punched it through the canvas. He raised his hand as if to try and stop her, but he knew there was only one way to do it. She wanted him to fight back and he could never give her that satisfaction. He remembered her words: 'Does this hurt? Do you finally feel something?'

The next morning, Luke started divorce proceedings. He asked his divorced business partner for the contact details of his lawyer. Luke told the lawyer what Emma was doing to him. He was the first person he told. Forty-eight hours later, Luke had a preliminary injunction in place and temporary custody of his children, pending the court case. He rented an empty house near the office. The following Saturday, he went with Ella and Finn to Lots Road and bid for a houseful of furniture.

'One more?' Luke spoke hesitantly into the silence between them.

'Yes, why not,' Connie said quickly.

Luke leapt up to find the barman. He was in the storage room behind the bar, getting changed into a pair of jeans. He gave Luke a friendly wave and suggested he help himself, as he was getting changed to leave for the night.

He heard Connie's giggles and looked up with a self-conscious smile.

'You're not a student now. What are you doing?'

He grinned back. 'The barman told me to help myself.'

They both laughed. Luke was beginning to relax. He sat down closer to her this time. 'Yours is large, after that comment.'

'Thanks. Are you trying to get me drunk?'

'Not difficult,' Luke bounced back, 'Only you can't steal my glass.' It was their joke after that first formal dinner. Luke was grateful when she smiled broadly.

'Connie, thank you for organising this trip. I love it. I might marry a giraffe next.'

They giggled. Connie stopped first. She rubbed her hand along his arm. He tried hard to look unaffected by her touch.

'Luke, tell me what happened with Emma. I thought you were well suited and happy.'

He frowned. He didn't want to talk about Emma. He wanted to enjoy being with Connie. She was watching him, the way she did. She read him as if he were transparent glass. His emotional nakedness in front of her excited him.

He put his elbows down on to his knees and rested his hands on the back of his head. 'Connie.' He mumbled, 'It was my fault.'

She looked solemn and dreamy, how he always thought of her. 'It was never your fault, Luke.'

They stared at each other, digesting what she had said.

'Yes it was. I never told you that I loved you. I don't know why.' He hadn't meant to talk about them. He didn't want to start this conversation. It couldn't lead anywhere positive. 'My big mistake.'

Connie blushed and looked away.

Luke pursued it. 'Julian said he loved you immediately, didn't he? If he hadn't, you wouldn't have left me.' Stop. Why are you doing this? You are friends again. Don't ruin it. She'll leave you sitting alone and unhappy.

Connie didn't leave, but she didn't answer the question. 'For the record, I should never have ended it the way I did. I always have felt deeply ashamed about it.' She turned to lightly touch his knee and quickly added, 'Not that it matters now, of course. It was a long time ago.'

'It was a long time ago,' he echoed.

'Luke, tell me about Emma.'

He remained resolutely silent. Luke felt a deep yearning for her and a huge sense of loss. She leaned back against the arm of the sofa. She took off her shoes and bent her knees up. Then she waited. She didn't say anything. It was the great joy of Connie, she always knew when he needed silence. It was a tremendous relief, like the end of a migraine.

'Okay. So tell me, Luke.'

'Tell me why you put up with Julian's affairs, and I'll tell you about Emma.'

Luke could see from the wrinkles tightening around Connie's eyes that he had overstepped the line. But he wasn't worried. She knew him well enough to know the question wasn't a gratuitous tit for tat. Luke wanted to know why Connie let Julian get away with it. What hold did he have on Connie that had eluded him?

'It's complicated.' She paused.

'I know.' It was complicated with Emma. He couldn't begin to unravel it.

'I was Julian's first girlfriend. He had never slept with anyone before me. He focused entirely on his future, even when he was a schoolboy. Then he became powerful and realised many women found him attractive. It flattered his ego.' She looked up brightly.

Luke shook his head. 'You are giving me his justification. I'm not interested in him. I want to know why you put up with it.'

'You sound like Sara,' Connie said.

'The children?' she said in a way that made it sound like a question.

Luke was silent.

'Okay, Julian and I have history. I have spent half my life with him. I cannot erase those experiences or that time. We have created a large family together. It's a profound experience. Julian has sex with lots of women, but he only has all those reference points with me.' She looked up at him, pleading for his understanding. 'I'm not saying that it doesn't hurt. It's incredibly painful at times.'

Luke gently nodded.

She continued, as if desperate to convince him. 'But we are a clan: unbeatable together, destructible apart. Julian is an amazing father and husband. We don't work without Julian. He's the lynch-pin. He drives us together and forward,' she paused and looked down. 'I'm ordinary without him, Luke.'

Luke was angry. 'Rubbish, Connie.'

She shook her head. 'Emma?'

'I divorced Emma because she was violent.' Luke was calm, though he didn't risk looking at Connie. 'Never with the children. But it's why I have custody.'

She was the only friend he could ever have told. Matt would be ashamed for him, Sara aggressive, Lizzie dramatic, Dan too empa-thetic. There was only Connie. She hugged him. He instinctively flinched but she continued to hug him and finally he relaxed. When she pulled away, he saw the strain around her eyes. It hurt her, per-haps, as much it had hurt him. She linked arms and stroked his right shirt sleeve with her other hand.

'I'm sorry, Connie. I didn't want to tell you.'

She shook her head vigorously to signal to him that she was okay, though clearly she wasn't.

Luke tried to make sense of it all, if only for her benefit. 'I am partly to blame.'

'Don't be ridiculous, Luke.' She sounded uncharacteristically vehement.

'I didn't love her. But I said I did. It wasn't the truth. I couldn't share my feelings with her. She hurt me to get a reaction from me.'

'What did she do?' Connie's voice was small.

Luke hesitated. The details were incredibly intimate, like sex. How wrong was that. 'Connie, I'm not sure that I want tell you.'

'What did she do, Luke.' It was no longer a question.

'She hit me with things,' he paused. Luke ran his hands over his forehead. 'With china, heavy books, furniture legs, stone pots, even a drawer from a wardrobe.'

He added that last detail in the hope it would sound light-hearted, but he hadn't realised how hurt he would be all over again, speaking about it out loud.

Her arms enveloped him. 'Badly?'

He nodded. Pain was complicated. He stared at the palms of his hands. 'Internal bleeding, punctured bladder and stitches everywhere. The worst scars are on my back. It's a mess.' He looked up at Connie. She was watching him. He felt brave. 'She didn't want anyone to know, which is why she saved my face.' He smiled to give her relief.

Connie ran a hand gently down his cheek. He took her hand and held it.

'My head still pounds all the time,' he paused. 'I started running to regain ownership of my body. It does make me feel better.'

'I want to see your back.'

'Connie.' He looked up confused and scared of her reaction.

'I want to see what she did to you.'

He shook his head, trying to laugh it off. She kept her solemn eyes on him.

He stalled. 'I think that you are a little drunk, darling. I know I am.'

'I've totally sobered up.' She squeezed her arms even more tightly round him. 'And I want to see what she did to you.'

Men stared at him in the changing room at the gym. He had avoided the pool at Gae, wondering who would be the first to ask him why he didn't want to sunbathe, or even dip into the pool in this heat.

She held his face in her hands. 'Everyone's in bed. Take your shirt off.'

Luke was terrified and aroused. Everything was complicated in his head. He wanted to scream. He had never cried, even when Emma had burnt him with her cigarette. A tear appeared. He hastily wiped it away with the base of his wrist. This was his cue to go to bed, take some more codeine and knock himself out. Forget it all.

'I'm going to crash, Connie.' He didn't stop to linger, or risk kissing her goodnight. He headed towards the door without saying a proper goodbye. He expected her to get up with him. She didn't, nor did she watch him go. He got halfway down the path and stopped. He crept back to look at her. She was staring out across the bar. Luke walked away.

Connie didn't want to move. Her physical control made her calmer. She was absorbing the pain Emma had inflicted on Luke, and the pain she herself had undoubtedly inflicted on Luke. Less visible, but deep-rooted.

Julian met her at Paddington station for their first date, which was great because it was busy and she was slightly overwhelmed. They went on the Underground to Victoria. He walked with her on the inside of the pavement to a French restaurant in Pimlico. She talked too much, which was liberating. She didn't need to try to express herself with Luke, because he understood her totally.

Julian made it clear from the start that he had a gut instinct about Connie, which he intended to follow. She found that extraordinary. He was so certain. He told her funny stories about Conservative Central Office and about the constituents in the seat where he was volunteering. He kept up a steady flow of humorous anecdotes. He shared his hopes for his career in politics and why he wanted to be a politician. He was generous – he ordered an incredibly expensive bottle of wine – solicitous – insisting they move from their table near the door when she started shivering – and bashfully charming – he bought her flowers at the station before she left. She was flattered when he didn't kiss her. Instead he declared he loved her. Did she fall for him simply because of that difference? She slept with Luke after the first formal dinner; Luke never said he loved her, though he certainly did. Julian's vocal certainty guaranteed Connie's. Luke didn't stand a chance.

When she got back to Harley Place at one in the morning, she stumbled up to their room, fully expecting Luke to be there. She was shocked by the half-empty room. She had never been quite sure whether it was Julian or Luke who forced the situation.

At the time, she didn't care. She fell for Julian easily and willingly. He was charming, expressive and attentive. He gave her a sense of direction. How could she know if she fell for Julian, because he was utterly different from Luke?

If Luke had declared his love, fought to keep her, she would undoubtedly have stayed, have married him and had children with him. It would have prevented the scars that they both shamefully hid from sight.

Chapter 16

A loud noise. Connie rolled over. Julian was snoring. She closed her eyes again. A thudding sound was coming from their sitting room. She panicked. Perhaps some kind of antelope had got inside? She stumbled out of bed. The banging was coming from the other side of their front door. Had they overslept? It was still dark. Her feet flinched from cold on stone floor blasted by the air-conditioning. She fumbled with the vast iron key attached to an equally vast wooden key ring carved into a rhino head. She managed to heave the door open. Dan was luminous in the dark in steel grey boxer shorts and a white T-shirt. He held up Matt, though she would have imagined it was a physical impossibility. Matt's shoulders were slumped forward, parallel to his waist.

She reached for him. It had to be the baby. She took him in her arms as she did with her children when a crisis shrank them back down to needy toddlers. Matt allowed them to lead him to the sofa. They placed him down gently. He didn't speak. The noise he was making was eerie. It was hard to believe that it wasn't coming from outside on the reserve.

'Dan?' she looked anxiously at him for answers.

He spoke gently. 'I don't know exactly, but Dawn was rushed into hospital for an emergency C-section last night.'

She nodded. They were both silent, sandwiched on either side of Matt, trying to relieve his pain by shouldering his bulk. He was wailing in anguish.

'Katherine?' she mouthed to Dan over his hunched body.

'I don't know. He banged on my door.'

'Matt,' she tried to lift his shoulders. Failing that, she lifted his head holding his face in her hands. His cheeks were red hot. 'Please, Matt, talk to us.'

Matt's face was scrunched up; his fingers dug mercilessly into his palms, as if he was trying to transfer his internal pain outside of himself. 'Isobel, Isobel.' Once he started, he seemed unable to stop. 'Isobel.'

'Isobel?' Connie asked quietly, deeply disturbed to see Matt cry.

'We were going to call her Isobel.' He looked down at his clenched hands, shaking his head vigorously. 'She was stillborn.'

They didn't move. Tears came to Connie's eyes, and she and Dan squeezed Matt, both equally determined to hold him together. No one spoke. Matt was numb, shivering and slumped. Connie gently extricated her arm and reached across to the other sofa and grabbed the throw. She wrapped it round Matt's shoulders. He leant back against it. They moved to the edge of the sofa to allow him to lie down. He curled up into the foetal position. His eyes closed. They stood up. Dan gestured her towards the terrace. The air was starting to warm up, even though it was pitch black.

'It's awful,' Connie mouthed. 'Poor Dawn, can you imagine. The pain she must feel, poor woman.'

'Horrendous,' Dan sighed. 'I'm worried for Matt. How can he cope with another divorce?'

'Do you think that Katherine will leave him?' Connie was horrified. She hadn't thought about that.

'Well, I don't know. What do you think?'

'He's got to tell Katherine the news first. Or maybe we ought to tell Katherine. For Matt's sake.'

Connie didn't respond. They were in no rush to face Katherine. Connie wanted to savour the easy silence that she had with Dan for a moment. When she turned to face the sitting room, the sofa was empty. She looked at Dan. 'Should we find him?'

Dan shook his head. 'He would have said if he wanted us to be around. You know what Matt's like. Sometimes he just needs to work things out on his own.'

Connie was struck by Dan's insight. She squeezed his arm. 'What about a cup of tea?'

He nodded. They sat in silence while the kettle on top of the minibar boiled.

Finally Dan spoke. 'It's an awful thing to happen, but at least they are here with us on this amazing holiday.' He reached for her hand. 'It is great being together again.'

Connie tentatively added, 'And Alan?'

'He prefers Ibiza.'

They both laughed.

After a moment Dan sighed. 'Connie, I don't think that it makes any difference whether we are in south-east London or the Kalahari. Except being with you all gives me the courage to move my life forward. Alan doesn't want us to have a more grown-up life. He's an overgrown teenager.'

Connie handed Dan a cup of tea and sat beside him on the sofa. She moved her arm gently on to his shoulder.

'I'm not sure what exactly it means, "moving my life forward", except that I want to feel more settled somehow.'

Connie smiled encouragingly.

'Do you know what I think I want to do…' he paused, qualifying it. 'Well, I'm wondering…'

She nodded again.

'I want to leave London. Buy this land in Tuscany,' his sharp eyes scanned her face. 'I want to create real roots, grow things on my own land. For myself, not just for rich clients.'

'What a brilliant idea.'

He paused, 'I thought that we could sell the house easily. Of course, we'd need to raise a lot of money. It's seven hundred thousand pounds without even the cash to do it up. It's derelict.'

Connie wondered whether she could leave London, move permanently to their cottage in Oxfordshire, or abroad? She never thought about it. This holiday was the most adventurous thing she had done for twenty years. Of course, there had been the dark side of her marriage. But she believed that what drew them together was greater than what pushed them apart. Despite Julian's flings, they were side by side at the heart of their family, involved with each of their children. They were a strong, confident clan. However many quick fixes he had, he would never share that kind of relationship with someone else: the joy of having children together and the intimacy it nurtured. She had this unbreakable bond with Julian, which sustained their love against regular assault.

Thinking about Matt and Katherine was a timely reminder of how lucky she was. Did it matter that Sally was leaving? The children were growing up, but at least she had them in her life. Her empty nest worries were petty. First world problems.

Dan watched her. 'Are you all right, Connie?'

'Yes. I have my family. When I look at Matt's situation, I realise that I'm so spoilt.' She paused. 'And Luke's...'

Dan didn't pick up on Luke. Connie was thankful.

'I don't know, Connie,' Dan said slowly, 'You work hard at it, even though you make it look easy.'

'Do I? Well that's good.' She thought of his idea again. It was the perfect plan for him. Dan loved space, nature and a simple life. She knew he was waiting for her to ask the obvious question.

'What does Alan think about Tuscany?'

'Well, I haven't talked to him about it. Yet.' Connie could see his effort to look cheery. 'I wanted to try the idea out on you first.' He lent forward and squeezed both her hands tightly. 'I value your opinion Connie.'

Yet again tonight, she felt appreciated and nurtured by her close friends in a way that Julian never did.

Matt watched Katherine sleep. She was beautiful. She had an ethereal grace that English women, in his limited experience, couldn't rival. His eyes followed the fine line of her pale jaw from her towering cheekbones down to her fulsome mouth. Her eyes were unnervingly half-open when she slept, glinting at him.

He was numb and drained, but calm. His utter devastation had bestially burst out of him. He was thankful it exploded with Connie and Dan. Whatever the outcome of the conversation he was about to have with Katherine, he was going to be okay. He had friends, best friends. He didn't want to wake her, to break this beautiful peace with her hysteria and accusations. Yet there was a cruel side of him that wanted her to experience some of the pain that he had endured over the last twenty-four hours.

'Katherine.' He touched her lightly on her left arm, which was exposed in all its fragility on top of the sheet. 'Katherine. Please wake up.'

Her eyes sprung open, though she didn't move. His stomach lurched. He didn't feel strong enough to take her on. She focused on him, trying to get her bearings.

She gently moved her hand into his, 'Are you all right?'

The unexpected gentleness of this moment unnerved him. His tears burst from him, water falling down his cheeks. He shook his head vigorously. He didn't want to tell her yet. He wanted to suspend their life from the next stage for a few moments more.

Katherine sat up and, in one easy flowing gesture, hugged him tightly round his neck. 'Oh, Matt.'

Matt couldn't believe it. She simply held him tightly. His fear overtook his grief. She didn't understand what had happened. He had to tell her. He pushed her away. He couldn't order his thoughts into sentences.

'Dawn. It was an emergency. Isobel—'

'Dawn is okay?' Katherine asked. 'I mean, physically. She's going to be all right?'

Matt nodded silently.

She hushed him, as Connie had done, and took him back in her arms again. He thought he couldn't cry any more. The tears exploded. The stress, the grief and the pain, not only in the last twenty-four hours, but the last few years of trying for a baby.

Katherine spoke softly. 'I had this terrible feeling. It was wrong to me. Right from the beginning. It was wrong to ask Dawn to carry a child for us. I tried to hide it but I felt guilty. Thank God, she is okay. I couldn't have lived with myself if anything had happened to her. How must she be feeling? Oh my God, Matt, what have we done?'

She cried. Her tears weren't angry, but remorseful.

Matt was overwhelmed with gratitude and the realisation of Katherine's inner strength. He was in awe of her, as he had been on that first night in Minetta Tavern. He saw what he had loved in her:

beauty, intelligence, physical fragility and mental strength and sure-footedness. Matt was emotional and physically clumsy. Annabel had only exaggerated this weakness in him. Katherine made him feel light on his feet, light in his soul. How had he forgotten it?

'It's totally insane. But it is a kind of relief,' she said gently. 'I don't mean that I wanted Dawn to lose our baby. Oh God, no. But it is a sign to me that it was never right. This baby was not meant to come into the world. Do you see?'

He whispered into her neck. 'I thought you'd go mad with grief and dump me.'

'Oh Matt. Don't be crazy,' she lifted his head to hers. 'I love you. I couldn't survive without you, Matt. We will be all right. Really, truly. I promise you.'

They were silent.

'Matt, honey, I have to call Dawn. We have to be there for her. God knows. How can I ever make amends?' Katherine's eyes watered again.

'Of course. You are right,' Matt nodded numbly. 'I'll talk to her as well.'

'Well, honey, if you are up to it. I think that it's really important.'

'Yes. Of course,' Matt paused.

He was ashamed of himself for telling his friends first, even if it was Dan, Connie and Luke. What had he been thinking? 'Katherine, I was out of my depth... I lost a sense of what was important.'

Katherine reached for him and was about to speak, but he stopped her. He had to finish.

'It's you, Katherine. When you floated up to me in New York, you changed my life. I have been incredibly happy since I met you. Somehow in this fight to have a baby, I lost sight of that. I love you. I am proud of you. Especially now.'

Katherine wiped her eyes. 'Oh, Matt. You have such a big heart. That is why I married you, honey. No man has ever been as good to me. I thank my stars ever day for you.'

As they kissed, Matt knew what he wanted to do. He couldn't make a baby, but he could make love to his wife.

Chapter 17

L uke watched Connie from the top of the spiral stairs. She was sitting cross-legged on the floor, poring over a large old book. Her knees were pointing sharply out of her leggings. Luke had been looking everywhere for her. He wanted to see her alone. He hoped to make sense of last night, before they went out riding together.

He woke early with a sense of dread. Why had he told Connie about Emma? It was humiliating. She was bound to share it with someone. As his head pounded, he imagined her telling Julian. He avoided breakfast and had two large coffees in his house. After the second one, he walked into the bathroom. He took off his T-shirt and turned to look over his shoulder at his back. At least he hadn't been drunk enough to show it to Connie.

Connie was absorbed by the book she was reading. Part of him wanted to leave her in peace but his fear of exposure pushed him forward. 'Connie.'

'Luke.' She didn't look up.

She clearly couldn't bear to look at him. 'About last night…' What a cliché. He was a cliché of a battered man.

She slowly lifted her head from the book. 'Can I show you something?'

He nodded numbly. He sat down on the edge of the sofa, conscious yet again of her legs. She moved the book on to his lap. It was a photography book open at a page with a large black and white photo. A desolate, neglected African bush scene spread across the page.

'This was Gae in the 1940s, before my grandfather bought the land.'

'It's been totally transformed,' Luke acknowledged. 'Was he responsible?'

Connie nodded enthusiastically. 'The most amazing thing was he bought it as a hunting lodge, but then fell in love with the place. He was one of the first proper conservationists in Africa.'

'Amazing. Really impressive. Why did he do it? He must have left notes or something.'

'Yes, I was thinking exactly the same thing. I have asked, but I am going to keep looking through these shelves.'

Luke wondered whether he should pretend that they never had the conversation about Emma. It was perfectly possible. They had shut out most difficult conversations.

'Luke, I have to tell you something.' She looked up at him.

Luke was fearful, but he held her gaze.

'Matt lost his baby. He was going to call her Isobel.'

He was appalled. He hadn't even thought about Matt. He had only thought about himself. 'Poor Matt and Katherine.'

She nodded. 'It's awful. I've been sitting up here trying to distract myself – though I do want to know what drove my grandfather to become a conservationist.'

He waited.

'I've been thinking about poor Matt obviously,' she continued.

He nodded to acknowledge it.

'And about your situation.' There was an uncharacteristic firmness to her tone, which Luke took as a warning.

'Connie, I don't know why I told you what I did last night. I was drunk, definitely. I exaggerated. Please, don't start thinking—'

She held up her hand in a way that she might with one of her children. 'Don't insult me.'

Luke decided to come out with it. 'Please don't tell anyone, particularly Julian.'

Her expression was pained as if he had slapped her. She uncrossed her legs and quickly stood up.

'Connie.' He was pleading with her, but for what?

She obviously thought better of storming off. 'I was going to say, I was thinking about Matt and you, and reminding myself that you have Ella and Finn. Even Emma's extreme cruelty cannot take them away from you.'

Luke thought about the children a lot when he was low about Emma. He paused. 'And you have your children, Connie. Julian's affairs cannot take them away.'

Connie blushed and walked past him down the stairs. Luke stood there for a few minutes, giving her time to get away. Why did he have to have a dig at Julian? It was becoming a compulsion. Did he selfishly wish Connie's marriage to be as unhappy as his own?

He sighed, but moved on to the immediate issue: he had to find Matt. As he reached the red brick path leading down to their houses, Julian walked briskly towards him. He didn't see Luke.

'Julian?' Luke was hesitant. It was the first time he had been alone with Julian, even for a brief moment.

Julian looked up, but didn't slow down.

'Aren't you coming riding? We're both rather late.'

Julian unusually frowned. 'No, I'm not. Work crisis. Will you relay to the others?'

Luke nodded.

Matt opened their door only because he didn't want Katherine to be woken by the knocking. He didn't want to see Connie or Dan, whom he could visualise on the other side of the door. Matt wanted to stay wrapped round sleeping Katherine. She was the only comfort he needed now. But it wasn't Connie or Dan. It was Luke.

'Connie told me,' Luke started. 'How's Katherine?'

Matt sighed. 'Asleep.' He paused, wanting to get rid of Luke, but then remembered their conversation in the bar last night.

'Come in.' He opened the door wider to let him pass.

Luke didn't move. 'Would it help, Matt? If not…'

'No, please stay.' Matt realised he meant it. Luke's presence was soothing.

Luke walked as far as the terrace door. 'Why don't we sit out here? Then we won't disturb Katherine?'

136

Matt appreciated his sensitivity towards her, which he rarely experienced from his friends. 'Good idea. Coffee?'

'Yes, but I'll make it. You go outside.'

Matt watched him quietly busy, opening up the bar and plugging in the kettle. He had always been more at ease in the kitchen than Connie. Luke joined him, bearing two coffee mugs and a pile of biscuits on a tray. He handed Matt a milky coffee. 'I've added three sugars.'

Matt smiled. 'Katherine has made me cut down to one.'

Luke sat down beside. 'Well, I'm allowing you three today.'

'Thanks, mate,' Matt lifted his mug to clink Luke's.

'You must be devastated.'

Matt nodded. 'We were going to call her Isobel.'

'A beautiful name,' Luke said quietly.

'I'm gutted, Luke. It's too large, you know, to really process.'

Luke nodded. 'Too raw.'

'Do you know, Luke, it's strange how things work out. We're going through this terrible ordeal together, but I feel closer to her.'

'That's important.'

'I realise she needs me as much as I need her. A revelation really...'

'No surprise, Matt. You're a rock. Any intelligent woman can see that.'

Matt smiled. 'Thank you, Luke. You are too.'

Luke gave his closed smile and shifted his gaze out to a couple of impalas grazing nearby.

'Look, I'm sorry about Emma, Luke. Do you want to talk about what happened?'

'Not now,' Luke stood up. 'But I'm happy you found Katherine, Matt. Promise me, you won't let her go.'

They hardly saw a single animal on their way to the stables, shortly after Luke had made Julian's apologies. The fall in air pressure had compelled them to crouch low, close to home. All hunting trips cancelled until the storm blew over. The wind was whipping in. There was a warning grey shock of thunder on the far horizon. Gus was confident they would get their ride in before it reached Gae.

Connie explained to the rest of the group what had happened to Matt and Katherine and that they wanted to be left alone at the lodge this morning.

'Fucking awful,' Sara said glumly, leaning over their seat.

'It's terrible, isn't it?' insisted Lizzie, who was sitting beside Luke. 'Can you imagine? Well, Luke, you probably can't. You have Ella and Finn.'

Lizzie was right. Luke was lucky to have Ella and Finn. And he was glad he was here for Matt. They had been close at university, but their friendship had drifted as their lives had taken them in different directions. The more successful his company was the more Luke was absorbed by it, while Matt worked methodically but uneventfully through several jobs in City law firms. They had married different kinds of women. Unsurprisingly, Annabel and Emma had disliked each other; Katherine and Emma were even more antagonistic. It made Luke happy to feel close to Matt again.

Gus dropped them at a low, immaculate building with three neat paddocks creating a tight L shape around it. Gus wasn't riding with them. Instead, he settled into his seat beside Ben, confident to wait in the vehicle with absolutely nothing to do until they returned. Jason was leading their ride. Jason was tall and young. Jason stood too close to Connie and leaned forward too eagerly. 'Hi, Luke, I'm Jason. More Farmer Brown than City Slicker, I'm afraid.'

Luke smiled tightly. He found himself looking at Connie again. She was wearing tight beige jeans and brown jodhpur boots. Her white cotton blouse was decorated with evenly bunched holes, which exposed a glow of tanned skin.

He looked away too late. Sara was definitely watching him.

A couple of other stable hands emerged. Chaps were found; hats and boots fitted and re-fitted, as the group sat relaxed on two wooden benches, which backed on to the white washed side of the stables. Varying factors of suncream were produced, along with a dripping bottle of water, chilled short of freezing, for each of them. They were ready.

Jason gathered them in a loose circle around him. 'You are nine?'

Connie replied quickly. 'No, we are down to six, I'm afraid.'

'I have your questionnaires on your riding skills,' Jason gave a slow smile. 'Interestingly, the men said that they are intermediate or advanced. And the women beginners.'

Riding was an interest that Luke had once shared with Connie. 'You are certainly not a beginner,' he said to her.

Connie murmured, 'It's been a long time. I don't think I've ridden since I was up at your parents' in Dartmoor.'

'Why don't you ride in Oxfordshire?'

She shrugged. 'I don't know. Julian and the kids aren't keen.'

Luke was chuffed. 'You won't have forgotten anything. If you have ridden Sheriff, you can ride any horse.'

'Unlike this pair of Black Beauties,' Sara joked, 'I am an absolute beginner. Nothing understated about my testimony. The truth and nothing but the truth.'

Jason interrupted. 'Okay, I think that I've got the picture and hopefully the right horse for each of you.'

'A knackered, slow moving beast for me please,' interjected Sara.

It took quite a while for them to mount, fit their water bottles, cameras and phones in the storage pouches behind the saddle, adjust their stirrups, find their reins, measure them up in length, practise holding them in one hand cowboy style, and move backwards and forwards to get out of their parallel line. They slowly walked, pushing each other's horses out of the stable.

Sara caught up with Luke, less by design than by luck.

'We must stop bumping into each other like this,' she quipped. Her face reddening.

'Sara, you look like you have been exercising.'

Luke had forgotten how much he loved riding. His horse, Mamello, was almost seventeen hands, but otherwise reminded him of the dark bay Dusty he had had as a child.

'Ha, ha, gym bunny. I don't think this is quite the docile nag I had in mind. Do you think that Jason's got a sense of humour?'

Luke smiled. Sara got her overweight grey's head out of an acacia tree and once again bounced alongside him. She shot him one of her knowing looks.

'Luke dearest, please tell me that you are not going to do anything rash?

Luke didn't say anything. He wasn't sure that he knew what Sara was talking about.

'Think pragmatically rather than emotionally,' Sara urged. 'I always do. I can highly recommend it as the safest course of action.'

Luke didn't respond. His default position was saying nothing, particularly with Sara.

Sara quietly eyed him and spoke softly. 'Oh Luke, the only way is forwards. Going backwards is an act of pure nostalgia. It doesn't lead anywhere. Believe me.'

'Why not?'

Sara repeatedly jerked on her reins to try and get her horse's head out of another bush, but to no avail, except to make her breath laboured and her face close to purple. 'Connie will never leave Julian. She loves him. He gives her a sense of purpose she doesn't feel herself. Alpha males do that – they carry you along on their wave.'

Luke was cross with her for ruining his great mood. He didn't want to think about anything, certainly not Connie. He wanted to ride. 'I'm not interested in Connie in that way.'

Sara yanked up her horse's head to stop him from eating and they trotted quickly to catch up with the others who had set off through the deep grasses towards a gentle slope. Neither spoke. Once they were a few metres from the backside of Dan and Alan's horses, their two rides abruptly slowed to a walk.

Luke tried to focus on the vast, open grassland bare without an animal or mountain in sight, yet rich with the ochre soil and grasses. Only a gentle hill stroked the foreground to their right.

'Luke, you are cross with me. I don't want to spoil your ride,' Sara continued, 'But remember, I lived with you both in Harley Place, as Lizzie tirelessly reminds me. I know you are both at a crossroads, but running back to each other is not the answer. Who else is going to be frank with you? It's why you love me.'

'Do I?' he joked, before squeezing his horse's thighs and moving away from her.

Ahead, Jason was busy organising them into two groups. One would canter over the hill with him first while the other waited until he returned to accompany them along the same track. Luke led his horse right up to Connie's grey. 'Shall we ask Jason if we can break away for a proper ride?'

He could imagine Sara watching him from further back in the line, but he didn't care. He wanted to enjoy this wonderful feeling of being out on a ride in Africa. How many more moments like this was he going to have?

Connie smiled silently in agreement. She trotted over to Jason's side. She talked briefly to him and then rode back to his side, but she didn't stop. She started cantering off the path ahead. He cantered after her. His horse had an easy stride. As its hoofs hit the ground, Luke felt the joy of that movement, the wind stroking his face. He was utterly free. Connie didn't slow down to direct him round behind the hillside. She gave a loose wave of a hand as she pulled her horse's mouth round with the other. He followed her. Once they were out of sight of the others, she accelerated into a gallop. Luke urged Mamello on. Riding was effortless; it made Luke feel light and high. It was his definition of total freedom.

It was Connie who slowed to a trot. Her blouse was wet with sweat. They both started laughing.

'Whoa,' Luke heard himself shouting, 'Bloody marvellous.'

'Bloody marvellous,' Connie echoed.

Chapter 18

The sky was shouting with rage. Its charcoal fury was matched by a wind, which whipped over two umbrellas, even a sun lounger. The first fine drops of rain were already cooling the air. Despite the climatic chaos unfolding around them, Matt and Katherine were calm, leaning against one another on the sofa furthest from the terrace. Their own personal storm made this climatic one comforting and an excuse for them to sit and contemplate. They had two separate pots of tea in front of them and a large plate with only two coconut and date balls left.

Matt thought about their honeymoon in the British Virgin Islands. They had spent a whole torrential day inside their beach house. They had made love, talked, read, while watching the rain flood the beach. It was one of the happiest days of Matt's life.

Their conversation with Dawn had been difficult and painful. Matt and Katherine made a huge effort to be supportive and understanding of her loss; Dawn had been equally sensitive to theirs. It had been uncomfortable all round. Matt realised that they weren't the best people to comfort Dawn. She needed her family. Matt had been left thinking that they wouldn't keep in touch with her long term. They weren't friends, merely drawn together by their shared goal.

As he poured Katherine more tea, Matt tried to share his thoughts with Katherine. 'It's strange, isn't it? We've been so close to Dawn. Yet she couldn't wait to get me off the phone once we had sorted out the practical details.'

'Yeah, but it's totally understandable. Who are we really to her? We don't know her. It was an artificial situation.'

'You're right, darling,' Matt sighed, re-wrapping the throw around Katherine's shoulders. 'In a strange way, none of it feels real. When we see Isobel, it's going to hit home.'

Katherine squeezed his hand. 'You know, I'm really dreading it.'

Matt pulled her close. 'Yes, me too. Though I think it's important. I want to see her.' He paused. There were many thoughts slushing around his head. Matt was finding it difficult to focus on any one. 'Katherine, are you sure that you are all right about staying out here? We could fly out today. Connie would totally understand. It might be better.'

There was no right or wrong ultimately. Dawn made it clear she didn't want them to rush back in the UK and bother her.

'Honey, what can we do at home? Stare at our beautiful nursery?' she sighed. 'No, obviously we will be back in time for her funeral, but you know...' She trailed off.

Matt knew that it hurt Katherine that Dawn insisted that she organise the funeral. It was on her terms, on her territory in Manchester. Whatever the legal rights and wrongs, they had agreed. They were hardly going to fight her over it.

'We couldn't easily organise the funeral for Monday from here, Katherine,' he said gently.

'Yes, of course. I know you're right,' she said hastily.

'I'm not saying it's easy. Isobel was our baby.'

Katherine's eyes watered but she stared fixedly over the overflowing pool as if the storm could renew her strength. 'Yeah. She was.'

As Matt was trying to pull himself together, his tears welled up again. 'The funeral is for Isobel. And we are both going to speak at the funeral. You know, it's all right this way. Really.'

Katherine squeezed herself to him. 'Oh Matt.'

Matt looked up and saw Connie. She was in her tan jeans, which were dusted in Namibian sand. She hovered a few metres away. She was his closest female friend, and he would never forget the physical support she gave him when he found out. However, Matt wanted to

143

be alone with Katherine. How could anyone else truly understand? Connie had her four teenage children.

'Connie,' he said as she slowly approached their table.

She looked uncomfortable. 'I thought that you might have left already?'

Katherine answered quickly. 'No. We are not leaving. We've talked to Dawn, but she needs to be with her own family right now.'

'How is she?'

'Devastated.' Katherine's face fell. 'Naturally. Like any mother who has lost a baby.'

His chin wobbled, but he quickly spoke to Katherine. 'Though Isobel was *our* baby girl.'

Connie nodded. 'Of course.' She reached out and took both their hands in hers.

'Do they know exactly what happened?'

Katherine squeezed Matt's arm, leaving him to explain. She already knew that he derived comfort from the facts.

'It points to the pre-eclampsia. It was a strong contributing cause, combined with birth complications. Dawn unexpectedly haemorrhaged. They might know more after the post-mortem. It is hard to establish the cause of a stillbirth. Often they never know.'

Katherine squeezed his hand and continued for him, 'The funeral will be on Monday in Manchester. It's going to be special. Dawn's whole family is coming. I think that we will be able to share our grief with them.'

Connie took her hand as well. 'We will all be there, of course. If you would like us?'

Matt could only nod. Katherine squeezed his hand harder. 'We need you all, our close friends.'

Connie crouched in front of them. 'I know it's a terrible thing to happen to anyone. I can't begin to imagine what you both feel. But I know that you have each other.'

Matt turned to Katherine. She gave him that secret little smile, he remembered on their first night together. 'Yes we do, Connie. You are right,' he said, kissing Katherine.

The rain was light as Connie went back to her room. Her legs were stiff, particularly her inner thighs. She hadn't ridden for years. She had loved every minute of it. The total escape. They had seen hardly any animals, but it hadn't mattered. Connie felt liberated by it.

Their front door was ajar. There was no sign of Julian. She looked out on the terrace. He wasn't there either. She sighed. He had probably slipped back to the phone without Matt and Katherine noticing. She walked through to their bathroom, desperate for a cool, long shower. She gave a short cry. Julian was sitting on the closed loo seat.

'Julian, hello, you gave me a shock. Busy morning?'

He didn't respond. Julian would brood through an impending crisis, working out his own position, before bursting out with a detailed explanation of the Chinese whispers that had led him down the latest dark corridor. She glanced casually at him as she unbuttoned her jeans. His skin had a tinge, despite two days of sun. She ought to be the good wife. Ask what was wrong. But she didn't want to delve into the human entrails of yet another political situation after such an uplifting ride.

'Connie,' Julian said as if trying out her name. His voice sounded dry. 'How was your ride?'

'It really was exhilarating. I love riding. It makes me happy. Why don't I do it in Oxfordshire?'

'You must.'

When they were first married, Julian had encouraged her to do the things she loved. He was as proactive and as enthusiastic about the small details of their life together as he was his career. Not so any longer. When had it changed?

She dismissed the idea of telling him that she might have found her grandfather's notes. She spotted a pale tan school-style exercise book with his name, George Sanderson, written in loopy black, smudged ink on the cover. It was in a cabinet in the library. Of course, it might be sketches or more photos. Still, she was excited by the discovery. It reminded her of the thrill she felt researching history at university. The sense of adventure into an unknown past.

'There has been a coup in my absence.'

She sighed. She was right. She distracted herself by trying to

145

peel off her jeans, which were cellophaned to her legs by the extreme humidity.

'I can't work out who briefed against me,' muttered Julian, leaning heavily on his arms. 'My instinct is it's Susan. She benefits most from me resigning from the Cabinet. The PM would offer her Chief Secretary.'

He stood up, towering over her. She tried to inch her jeans down her thighs.

Connie guessed he was already in Westminster, fast-forwarding to the next cabinet meeting.

'Susan's a bitch,' he continued as if Connie had made a comment. 'She had it in for me.'

She looked up. She could only guess why. She didn't respond. Julian didn't require political feedback. He needed to vent his anger, work out his own solution and move swiftly to exact his subtle revenge. It was the way politics worked. Of course, even from the Kalahari, Julian would trace the mole. It was extraordinary he didn't already know for certain. Susan, if indeed it was Susan, would rue the day she started a war with Julian Emmerson.

Connie resorted to crouching with her bottom resting on the floor and pulling one leg at a time up thirty degrees, as she rolled the jeans painstakingly inside out and down her calves.

'I'm sorry, sweetheart,' he lowered his eyes to hers. 'I've rather botched up.'

She looked sharply. It was one of those idiosyncrasies of any long-term relationship: the tiniest things gave the greatest away. Sweetheart was a decidedly un-Julian word.

He raised his arms in a gesture of helplessness, gave a dramatic shrug. She had seen this act many times before.

'I'm sorry, Connie.' He sighed deeply. 'We have to go home. Face the music.'

'You are not talking about leaving now?'

'Well,' he sighed. 'The story is going to break in the *Mail on Sunday*. I need to be back before it goes to print. I need to counter it. Otherwise they will write: *Julian Emmerson is hiding from the press on safari in the Kalahari. Privileged bastard.* It will make it easy for PM to be bullied into letting me go.' He gave her the strong, purposeful look that had won her over in that French restaurant.

With a final, desperate shake of her right leg, she hurled the jeans across the white tiled bathroom floor. 'I am sorry, Julian, but I'm not leaving my friends in Africa on my fortieth birthday celebrations. Not to mention Matt and Katherine after they have lost their precious baby.'

She was taken aback by the vehemence in her tone, but delighted by it.

'I heard,' he murmured. 'Awful.'

'How could you ask me to leave them now?'

She stood up, sweaty and rather deliriously confident. It was probably the pre-storm humidity that had yet to completely melt away.

'It's…' Julian trailed off.

Such a tiny pause, yet such an obvious clue. When was Julian ever lost for words? Connie started to worry she had misjudged the severity of the problem.

'I've been tormented, Connie. You have no idea what I've been going through for the last seven months.'

She searched his face and saw his lost schoolboy look: *I've got into trouble, but it's not my fault, honest.* Connie wasn't about to break a habit of twenty years and ask him if his latest fling was breaking in *Mail on Sunday*. She had been publicly humiliated before, and she would be again, but she would rather sit it out in the Kalahari than in west London. Nothing would make her ask Julian about it; he would never volunteer the information. It was the power she had over him.

'Well, I am certainly not going home for that reason. In fact, that is a perfect excuse to stay.'

She turned her back on him and moved towards the bathroom door leading to the outdoor shower.

'Connie, we need to outwardly present a united front. There can't be any ambiguity,' he was pleading with her. 'This time.'

She frowned. She was angry with him for breaking their code of silence on the subject of his affairs. She couldn't help thinking of Luke's probing. She hated her friends being here to witness her latest humiliation. It would make it far worse.

'Why is it worse this time, except for my friends being here?'

'Connie, you know, I never, ever set out to hurt you.' His eyes were watering. 'It's Sally.'

She squeezed her hands, one on top of the other over her mouth, but a sound escaped somewhere deep in her throat.

'Connie, please, look. We both feel hideous. I didn't know how to tell you. I kept trying. It was never the right time.'

She looked down confused, expecting to see blood dripping down her leg.

'I was sorry for her. You know her story: late thirties and desperate for a baby. We both did, didn't we?' He lurched forward, trying to take both her hands and draw her back to him. 'But I love you, Connie. You know I do. God knows: I'm entirely in your hands.'

She backed away from him, hitting her head on the corner of the Yellowwood cupboard by the door. The knock made her dizzy, made her feel as if she might vomit. She went out of the bathroom. He didn't follow her. She stepped out uncertainly on to the path. Her bare feet touched the brick, but her body swayed, loose and lost. She kept looking at her hands. She was drenched by the time she reached the lodge. She walked round the back path to the deck. The rain was overpowering everything. She could feel it, seeping into her bra, down through her T-shirt, her knickers, her legs, pouring down her skin like blood. Blood everywhere. Blood thumping in her head. She walked slowly into the pool, down the steps, wading right into the centre. The water was part of her, it seeped into her skin until she was fully submerged. She was safe. But she couldn't let herself breathe. Her heart was bounding somewhere. She held her breath to suspend this moment. The longer she held her breath, the safer she was. The longer she held it, the greater pressure knocked against her eye sockets and against the back of her head, and the better she felt. Make it go away. Then slowly her mouth opened and she filled it with water. Her body was sinking as happily as her mind. She was where she wanted to be. Beyond consciousness.

She was being yanked up by her armpits. She resisted, trying to shake the hurt off. There were voices. Loud, insistent shrieks forcefully interrupted her calm. The soaked decking was beneath her. She heard someone being sick, repeatedly, until vomit swilled around her face. The voices sharpened.

'Give her some air, some space.'

'Connie.' Not Julian. 'Connie.' Definitely Luke.

She looked up at him. He smoothed her hair back from her face, as Dan wiped her mouth. Luke propped her head up with a towel and then moved her legs into the recovery position. He tucked a blanket around her shoulders.

The voices were too loud. She closed her eyes again, willing the shouting to stop.

'It's all right, Connie. I've got you.' She opened her eyes. Luke was crouched in front of the group, his face close to hers. They were all watching her with such concern, such tenderness. Here they were her oldest, closest friends. She wept for the first time in a long time.

Chapter 19

Lizzie spotted Connie slipping on to the deck in only her T-shirt and knickers. She was soaked. She waded into the water. Sara was thrashing everyone at whist and Lizzie was distracted. It was only when she looked up again at the end of the game that she spotted that Connie was still in the pool, under the water. It took Lizzie a second more to fully understand what she was witnessing. She stood up quickly to double check that she was seeing what she thought she was seeing. Then she screamed. She pointed madly, terrified that the others wouldn't understand the emergency. For once, her panic made everyone move. They jumped up as one from the table. They jostled each other down the decked steps, pushing past each other to get to Connie first. It was Luke who lifted her out of the water. He heaved her up the three steps leading to the decking. He wedged the towel under her head, moved her swiftly into the recovery position, banging her on her back to force the water out of her.

Lizzie was too shocked to do more than circle Connie, watching her repeatedly vomit. First water, then breakfast and lastly bile. Lizzie closed her eyes and then blinked several times to stop her own tears. Connie finished retching. She half-opened one eye and started weeping. Connie was weeping.

Lizzie was horrified. What could possibly have happened to make Connie try and drown herself? Something must have happened to one of the children.

Luke held her close to his chest as he carried her to a sofa; Dan ran to find a member of staff to call for a doctor. Luke sat holding her hands while Sara hurried to find water from the bar. Lizzie wanted to do something, but she couldn't think what to do. She was helpless and useless.

Luke gently cradled Connie's head in his hands. 'Tell me what happened.'

'Sally, my housekeeper, is pregnant. It's Julian's,' Connie spoke quietly to Luke, but they all heard. She was shaking uncontrollably, but turned to Matt and Katherine. 'I am sorry.'

Lizzie was shocked but equally appalled by her own self-deception. What on earth had she been thinking? How could she have intended to inflict this kind of pain and horror on Connie, her dearest friend? Considering how many years her fantasy about Jules had festered, her realisation was quick and utter. She was immediately ashamed.

'Connie,' she took the water from Sara and held it to Connie's lips. 'Here.'

'How fucking warped,' Sara gestured gently towards Matt. 'When you have lost your precious baby girl.' She reached to squeeze Matt's hand. 'He is a prize cunt.'

'Oh my God,' Matt paled. 'I don't think that I can deal with this.' He collapsed on the arm of the sofa and put his head in his hands. Katherine moved rapidly in beside him. 'I cannot believe that I'm hearing this.'

'He's a bastard.' Lizzie didn't think she had ever heard Luke swear before.

Lizzie had been living in a fantasy world, where the reality of secret sex didn't have consequences or ruin lives. Of course, it did. Everything had consequences.

'Okay, we need to think straight.' How like Sara. 'First question: is this whore out of your family home?'

Connie looked blankly at her. 'I don't know. No, I don't think so.'

'Don't worry. I'll sort it. I'll call your parents and get them go up there right now.'

Lizzie wished she had come up with the idea. They both knew Connie's parents. They had stayed with them numerous times in their university holidays and after they had left Bristol.

To make up for it, Lizzie insisted, 'I'll call them, Sara. You'll be far better dealing with Sally.'

Sara nodded. Connie appeared happy to delegate all responsibility. She let Dan and Luke comfort her. Dan held Connie's hands while Luke stroked her hair.

Luke murmured, 'Why did he tell you now?'

'It's going to break in the *Mail on Sunday*.' Connie said blankly.

'I don't understand,' Dan asked gently. 'How does Julian know it's going to be in the *Mail on Sunday*?'

'Politicians know what's coming up in the papers before the rest of us. They get tipped off.'

Connie spoke without a trace of bitterness, which disturbed Lizzie, but not for long. Julian walked in. His face was drawn. He anxiously scanned the room. Lizzie immediately could see he had been told, possibly by a member of staff, what Connie had tried to do.

Lizzie walked up to Julian and slapped him as hard as she could across the face. She had no idea she was planning to do it. A welt rose under his eye.

He looked genuinely hurt. 'Lizzie, I thought we were friends.'

'My friends don't behave in this despicable way.' Lizzie heard an alien steeliness in her voice.

'God, Emmerson, you think that you can talk your way out of anything?' Sara looked visibly upset. 'You are a vile coward.'

Matt interrupted Sara. 'Jesus, Emmerson, do you feel no shame? After what has happened to Katherine and me? There's you, cavalierly fucking your housekeeper and getting her pregnant?'

Julian tried to make eye contact with Connie. Luke was sitting in front of where she lay, while Matt moved to perch on the arm. Katherine was hugging him from behind, as if she wanted to shrink away from Julian.

'I love you, Connie,' Julian threw out into the room. 'You know that. And I'm not leaving here without you.'

'You are, Julian,' retorted Luke who seemed to be gaining confidence from the situation.

Julian turned on him. 'You've become very righteous all of a sudden. You ran off and left your wife, poor Emma, in not-so-sweet suburbia. Took her children away from her. You ask Connie what she thinks about that!'

Luke was shaking. 'I never lied or cheated on Emma or anyone. I have a conscience, a moral code.'

Julian sneered. 'Right. If you believe that.'

Luke spoke calmly. 'I've only slept with three women in my entire life. Connie was the first. I don't have such a fragile sexual ego that I need to fuck around.'

Lizzie was proud of him for his honesty.

'You took Connie from me to do this to her.' Luke whispered, barely getting the words out. 'Her own father describes you as an utter cunt. It destroys him to see how you treated his only daughter.'

Lizzie was shocked. She never imagined Luke was still in touch with Connie's parents.

The last person Lizzie expected to speak was Connie.

'Luke,' her voice was stronger than she looked. 'I made a terrible mistake for both of us.'

Julian tripped backwards catching the edge of the woven matt with his foot. He recovered his balance and strode out of the room.

Connie made an effort to sit up. Lizzie ran forward with cushions and support.

'Lizzie, I wasn't trying to…' Connie's voice was definitely her own again, which was such a relief. 'You know, I was in shock.'

'Of course, we know that Connie,' Lizzie held her tight. 'My dearest friend.'

Lizzie didn't believe her, but she accepted her denial thankfully. Connie was strong. How she could keep up appearances when her life was so bloody?

Lizzie was so lucky.

Connie sat dangling her legs into the pool, rocking them rhythmically up and down until her scarlet toenails winked out of the water. Her white vest had dried out. She was only wearing her knickers underneath. It was blazing hot. The storm might have never happened. The water stopped Connie from overheating, though she wanted to bake. Empty and free. She took several deep breaths and stared at the far horizon. Miles and miles of wild flowers, wild shrubs, wild life, freedom and space. It was achingly beautiful. She was emotionless. She had been rubbed out from the landscape and her own life. She couldn't stop her hands from shaking. The rest of her body had calmed down, but her fingers wouldn't. They quivered as if to remind her she was alive.

Someone sat down beside her. She didn't look round. The sun was overpowering, the sky deep blue and the wild life teeming and she wanted to sit it out in this heat on her own. Stay here until she was ready. She resented the invasion of the long slim legs that splashed into the water right beside her. Katherine, she assumed.

'Your husband's a bit of a handful, I hear,' stated a voice, matter of fact with not a shade of sympathy.

She looked up. It was Helen, the wife of the ex-head of the British Army. Connie had already forgotten their surname. She was in an ancient swimming costume, the type that slashed Union Jack coloured stripes unflatteringly straight across the thighs without a nod to a curve. She must have been in her sixties, but she had lean legs and boyishly short hair.

Connie didn't say anything. What was there to say? Helen's statement didn't seem to demand a response. Helen repeatedly dipped her hands into the water, pouring it over the loose skin under her arms.

'Political ones are the worst, I find. It's a haven for emotional cowards. They crave the power they don't feel inside.' She added wryly, 'Though, believe me, army men are a close second.'

Connie tried to smile. This straightforward conversation was a relief. The horror she couldn't acknowledge was being given ironic context.

'He is having a baby with our housekeeper, Sally. She's been living with us for ten years.'

She expected that would shock Helen. It would shock everyone in London. Can you believe? Have you heard? What kind of woman would put up with that? How low can he stoop? They would never know how it was at home in their daily life together. Sally was not some slut. She had been Connie's most trusted friend: a warm, unthreatening brunette who had been intimately part of her life journey, helping her bring up their children.

'Chekhov wrote, "No one can know the joys and the horrors within a marriage." Well, something along those lines,' Helen said.

Connie looked into the older woman's face.

'I've got my own saying: marriage is like hacking out,' Helen continued. 'You turn up at the stables and pick your horse: the constant grazer, the slow-moving nag who needs to be whipped into action, the frisky, high-maintenance thoroughbred and so on. The last will probably knock you for six at some point,' she paused, letting the thought sink in. 'You decide.'

Connie thought of Luke. Helen was right. She made her choice. She chose Julian. She turned to look at her. She wondered whether the army chief with his obsession with close up wildlife photography was the high-maintenance thoroughbred.

Helen continued, 'When you fly off, land heavily, bruised, your pride in tatters, your buttocks sore, do you get straight back on the horse? They say you should.'

'My husband Julian's going to back to London. To try and clear up the...' What was it? Connie wondered. How could a new life be a mess? It was a baby. Her shaking intensified and she crossed her arms over her belly.

Helen looked at her calmly, ignoring her state. 'Are you going with him?'

'No. I'm staying here with my friends. They've come all this way especially for me.' Even now Connie was hiding, only this time behind the group. Had she always been a coward deep down?

Thankfully, Helen didn't comment. 'You are lucky. You have a close gang of friends. I never quite managed that. We moved too often. Friendships came and went.'

Connie nodded. She was lucky. She appreciated Helen for sharing some confidence, however small.

'I suppose when your holiday's over,' Helen said, 'you have to make a decision: do you chuck him out or not.'

Connie stared at her. She was disconcerted by having her choice put so crudely. 'I might stay on here for a while.'

'Well, it's the most beautiful place on earth. We come here twice a year.' She looked out across the horizon. 'Although, I don't know about you, but I couldn't hide in paradise forever.'

Why not? Connie was tempted to ask.

Chapter 20

Sara hovered anxiously in the sitting room, watching Connie by the pool. How on earth would she survive this? When the army wife appeared and settled down beside her, Sara sat down, but continued to eye Connie protectively through the window.

Gus silently appeared, standing in the middle of the room. 'Ready, Sara?'

The sleepover. She had no desire to bounce back a witticism. 'Gus... how can I put it?' She paused. 'Something shocking has happened.'

Gus looked at her concerned, though he didn't ask what was wrong, or superficially fill the space she had left.

'I understand,' he said calmly. 'Why don't I wait round, eh? In case I can help in any way.'

She nodded.

He crouched close enough to the other end of the sofa to make it sag. It was the first time they had found themselves together without the group or the vivid backdrop of the safari. She could do smart retorts, but she didn't have an easy repertoire of small talk. She hadn't grown up around it. Sandra, her mother's best friend, only did gossip. This was why Sara stuck to asides, which involved her in conversation without complication or intimacy. One to one, she was lost. Only Gus didn't seem to be worried by her silence, or his own.

'You're a criminal lawyer?'

She nodded. He must have gleaned it from the others.

He smiled. 'High-flying, eh?' From anyone else, his tone would have been mocking.

'Not sure about that,' she retorted, back on comfortable territory.

'Connie said that you've won a big high-profile case, eh.'

He shifted his arm. His hand stretched towards her shoulder. His left knee was bent up and his boot missed the cream cotton ribbing. The thick tread of its sole turned up. His groin glared at her. Why were men oblivious of forcing you to stare into their crotch? She thought about escaping to lie down in her room, but she was worried about leaving Connie.

She didn't want to talk about the Jade Sutton case, let alone explain it to someone who knew nothing about the British legal system. Yet again, she tormented herself: if only she had never boarded that First Great Western train from Paddington.

She paused. Then, in a voice she hoped was sufficiently light, she said, 'Yes. A couple accused of murdering their child. They were found not guilty. I was representing the woman.'

Joanne Sutton. Would she ever get away from her?

Gus cut into her reverie. 'How did you know she was telling the truth?'

She stared at him. She was about to formulate a platitude, but decided against it. 'Why do you ask?'

He shrugged. 'Well I'm curious. I imagine it must be a problem for lawyers, eh. Locating the truth.'

She nodded.

He waited for her to reply, before elaborating as if she had failed to understand him. 'Is it the truth? You must always ask yourself that, eh?'

She answered automatically. 'The law is not about truth. It's about proof.'

'Maybe. But you, Sara Wilson, are a member of the human race. The truth matters to you, surely?'

'My only duty is to put my client's case forward, and not to mislead the court,' she insisted, trying to imagine he wasn't such a gentle, thoughtful person.

Sara had been sure the Suttons were innocent. Obviously. She didn't press Joanne Sutton as hard as she might a woman who was more deprived and desperate. She didn't question the middle-class perfection of Joanne Sutton until it was too late.

'Sure. I get that. As long as they tell you they are innocent, you're in the clear, eh,' Gus persisted.

Back with the cake in the garden. It was too much. 'It's far more complicated than that.'

There was the fear she had drowned in whisky chasers in The Elephant.

He paused and eyed her thoughtfully. Unlike Julian, who picked apart the facts, Gus was probing beneath the points of law to a place Sara couldn't go.

'Go on, try me.'

Sara saw a stubbornness she recognised and admired. When he wasn't working he was probably opinionated and headstrong.

'It's boring legal stuff.'

'No, I'm genuinely interested. Tell me what happens.'

'Is this some sort of out-of-court confidential?' she quipped, trying to avoid being drawn into the determination in his green eyes.

'Let's suppose they say they are innocent, but then change their minds? What happens then, eh?'

His stare was unfaltering. Something in Sara wanted to confide in him. Try out the truth on someone disconnected with her daily life.

'Well, I would have a duty to tell Joanne Sutton's—' Sara noticed her slip a second too late. 'My client's solicitor.'

He shrugged. 'What if you didn't?'

'God, Gus. You're getting down into dirty law.'

'Or dirty morals?'

She felt the blow. She thought of her mother and her considerable sacrifices she had made for her daughter's career. How could she explain to her that she had let her down? She knew Gus had no idea what he was talking about. He was simply making conversation. It was not meant as a criticism of her career or her behaviour. He knew nothing about the Jade Sutton case. Yet it was as if he could sense her discomfort.

She avoided his eye contact. 'Planning on retraining?'

'My cousin's a lawyer in Cape Town, but no, it's not a job I would ever consider.'

She tried to joke. 'What, the law's beneath you?'

He answered it as if it were a serious question. 'You know it's difficult to explain. My family is unbending. My father's a man of huge integrity, strong and inflexible. Not designed to be beholden to a set of rules, certainly not anybody else's. I am exactly like him,' he leaned forward. 'I know what I believe and what I feel. And I draw huge confidence from that.'

People didn't usually confide in Sara. Unless they were clients.

'We are a strong clan, who are extremely close. Farming families grow up together in the middle of nowhere. Integrity is our cornerstone. My dad or my brothers would horsewhip me for doing wrong.'

Wrong was a word that Sara hadn't heard in a long while.

He smiled gently. 'My dad is the strong, silent type with a dry humour. If he's unhappy about anything we do, he lets us know.'

'You're like him,' she smiled. 'You are hauling me up.'

'No I'm not. I admire you, Sara. The downside of a big happy farming family is you never have to make your own way, because it's expected you will eventually go home and farm the land. I am too comfortable to make the extraordinary effort you have for your career.'

She paused and spoke quietly. 'I had to make my own way.'

'Sara, I'm not knocking you, eh? Believe me, far from it. You are super smart, funny, strong and you care deeply about your friends.' He blushed faintly. 'They are clearly proud of you, eh. I've been wondering, why do you look deeply uncomfortable whenever they mention your victory?'

She searched in her mind for the appropriate response.

'I'm assuming that something went wrong?'

She almost confided in him, but she resisted.

'Are you going to be a farmer?' It was a diversion from the mess of her own life, but she was genuinely curious. She had never met anyone like him before.

He sighed. 'Eventually, yes. My family is one of the oldest farming families in South Africa. It's an estate, really: animals, crops and a vineyard. It's a huge undertaking. The Hamiltons are farmers. It's the way it is. My younger brothers already run the estate with Dad. They are expecting me back.'

She smiled. 'Rangering is a gap-year holiday?'

'Only I've been doing it for nine years. More escapism, eh.'

'What are you escaping from, Gus Hamilton?' she was imitating his tone, only he refused to deviate into pointless playfulness.

'Commitment, in all ways.'

'Oh, that old chestnut.' She smiled easily. 'Well you've come to the right person.'

'My life is mapped out. I can wait before I get on with it. I've always said that I'll go home when I fall in love and get married.'

'Settle down. How ghastly. Well don't do that in a hurry.' Sara mocked, 'No girlfriend then?'

'Jess and I split up. A few days ago, actually. She used to work here. We were properly together for five months and we've been trying to make a go of it long distance, but we've drifted apart.'

He blushed. A deep red that spread right under the roots of his thick hair.

'Oh dear. I'm sorry and all that.' Christ. One thing Sara couldn't stand was men who confided their emotional heartache. It was going to be worse because Gus was decidedly younger than her.

'No. It's fine. I wasn't in love with her.' His green eyes were straight. 'And she finds me too reserved and cold.'

'Are you?' Sara considered him for a moment. 'You don't strike me like that. Anyway, don't worry about it. The world's not reserved enough in my opinion. Why people go sharing their innermost thoughts with randoms, I've never understood.'

His face lit up. He was definitely shaggable.

'What about you?'

'What about me?'

'Have you got a boyfriend?' He was tugging at his leather bracelet, his head buried beneath his floppy hair. He was boyish, which made Sara more relaxed than she usually was one-to-one with a bloke.

'Do I look like the kind of woman with a boyfriend?'

He didn't answer.

She relented: 'No, I don't do boyfriends: tiresome little shits the lot of them.'

He eyed her drily.

'Nothing personal. I'm sure that you are the exception.'

He changed the subject. 'What about your family, eh?'

Sara gave him a warning stare. He completely ignored it and waited for her answer. She breathed in to affect that breeziness she had perfected.

'Once there were three: Mum, Dad and little me. Now there's two: Mum and me. Next question.'

Gus didn't say anything. He didn't move either. She was irrationally angry and knew she was going to say something she would regret.

'Not like your cosy clan of comfortable farmers communing on their chunk of South Africa. My mother has slaved at Manchester airport for years, doing all the shitty shifts to pay for my education, and paying the rent on a minute flat above a shop in the wrong part of Hume. She won't let the job go. Too proud, too independent to accept help from me.'

Sara couldn't shut up. She rarely talked about her childhood that she couldn't get away from her deep-rooted anger.

'No gap year for me. I had to make my own way, the hard way. Which is why this case is difficult and important for me in a way you cannot even begin to understand.'

He touched her gently on her shoulder. 'Okay, I get that. Let's return to the easier question of your legal morality.'

His gentle teasing gave her a way out. She was grateful. A rare emotion.

'If your client said don't tell my solicitor, what would you do?'

'I would be in serious danger of misleading the court,' she paused. She heard her voice fade. 'I would have to walk away.'

'Walk away?'

'Drop the case.'

'Okay.' He was subtly intelligent. 'I see.'

'Do you?' She whispered. 'Do you really?'

Gus frowned, reflecting the anxiety, which must be wrinkling round her eyes.

At that point Connie wandered in, protectively wrapped in a thick beige pool towel, which only made her look thinner and more fragile. She reached for Sara and hugged her gently.

'Oh, Connie.'

Connie didn't make eye contact. She nodded quickly and then looked at Gus. 'When are we leaving?'

Sara started, 'Look, Connie, I don't think…'

Gus segued, 'I was saying to Sara, you guys have got three more nights. The sleep out doesn't have to be tonight. After a storm's come in, maybe it's better not going down to the deck, eh?'

'No, we are keen,' Connie half-turned towards her. 'Aren't we, Sara?'

She was trying to work out if Connie really wanted to go.

'I am, anyway. Let's go. I might have a cold bath now. Half an hour?'

'Sure,' Gus soothed. 'Don't rush, eh?'

Connie nodded. 'Gus, can you do something for me?'

'Sure, Connie.' Sara was grateful for his warmth.

'There is a notebook of my grandfather's in the last cabinet in the library, furthest from the spiral stairs. I would really love to read it. Might I be allowed to do that?'

'No worries. I'll bring it with us, eh.'

Connie's wet feet marked the brick path. Sara turned to thank him for everything, but he had gone.

Chapter 21

Dan carefully considered which photo to show Alan first. Logically, it would be their generous landscape of olive trees, stretching suggestively into the middle distance with only a hill top hamlet peaking through the morning mist. The olive tree in the foreground looked like a menorah. He would gratuitously point this out to Alan, creating a spurious link between their Tuscan countryside and Alan's Jewish ancestors. He would try and create a sense of destiny about this move.

He changed his mind. He imagined an estate agent would try the same trick. Focusing on the land would mean one thing: the house was derelict. Alan would immediately ask and it would be a let down. He must show him the close up of the house first. The angle of the photo that Josephine had taken showing twin poplar trees planted far too close to the building. It meant Alan could guess at the marvels of the surrounding land.

Dan mentally listed the house's attractions: chimneys cornering the squat tower with arched windows offering spectacular views across the Tuscan countryside; the tiled roof ranging over the house, demonstrating its size and solidity; the deep wooden front door pointing to the weightiness of its history.

He looked again. He sighed. Alan would see that 90 per cent of the outer plaster peeled back to the brick; the windows were mere holes without frames; the roof tiles were either missing or unstable and all coated in lichen. Dan would try to compare it to a Surrey cottage in need of urgent updating: rewiring, possibly a new roof, kitchen and bathroom, a wall knocking down to make it more open plan, even some re-plastering. Only this Tuscan house didn't have electricity, or gas, possibly even a water supply. There probably weren't any rooms, even floors, certainly no fixtures or fittings. Except damp, woodworm, rot, decay, neglect. It was a soggy shell. No more than a very expensive Tuscan statement. Their home.

Given his obsession with home comforts, Alan wouldn't consider camping overnight. How could Dan believe he was going to persuade Alan to sell their modern home, move out of his linguistic and cultural comfort zone, borrow a fortune and more, only to sink it without a trace into this quicksand?

Dispirited, Dan was about to shut down his laptop when Alan appeared to find him. He bent down, coiling his arm about Dan's shoulder and whispered in his ear. 'Come on, you. I'm feeling horny. Let's go back to the room.'

Alan leant down further to kiss him, and Dan met his lips for a much-needed reality check.

'What the hell's that?' Alan was staring at the close up shot of the house. 'Don't tell me: Josephine is setting up some sort of artists' squat. Ha, ha.'

Dan's mind was blank as they both looked at the photo. The Clash's 'Should I Stay or Should I Go?' beat into his brain and wouldn't budge.

Clearly Alan wasn't interested, Dan saw. What was he thinking? Why had he become so madly optimistic, he asked himself. This was some sort of mid-life crisis. He had to shake out of it. Alan couldn't hear the strumming in his head. He wanted to have sex, siesta and a slap up dinner, hopefully reduced down to the two of them, which was what they had done on holiday for the last ten years. Dan could easily enjoy every step of this three-stage plan. Happy holidays. Like Ibiza.

Alan stretched, yawned and stood waiting for him to close up his laptop and come with him to the room. Dan dreaded this moment. He hated confrontation.

'Josephine sent me that photo. It's a house for sale near her village.' He waited, but Alan wasn't going to help him out. 'It's got a huge plot of land filled with olive trees.'

'Oh yeah?' He pinged the string ties of his board shorts and then rubbed his balls.

Dan breathed in. 'I really want us to buy it.' Oh God. How ridiculous. He cringed at his own lack of subtlety.

'You are kidding me?'

Dan remembered the vegetarian Moroccan couscous dish that he had made many times, and kept making because Alan had never told him he hated it. It was only a friend who had eventually told him. It had been the start, the hairline crack in the egg still in its box. Alan had told Michael that his vegetarian couscous was like gerbil food. Dan's favourite meal, his Sunday-night supper, was only fit for a gerbil. Why had it mattered so much?

'Oh my God, I'm not joking.' Dan heard the acidic note in his voice. 'I want to buy that house and land. It's very important to me.'

'How much is it?'

'Seven hundred thousand pounds.' As he said it, he realised how ludicrous it was.

Alan's face relaxed again. 'Have you won the lottery, or something? We don't have a million spare cash lying around, Sunshine, cos that is what it would cost to get that dump habitable.'

Dan knew that he would regret this exact moment. It reminded him of the time he had purposefully smashed a crystal vase his mother had been given by her maid of honour. He had held it above their stone kitchen floor. His mother screamed, 'Don't you dare drop that, Daniel.' And he let it go. Afterwards, he cried as much as she had. Something had been lost that he could never get back.

'I was thinking that we could sell the house.'

Alan's outrage was limited to his eyes, which darkened. 'What? Sell our gorgeous home and move to Italy?'

Alan walked round the corner table and towards the glass door leading to the brick path.

The discussion, if it had ever been that, was over. Dan took one last look at the photo and shut his laptop. After what Julian had done to Connie, he should appreciate what he had. Alan would never ever cheat on him. He was a good, decent person. Dan was lucky. It was a crazy idea. It could be straight off one of those reality TV shows Dan watched incessantly.

We moved from Esher to Casolare with no Italian, barely any previous trips to Italy, not enough cash, no job, less sense. Surprise, surprise, we got divorced in the process. Here we are to share the horror of our mad life change. You can feel happy and righteous staying right where you are. Here's what we learned: you can take the boy out of east London, but you can't take east London out of the boy.

Dan didn't embrace change for change's sake. He relished stability. It was the truth.

He wasn't going to leave Alan.

Chapter 22

St Mary the Virgin church squats on the brow of Worldham hill in East Hampshire. It is an unexpected find down an ancient forest track, un-Tarmac-ed. Church Lane slips past a couple of Grade II listed cottages and on to the church. It was built in the early thirteenth century, probably on the ruins of a Saxon predecessor. The South Porch was a nineteenth-century addition, veiling a much-admired early English doorway, while the triple lancet windows inside were listed features in the church's history pamphlet on the shelf inside. Connie loved the tower, reconstructed in 1864. It was one of those short, square structures with a wooden bell cote. A rural note rising from its roof. The bell cote was added to an earlier tower in 1660. It was typical of many Hampshire churches. And to her, it was a symbol not only of Hampshire, but home.

Her dad had been a church warden at St Mary's for thirty-eight years. And Julian had been as eager as she was to get married there. A historical setting with chic London guests, a beautiful, skinny bride in an Alistair Blair wedding dress, bridesmaids (Lizzie and Sara) in Tara Jamon lilac shifts, and a circular marquee with retro food designed by Admiral Crichton thrown in. Her parents' vast English cottage-style garden was opened to the public once a year. It had been garlanded for the event. Connie's friends had danced the Ceroc into a dawn, which had seen Julian's awkward political types drunk enough to unknot their ties and stuff them into their jacket pockets, before flinging their sweaty bodies at her single girl-friends. Sara had ended up in bed with a colleague of Julian's from Conservative Central Office, whom she completely disowned at breakfast. Connie couldn't remember his name or face now.

Connie was sitting in the back row of the vehicle on her own. Lizzie and Sara had taken the front seat. They spotted animals and chatted to Gus, but discreetly left her out of the conversation. She leaned forward and shouted over to Sara. 'What was the name of that man you got together with at our wedding?'

Lizzie groaned. 'What a performance: you thumped against my wall all night. Do you remember?'

'Please, ladies, don't lower the tone,' Sara sounded embarrassed as she glanced at Gus.

'Come on, Sara, you must remember his name,' Lizzie persisted. 'How could you forget?'

'How could I remember?' Sara snapped. 'Some wanker wannabe politician.'

Gus shot Sara a look. He looked appalled either by her attitude or language, or both. Connie saw her spot his reaction and blush.

'Over there,' Lizzie pointed at a dazzle of zebras showing off their wider, whiter backside stripes as they trotted away from the vehicle. 'Great spot.'

Connie slipped back into the past. She wasn't sure why she couldn't stop thinking about their wedding. Their wedding photos shot outside the South Porch showed him smiling, charming, confident and in love with her. Maybe she was searching for clues. Should she have predicted what Julian would become? How he would disappoint her in the end?

On their wedding day, Dad had given a careful, thoughtful speech, which highlighted Julian's talents and charms. Though now she thought about it, he never said he was a good man. What use did she have for goodness in her twenties? She had her own happy, close family life, which was comfortably supported by stocks and shares. Her father cannily resigned as a Lloyds name a couple of years before the crash in 1992.

She stared at the dunes as they rose to welcome her. She couldn't locate the root cause of Julian's philandering. When she met him, Connie was probably more highly sexed than he was. He was the antithesis of Luke. Instead of getting it out of his system when he was young, he was too busy pushing to get a First.

Julian had his first affair shortly after Lou was born. Connie discovered evidence of it a year later. She was looking for some cash to pay the window cleaner. There was a pornographic note folded neatly into his wallet. Of course, Connie believed that it was merely a woman's fantasy about Julian. No more. She debated whether to mention it to him. Eventually she decided to hold it up, half a page of flimsy evidence, expecting him to roll his eyes and joke about it. His response shocked her more than the act itself.

'Connie, darling, God, I was such a wretch. I hate myself for it. Please forgive me.'

'Sorry?' She distinctly remembered she was holding Lou at the time. 'Did you sleep with this woman?'

He dropped his gaze and then looked up at her penitently. 'Darling Connie, can you ever forgive me? She meant nothing. Literally nothing.'

Connie was terrified, not by the act he had committed, but by the enormity of what this might represent. 'Why have you kept this?' She dropped the note to the floor.

'God knows. I probably put it there to get rid of it.'

Connie was silent. She was conscious her reaction wasn't typical. She should scream, thrust Lou into his arms, even though he was about to leave for work, and storm out. She didn't.

Julian dramatically swooped the note off their kitchen tiles. He tore it aggressively into tiny pieces, slammed his foot down on the pedal bin and scattered it down into its entrails. 'All gone.'

Without saying a word, Connie went upstairs to change Lou.

Julian had undoubtedly changed. His ego grew with his career. When she became a mother, she changed. Their relationship was incomplete and in the gap they both left, Sally took possession of the vacant space. The space, in fairness, she allowed to become available.

She thought about the consequences of Julian's actions. The public humiliation would be viewed as a personal slight by her mother. Her friends read the *Mail on Sunday*. Her father was different. He was a thoroughly decent man. He was hurt and bewildered by his son-in-law, by the grief that he could carelessly inflict on his only daughter. Her dad understood that her public show of strength, her universal silence on the subject, was a brittle charade, waiting for this moment to be fully exposed. He was the only person she talked to about Julian's affairs. She hadn't called him. She couldn't face his anguish.

She closed her eyes. The wind washed her face. She wanted to drift off; she wanted to sleep. She didn't want to think through the questions she needed to ask Julian and the conversation that they would inevitably have to have. She didn't want to think about what she was going to do.

They rounded a bend in the track, pulled off on to a small path leading to the sleep out deck. An elegant king-size bed dominated the raised decking. It was surrounded by three hundred and sixty degrees of reserve. The bed was piled high with gleaming white Egyptian cotton pillows on top of a gleaming white duvet. It looked more luxurious than their bed at the lodge, certainly than their bed at home. A weathered roof, supported by thin tree trunks, held up immaculately rolled protective blinds. The whole effect was imperial, like a royal litter.

There were white towelling robes hanging from a dark hat stand at one end; three pairs of slippers were lined up parallel with the foot of the bed. At the front of the deck were a wooden table and chairs and a pile of large ochre-coloured floor cushions.

'Serious glamping, Gus,' Sara exclaimed.

'I knew you'd love it.'

They smiled at each other.

Lizzie, who had already kicked off her cream Converse, was round the back, running down the narrow decked walkway. 'Do you see what I think I see?' She called out.

Connie and Sara followed her. The path was lined with tiny black uplighters, and led to a steel shower with a vast head, stylish in any London bathroom. A white china loo was plumbed in beside it. The white basin was carved into a polished rock, which had been sculpted into a shelf for bath products, towels and a hand mirror. As Lizzie flushed the loo and Sara energetically ran the water in the basin to confirm it was plumbed in, Connie wandered back towards the deck. She sunk back on to the pillows and looked up at the sky. It was deepening in colour in preparation for sunset. It was going to be an extraordinary view of what her grandfather described as the Green Kalahari. This area in the south got more rain than the central Kalahari. Thousands of kilometres of flat dunes unfurling into the distance.

At the front of the deck, Gus was unloading the khaki canvas holdall. One was piled high with cheese and bread, the other one had an array of miniature desserts: chocolate mousse, tiramisu, panna cotta, lemon mousse, blueberry cheesecake.

Gus glanced over to her. 'Sara thought you were done with big meals. Wouldn't want a chef here fussing away with a three-course meal, eh? He laughed.

'Girls love to snack, Gus.'

'Sara's lovely, you know,' Connie insisted lightly. 'A good and loyal friend.'

Gus murmured, 'Soft as Kalahari honey underneath all that carbon fibre.'

Connie unlaced her safari boots and released her feet.

'Gus, glad to see you followed instructions,' Sara breezed up, bending over the holdall to search for a bottle opener.

'Sara, I'll do it,' Gus insisted, crouching on the other side of the bag.

She stood up and over him. 'Gus, we can't have a qualified zoologist acting barman to three over-privileged, maturing London ladies.'

'Speak for yourself.' Lizzie landed heavily on the cushion beside Connie, who moved up to make room for her.

'We are going one way, Lizzie dear. Ageing isn't personal.'

'How can you say that when I haven't even got a boyfriend? Nor have you for that matter.' Lizzie looked at her slyly.

Sara paused. The subject of men had a habit of making Sara pause, before she doubled her defences. 'Christ, Lizzie, today of all days, give it a break. Don't you ever stop thinking about men? They are either A-list fuckers, I'm sorry to say, like our dear friend's erstwhile husband. Or domestic pets you need to put on a lead to take outside.'

Connie automatically leaned forward. 'She doesn't mean it, Gus.'

Sara gave him an impatient wave of the corkscrew. 'Gus, I'm obviously not talking about you.'

'Great. What am I, the safari eunuch?'

'That was funny. Very funny, actually.' Sara gave him a curious look. 'Gus, women of the Empire open their own bottles.'

Connie smiled. 'I would quickly escape, before you throw the corkscrew at her.'

Sara was squeezing the bottle wedged between her thighs, as she grunted to no avail. 'Gus, this corkscrew is useless.'

'Zoologists don't pack the kit, Sara,' Gus chipped in.

Sara laughed. 'Okay. Two–one to you, Gus.'

'Which point did you win?' He bounced back.

Sara's mouth softened. He seemed to have won her over somehow.

Gus coughed. 'If you are nervous, eh, your guide can sleep in the game vehicle round the back.' He looked embarrassed, doubtless preparing for Sara's visceral wit. 'Or I can come back at dawn with breakfast.'

'Are you planning to gawp at us in our underwear, Gus? I didn't put you down as a peeper.'

Sara spoke automatically and Connie sensed that she instantly regretted it. Gus blushed hard.

'Sorry, Gus, that was childish. Forgive me.'

'Ignore her, Gus, she has no manners,' insisted Lizzie. 'She's going to die a lonely lesbian in an old people's home in Florida.'

Gus started to walk away without saying goodbye. Connie moved after him. 'Gus, I apologise on Sara's behalf.'

He didn't say anything.

'Do you know, I've had a hell of a day and I would be reassured if you were here overnight, in case.'

'Sure, Connie.'

'Why don't you join us?'

He shook his head. 'I'll come back later.'

Connie went back to the others.

'Why do you give him such a hard time? He is our guide, you

should treat him with respect.' Lizzie prodded Sara, before pronouncing, 'You fancy him.'

Connie winced.

'Lizzie, don't be preposterous. Christ, I'm not some pubescent schoolgirl,' Sara said angrily. 'I'd rather shag a buffalo.'

'I don't believe you,' Lizzie pronounced as she spooned another mound of chocolate mousse. 'Don't look at me like that, Connie, I'm on holiday and the food is delicious.'

'Podgy people eat puddings,' Connie said without thinking.

Sara laughed loudly. 'Don't tell me, Connie, you've got that saying on a fridge magnet?'

'You can't say things like that, Connie,' said Lizzie, 'It's fatist. God you would get eaten alive at Channel 4.'

The snap of their banter had brought Connie briefly back, only she couldn't help sliding away from them again. This time to think about what was going to happen. Sally having Julian's baby. His baby; his blood. A headache started to tug at her temples.

Sara paused. 'Oh Connie. I'm not good at finding the right words to say.' She squeezed between Connie and Lizzie, 'But I'm so sorry. You don't deserve the little shit.'

Connie looked at the horizon. It was achingly sparse.

'Have you ever had an affair?' Sara asked.

Connie gave a closed smile. 'Why do you ask?'

'Years ago, I saw you in the bar at the Athenaeum with a hot-looking civil barrister.'

'I saw you,' she half-smiled.

'Connie, I am shocked,' Lizzie interjected. 'Did you have an affair?'

Connie had forgotten about that night. 'For once, I wanted to be the one to walk away. To be able to forget our family, leave it behind as easily as Julian does,' she paused. 'For one night, I was single again.' She breathed in abruptly. 'But I couldn't go through with it.' She looked up wistfully at them. She pointed at Sara, 'Seeing you reminded me of who I was, for better or worse.'

'You shouldn't have let me stop you,' Sara paused, 'Julian is unredeemable, Connie. You can't stay with him this time.'

Connie didn't reply. She genuinely had no idea what she was

going to do. She noticed that Lizzie was quiet. Connie was conscious it was the first time that they had ever asked her about Julian's affairs.

Connie eyed the horizon. 'The only difference is this time I've been truly violated. He has had sex in my own home with one of my great friends. This woman lived in my house, helped me to bring up my children and shared every aspect of my life, before having a baby with my husband.'

No one spoke. Neither Lizzie nor Sara could comfort her. They couldn't help her. It was the reason that Connie had never confided in them before. What could even her best friends say?

She brushed imaginary dust off her knees. 'I don't know what the answer is.'

The silence was restful. It was a pause before the certain madness of talking to Julian before he left for London. He had booked to take the plane back to Jo'Burg at midday tomorrow.

'Divorce, Connie.' Sara stood up and strode to the holdall, pulling out a bottle of water. 'I can heartily recommend single life.'

Connie squeezed Sara's arm. 'You won't stay single forever, Sara.'

'Oh please, I wasn't looking for sympathy. I am thankful to be on my own.'

Connie was surprised that Lizzie didn't add, what about me? She looked at her. Lizzie looked back at Connie.

'Okay, I need to get something off my chest.'

'Lizzie, go on,' Sara urged, spooning some panna cotta into her mouth.

Lizzie paused.

Connie knew what she was going to say. She smiled for the first time today.

'I've had a sort of crush on Julian. I know, it's ridiculous and wrong. I am really ashamed. Can you forgive me, Connie? It really matters to me. You and Sara are my best friends. I would hate you both to think badly of me.'

Sara's laughter was loud and unabated. She seemed unable to stop.

Connie smiled again, she hoped sympathetically. 'Lizzie, of course I do.'

'You knew?' Lizzie said anxiously.

'You're a mirror, Lizzie, much as we love you,' added Sara. 'The whole group knows.'

'How embarrassing. Even Luke?'

'What? Do you fancy Luke as well?' Sara raised an eyebrow dramatically.

Connie laughed for the first time. It was good to know she could. She took Lizzie's hand. 'You need to find a real, normal boyfriend. An available one.'

Unusually, Lizzie was keen to change the subject. 'What about you, Sara?'

'Me? I'm overwhelmed by the Jade Sutton case. God knows, by the time we get back in the morning, the verdict could be toast.'

'No, silly,' Lizzie tapped her playfully on the arm. 'You and men.'

'Don't belong in the same sentence. Next question.' Sara's quip wasn't convincing to Connie, but she would never argue her out of the position.

Sara continued: 'Lizzie, what are you going to do about getting a flat?'

'I need to sort out a mortgage first. It's a nightmare.'

Connie dived into the property discussion. What about her parents acting as her guarantors? Had she spoken to Michael Stubbs? He had his own production company. He might be looking for a commissioning editor. She would give her his number as soon as they got back home. She could then get a pay rise and the boost of a new job. The practical problems of Lizzie's life were a welcome diversion. This was what Connie did best. She was a mender, a fixer, a binder, the carer of her family and her friends. It was her role. Julian's baby couldn't change that.

The sun had been slowly bleeding, leaking out across the horizon, seeping into the corners. It was a complete painting. Blue-black thickly dubbed across the top, descending into a broken line of dirty oranges then hot pink into deeper red. The sky was a giant pad of blotting paper no longer absorbent, but evenly spreading out its colours. Lying on the decking gave Connie the feeling they were miniature, unimportant and uninvolved with the serious business of earth.

Chapter 23

Before the dessert was brought out, Katherine left Matt and Luke, pleading exhaustion. Luke knew stress was exhausting. The pressures of his business, Ella and Finn and Emma in the background, not to mention his ambition to successfully complete an Iron Man, a tough goal for an overworked, divorced entrepreneur who was turning forty, was overwhelming. He was knackered after running for an hour in the gym. He wanted to knock himself out for the night. His anxiety had been mounting since Connie's attempted drowning. He tried to block it out. Usually two vodkas fixed anything, only tonight they did nothing to assuage his nervous tick.

Dinner was intense without the girls to lighten the atmosphere. He missed Connie and Sara. Thankfully, Julian was nowhere to be seen. Luke was hoping that he had already packed himself off to London. Though he suspected this wasn't the case. Dan and Alan sandwiched themselves on either side of Katherine, leaving him to talk to Matt, who thankfully didn't mention his outburst with Julian. It left Luke feeling exposed. Connie's attempted drowning confirmed what he suspected: he still loved her.

He urged Matt to keep him company. They moved together across the terrace from the restaurant deck, up the couple of steps into the sitting room and across into the bar at the back. Luke was conscious of Matt's increased bulk and the way he walked, rocking from one foot to another. Matt grunted as he mounted a barstool, which was buried beneath him. They both ordered drinks which they finished desperately fast before they said a word to each other.

Luke sighed. 'Matt, you must be feeling shit.'

Matt stared at the grain coursing through the wooden bar. 'Do you know the strange thing, Luke? I'm the one who's heartbroken,' he raised his bushy eyebrows. 'Katherine's okay. She is strong, Luke. Women are.'

Luke nodded. He was thankful Matt hadn't gone through the gruesome details with him on the terrace and didn't do so now. He sensed that, like him, Matt simply wanted to be with a great mate and forget. Old friends were easy compared with women. A relief. Luke's chest was feeling tight. His body was completely exhausted.

Matt half-turned his head in his direction. 'You look drained, Luke. This afternoon, it was a real shocker, wasn't it?'

'I overreacted, but then Connie had tried to drown herself in the pool…' He trailed off.

Matt squeezed his arm sympathetically. 'I'd have socked him if Lizzie hadn't.'

'We're going to have another one, aren't we,' he confirmed without conferring and gave the bar man a definite nod.

With fresh drinks, the conversation could have gone off in a different direction, but he desperately wanted to talk to Matt. 'Okay, here's the mad thing, I think that I still love Connie.'

'Really? Surprise me,' Matt grinned and gave him a large bear hug that made Luke rock on his barstool.

When Matt relinquished him, Luke sighed. 'What do you think?'

Matt glanced at him. 'What do I think about what? Whether you really are in love with her? Or what you should do about it?'

'Both.'

They laughed.

'Christ, we're a fine pair,' Matt ruffled his hair. 'Here's the thing: you never stopped loving Connie. What are you going to do about it? Jesus, I don't know.'

Luke smiled.

'You know, she's fair game now, considering the circumstances, but not considering how vulnerable she is feeling. Am I making any sense?'

Luke nodded.

'You've got to grab happiness. I did.' Matt squeezed his hands together.

Luke loved Matt. He was down to earth, solid and reliable. A great bloke. A great friend. He lurched forward and gave him a bear hug across one shoulder. 'Why don't we see more of each other, Matt? When we're back in London, can we meet up soon?'

'I would really love that, Luke,' Matt nodded back. 'You're a great mate. I've missed you.' Matt lurched up. 'But if I don't go to bed now, I'm going to fall over.'

Luke laughed. 'Lightweight.'

Matt fell against the bar as he climbed down from the stool. 'Whoops…'

'Okay, wait, let me help you.'

With one arm round Matt's waist, Luke directed him across the bar and out towards the path. They were both giggling and shushing each other as they approached Matt's house.

'You better go,' said Matt in a dramatic whisper, 'Or Katherine will blame you for leading me astray.' He prodded him lightly on the chest, 'It's all your fault.'

They both laughed.

'Listen,' Matt looked at him. 'About Connie: go for it, mate. What have you got to lose? Nothing but your pride, which is worth shit. You said that to me all those years ago. You were right. Count to three.'

Matt shoved open the heavy door and shouted over his shoulder. 'Julian's leaving tomorrow morning. Actually, this morning. Night, night Luke.'

Everything made them hoot. They ate the rest of the puddings in bed, careless of chocolate on the duvet. Sara remembered Gus had shown her a stash of chocolate. They handed round the bar as they had done with other substances in the past. Lizzie mentioned she was on the Dukan Diet, which made Sara laugh until she complained she had a stitch. Lizzie exacted her revenge by repeating her claim that Gus fancied Sara, which exacted a long list of animals she would rather shag first. They taunted Lizzie for snoring and Sara for hogging the duvet, until they were asleep, bar Connie.

Lying awake with her stomach warmly lined, Connie had the kind of clarity that only comes to you in the middle of the night when everyone else is asleep. She reached into her rucksack, felt for her torch and her grandfather's book. She opened the cover. It didn't look as if he had written in it. The first eight pages were blank. Then Connie discovered his scrawled notes. They weren't in a diary form. More thoughts scattered at random angles over different parts of a page.

She read: *Dr Livingstone set off from the nearest town on his Moffat Mission into 'deepest Africa'.*

She turned the book sideways to read the other note on the page: *Kalahari comes from the Tswana word, kgala, meaning great thirst.* Perhaps, Connie thought, a bushman had told him that, and he had written it down. Not to forget it.

The ink had washed into the next page, but Connie could just about make it out: *Bushmen have been in the Kalahari 20,000 years. Imagine! BUT farming livestock impossible. Which is why it is the last great wilderness.*

Connie looked up, knowing the vastness was around her yet still darkly invisible. A wide, wild range of beautiful, even rare and endangered, species would be waking up in this safe haven, magically far away from the destructive nature of the human world. All because of her grandfather's understanding and commitment.

Connie knew exactly what she wanted to do. She went to see if Gus was still awake. He was dressed and sitting in the vehicle with a coffee. 'Hello. It is amazing out here.'

'Hello, Connie. Yeah, early on the reserve, it's something else.' He glanced towards the bed. 'The other two asleep, eh?'

'Lizzie would probably worship you if you make her a coffee in about five hours,' she paused, wondering whether to say anything. 'Listen, I absolutely love Sara. She is one of my dearest friends. But she can overstep the mark.'

Gus waved an arm dismissively, before looking up with the gentlest of smiles. 'Well, out here, we allow fires to rage, eh? We just keep an eye.'

Connie watched his expression curiously. In it, she read someone who wanted to know Sara, to truly understand her. Someone like Gus would be great for her. Calm with an understated intelligence. Connie sighed. She couldn't think of anyone remotely like him in London.

Connie paused not sure how much Gus knew of her situation. 'It's terribly early.' She looked at her watch to confirm that it was four in the morning. 'But I was wondering if you wouldn't mind driving me back to Gae, and then coming back to pick up the others later.'

They hardly talked on the way back. It was black around them, which made it easier. Connie was nervous about what she was going to do, half-wishing she was still buried under the Egyptian cotton duvet. But she had been a coward for too long. When they got to the path, Gus stopped the vehicle.

'I'll get back to the others.'

'Thank you, I'm sorry to drag you back here.'

'Connie, no worries. You take care, eh.'

Connie walked along the path. She pushed on the door, wondering whether he would have locked it. It was open. The wood scraped against the floor. The sound echoed into the silence. Connie waited to acclimatise her eyes to the darkness, before moving into the bedroom. He was asleep with one arm and the top of his shoulder visible over the duvet. Connie walked quietly to the side of the bed. She crouched into a squat and then sunk to her knees. Luke had always slept on his back. Now he slept on his chest with the abandonment of a child. His narrow head was tucked to one side. She had intended to wake him, though she didn't allow herself to think what would happen if she did. Now he was in front of her, she wanted him to stay asleep. She didn't want to have to articulate her thoughts. She raised her arms until her fingers touched the edge of the duvet closest to his shoulder. She gently lifted it up like a tent and folded it carefully down to the base of his back. Her breath was laboured. At first, she could only see the outline of his back, but she bent over, scanning it carefully. She knew the risk she was taking of waking him angry and hurt, maybe even disgusted by her tremendous invasion of his privacy. What gave her the right? Yet she had this irresistible urge to see his back. She stared at the raised scar crossing his lower spine and ran her little finger along it. He didn't wake. She got bolder. She ran her forefinger up on to what looked like a burn. His skin was shrivelled and whitened. Luke stirred. Connie instinctively removed her finger. He rolled over on to his side. As if he sensed his body's sudden coolness and exposure, he opened his eyes.

Connie stood up quickly.

He didn't move. He stared at her. Connie was terrified – she was totally in the wrong. What was he thinking? For once, she didn't know. She realised how much she cared about his good opinion, even after all this time. He said nothing. He would put it down to her grief over Julian's baby, if she could get out of here. She didn't move.

'What are you doing here, Connie?' he said quietly.

'I'm so sorry. I don't know, Luke,' she mumbled, looking away. 'Please go back to sleep, I'm going now.'

'Where are you going Connie? Back to Julian?'

She shook her head. 'No. I'm going to make him move into the basement flat, where Sally used to live. It's over in that sense, that much I know.'

He sat up, exposing his chest and leant sideways to turn on his bedside lamp. His movement, nakedness and the light all startled her. She stepped back, aware of the sensuality of the situation.

'Would you grab my T-shirt?' Luke pointed at a white one over the chair at the end of his bed.

Connie held it out for him across the bed. He couldn't reach it without leaning forward. He hesitated – he clearly didn't want to expose his back to her again. She moved round the bed to his side. For a second, they both held on to it and then in the next, Luke was holding the T-shirt in one hand and Connie's free hand in the other. His touch made her eyes water.

His face spread into a smile. 'Who would have thought we would both have ended up in such a mess?'

She was thankful. He was giving her a way out. She nodded, 'Yes, it's mad.'

He readjusted his hold of her hand, pulling it gently towards his chest. Connie had a choice: she could follow her hand or let go of his grasp. She briefly considered her response to Sara's question about having an affair. *I couldn't go through with it.* He spotted her reaction immediately and moved her hand back into her lap.

She pulled him towards her, running one hand gently over his back. She ran her fingers along each one. She knew exactly where the scars were.

Chapter 24

They were in the vehicle for their early drive out to walk into black rhino. According to a message laboriously relayed by Matt, who was looking rough, Luke wasn't feeling well.

Julian appeared dressed in safari shorts and shirt. He had some front to tip up for a ride with the group. What were they supposed to say to him? He looked anxious with a dramatically penitent expression. Connie completely ignored him. She was studiously reading an old exercise book. She was strangely calm since their night on the deck, as if she had come to some decision. She had left in the night. When Sara questioned Gus about it, he was surprisingly reticent. Was she intending to have a heart to heart with Julian? He insisted he didn't know.

Thankfully, Gus didn't stop talking. Sensing their awkward silence, he padded out rhino info. 'We have one third of the world's black rhinos in South Africa here, at Gae. We try to stop the poachers by putting notches in their ears, and microchips under the skin at their neck.'

Normally Sara would have dug into a discussion about the legal laxity of the South African government and their failure to protect their endangered species, but she was too concerned about Connie.

Getting no response even from her, Gus continued for his imaginary audience. 'You know, they are irascible, temperamental animals.'

He ruffled the front of his hair. He was attractive in a boyish way. 'We think that the black rhino are more aggressive than their white cousins, because they are smaller, eh?'

The silence set in, deepened and widened. The vehicle was too cramped for all of them. Matt shifted irritably; Connie and Julian stared out in different directions.

Julian turned to Lizzie and Sara. 'Did you three have a great dawn breakfast?'

Sara noticed Gus glancing at her in the mirror, but she quickly diverted her attention to Lizzie. She gave her a warning look she prayed she would understand.

'It was amazing. The colour and the light. We all had such a fantastic breakfast cooked by Gus. Thank you, Gus. I was saying to Connie, I can't believe how much I ate,' Lizzie said.

Sara squeezed Lizzie's hand. Where the hell did Connie go? She had a pretty good idea. She glanced over to her, expecting Connie to be studiously admiring the view, but she turned to look at Sara. She smiled at her. It was how she always thought of Connie, before Julian and her pile of kids. Serene and dreamy.

'They have a strong sense of smell. They can pick up human scent up to eight hundred metres away. Most of the recorded cases of rhino charging show that they stop a few metres away from their quarry. It's strongly believed by rangers that it's a form of curiosity, eh?' Gus nodded at no one in particular.

'Right, Gus.' said Sara. 'Curiosity might kill a tourist or two surely.'

'Not on my watch, Sara,' Gus said back. 'If they do charge, which is highly unlikely as we will be down wind, don't move, eh? Stay absolutely still.'

'Forgive me if I completely ignore you,' she snapped but then remembered Connie's reprimand about not torturing the ranger. 'And climb the nearest tree.'

'That would be a stupid move, Sara,' Gus intoned without his usual sheen of politeness. 'You can't outrun a rhino.'

'You should see me try,' she pipped back.

'They can charge at fifty-five miles an hour.'

'We've got a lot in common. That's me charging down Westbourne Grove.'

Gus ignored her. 'I would be forced to shoot, which, as I've told you, is a final resort.'

She tried to catch Connie's eye but she was staring out at the veld, Julian watching her intently from the other side of the vehicle.

Sara, quickly spoke to fill the silence. 'Gus, what would you do? Sling me over one shoulder with your rifle over the other?'

Lizzie joined in, 'The idea of any man getting away with carrying you anywhere. Sorry, that's a picture.'

Gus stopped the vehicle. 'Listen, guys, this isn't funny. It's about basic survival. I want to take every one of you back alive, eh?'

'If you leave one behind, we won't ask for our money back, I promise.' Sara said without thinking.

Silence descended again, even Gus took the hint. They drove seemingly on and on. The heat was unbearable. It fought to get under the canvas roof, striking Sara as they turned the corner. She was sweaty. Gus explained the temperature was higher after a storm. She was craving caffeine but she was dreading their coffee stop. She couldn't bear the idea of getting trapped with Julian or trying to make sense of Connie's behaviour. She could hardly ask her outright where she was last night. The whole situation was quite maddening.

When it felt like the journey might never end, Ben made a signal with his right arm and Gus veered off the track. Sara squeezed the bar, preparing for the lurch, which took them up and down into a small, shaded waterhole.

'Rhino only have three toes in their track – toes one and five are missing.'

No one reacted. Sara was conscious they were a tough audience today.

Gus ploughed on. 'They are plantigrades – that is, they put pressure on the whole foot rather than walking on their toes.'

The silence inescapably returned.

Sara tried to rescue Gus. 'How can Ben tell the difference between white and black rhino tracks?'

'Well, Sara, the front of a white rhino track is a pronounced W shape.' Without any warning, Gus took her left hand off the bar and flattened up her palm upwards and with his left index finger draw the shape across her palm.

She had to concentrate on not withdrawing her hand. Men didn't touch her, unless with serious intent. Then she was in control. If she wasn't interested, they would soon know it. She had slapped more than her fair share of drunk barristers in the last ten years. Sometimes she wanted sex but never at home, and she never stayed the night. It was too complicated, too personal. Sara obviously knew why she behaved this way. It was a hangover from her childhood, but one that she accepted. She enjoyed her own company; her life was full and exciting. There was no room for anything more.

'The black rhino's toes are smaller and more widely spaced, producing a gentle curve at the front like this.' There was something subtly presumptuous about Gus that was difficult for her to locate. 'And they hardly have any indentation at the back, eh.'

Instead of letting go of her hand, he took it and placed it gently back on the bar.

Sara blushed. Irrationally, she thought of their conversation about Joanne Sutton the day before. She suddenly wished she had confided in him.

Ben was staring at an unremarkable bush. He turned to a patch of bare fiery sand. He picked up some mud, crumbling some of it, before bringing the rest up to his nose.

Gus jumped down to join him. 'You see this bush.' He held a bare spiky branch. 'It is a different colour from the other side. The rhino has brushed it very recently. And this is fresh dung.' He kicked the pile that Ben had assiduously held to his nose. 'Look there is a lot of moisture in the dung and it's shining. It's a sign that the animal is very close.'

Ben walked round the other side and wandered back with his eye on the thick bush behind it. He spoke in rapid Afrikaans.

'Okay, Ben,' Gus responded. 'Ben says a mother and her baby and, possibly a male, were here early this morning. He is going to explore on foot. He's pretty sure that they are in this block. If you are happy with that, let's wait here and have some coffee, eh?'

Matt and Katherine stood close together holding hands, which didn't allow for a third, Alan and Lizzie chatted protectively to Connie, while Dan valiantly talked to Julian. Sara took her coffee away from everyone else so as to not upset the tenuous balance of the group. Gus wandered up to her.

'Don't talk to me, Gus, I'm under strict instructions not to upset you. Though I'm perfectly sure that you can look after yourself, despite being a young nipper.'

'Nipper? What's that?'

'Up north, we say nipper, meaning young boy.' She raised her eyebrows playfully. 'But it can mean a dog.'

He shook his head.

'How old are you anyway?'

He eyed her suspiciously. 'Thirty-four, Sara. I'm not going to ask you how old you are, because it's totally irrelevant to me.'

She blushed. She deserved that.

'Sorry, I can't help it.' She paused. 'Joking is a bit of an addiction, I'm afraid.'

Gus kept his eyes on her in the way that he did, before murmuring, 'Guaranteed to keep everyone at arm's length, eh?'

She struggled to think of what to say next.

'Sara listen. This isn't the right moment, but since we are on our own.' He looked concerned, reached for her hand and pulled her close to him. 'It's not great news.'

She had been about to shake him off, but instead she went limp. Her first thought was her mother. Had there been a phone call while she was out glamping? 'What's wrong? Tell me. I can take it.' Could she?

'Julian asked me to give you this note. He said it was urgent.'

She relaxed. 'He wants to intervene with Connie. He's such a bastard.'

'I don't think it's about Connie, Sara, eh. It's about your case.'

Sara unfolded the piece of paper and read it. 'Alistair Bent,' she murmured.

She looked up at Gus. He waited.

'He is a well-known legal journalist in London on *The Times*. And he is running an exclusive with the husband tomorrow. It's being pitched as a breaking story.'

'What could he say that would change things?'

She didn't answer. What would Nigel say to Alistair when he had been acquitted? Why would he implicate her? Madly, Sara imagined that Joanne Sutton had stage-managed the whole scenario. To destroy Sara and her record of achievement. She was getting paranoid on top of everything else.

She didn't notice Gus was holding her hands, squeezing them tightly. She could feel the warmth and pressure, but didn't consider where it was coming from. She anticipated the possible repercussions. Those jealous of her success would seek to bring her down. She shook her hands free and pressed her fingers into her forehead. She needed to share what had happened with someone.

'You can trust me, Sara.'

'I made a big mistake. I was cornered.' Her desperation burst from her. 'I've always done everything by the book, followed Best Practice always, always, always. I've worked so hard you can't imagine.' She was pleading for his understanding. 'All my life, ever since I was at school.'

She expected Gus to be embarrassed by her lack of control. Instead he hugged her. A strong, silent hug, unfussy somehow. She rested her head on his shoulder. With her head touching the brush of his cotton, she started to tell him what happened.

'Joanne Sutton called me. Literally hysterical. It was urgent that she saw me alone, she insisted. It's against the unwritten rules. I was stepping over a line, but I wanted to get her off the phone. I hate people getting emotional.'

Sara sighed out her regret. She could have rectified the situation, even at that point, but she didn't. As if he sensed it, he stroked her hair. It made it easier.

'You met with her?'

Back to the garden.

'She explained that her husband had done it. He had confessed to her. It was a mistake. He was giving Jade sleeping pills as they often did before they went out to the pub opposite their house. Only this time she didn't wake up.' Sara looked up defensively. 'The first thing I asked her was why didn't she tell me this straight away.'

Gus nodded reassuringly.

'She insisted that she didn't want to lose him as well. He was all she had. I asked her why she was telling me and she said...' Sara grimaced at Gus. 'She said she needed to tell someone. "Tell a friend or the Samaritans," I shouted. Can you believe that? She tells her fucking barrister?'

Gus nodded.

'Of all the people in the world, she chose me.' Sara shook her head. 'Hardly sympathetic. Her defence lawyer to boot. But there was more.'

'Tell me, Sara,' Gus gently prompted.

'She said that she thought I was the one person who would understand.'

'Why did she think that?'

'My dad disappeared when I was six. Jade's age.'

Gus was silent. She read his concern but he didn't expose it.

'He walked out one morning and never came back. Somehow Joanne Sutton discovered that. I don't know how she did. I never talk to anyone about it.' In Sara's experience, confessions held huge risks. She tried for levity in an attempt to build up her armour. 'Hardly your idyllic family set up.'

He said nothing.

'Are you shocked?'

'I'm shocked that a man could leave his wife and child. Not that it happened to you.'

'Why? Do I wear my heart on my sleeve?' she quipped.

'It's more like a film over your eyes.'

'Here's the bit that will make your morality pale. It would have been okay, if she had been prepared to sign a statement to that effect. She insisted she couldn't.'

'And you didn't walk away.' He was stroking her neck.

'I could have represented her, but I had to inform her solicitor of her change of evidence.'

He was silent.

'And I couldn't call her to give evidence.' Sara said. What she should have done. 'It would mean misleading the court.'

She looked up and saw his intelligence.

'What did you do?' He said it quietly. He couldn't possibly approve – she had let a man off the manslaughter of a defenceless child.

189

'Firstly, she had no idea where the body was. Secondly, she didn't see him do it.' Of course her self-defence was feeble. 'I persuaded her it was a mere supposition. Not based on facts or evidence. I wrote her script.'

'Otherwise, you would have been fighting against Nigel Sutton and his lawyer?'

'Exactly,' she seized on his words. 'To avoid what we call a "cut-throat defence". When nobody wins. And it's all about winning. It has to be. Do you see that?'

He was silent. She bowed her head and stepped away from him. Of course he was appalled. An eager ranger full of integrity, hope and a future with some untainted babe.

She realised she was rubbing her hands like Lady Macbeth.

'Sara. You're going to be okay,' Gus gently separated her fingers. 'You'll do the right thing, eh? You know that. Or you wouldn't be so tortured.'

He walked away from her. For the first time in such a long time, Sara was lonely.

Chapter 25

They were baking hot and dishevelled. Even Katherine. Tracking the black rhino was one of the week's highlights. Katherine had been keen to see 'rhino in their natural environment', as the brochure boasted, but as far as Matt was concerned the moment had passed. They were all low and distracted. Connie was a ghostly presence. Julian was immune to the tension he had created. Sara had had some sort of intimate moment with Gus – God knows what was going on there.

Matt had a slicing headache, a vicious reminder of the big downside to nights out with Luke, a surprisingly heavy drinker, considering his slight frame and evangelical exercise regime. It left Matt feeling maudlin, low all over again about Isobel. His baby girl.

Early that morning, while Matt nursed his hangover, Katherine had said out loud what he already knew. She wasn't prepared to try for another child. Her relationship with Dawn was too complex, too personal, she said. It brought up many issues for her. She couldn't do it again. He nodded bleakly. Deep down, he knew that they couldn't go through this again. It was clear they couldn't cope with surrogacy; it wasn't worth damaging their precious relationship.

But even so, losing Isobel, and the decision that he and Katherine had made, hadn't stopped the aching feeling he had for a child. He wanted to get back into bed, nurse his head and hurt in the latest twist in his fight for a family.

Instead, soaked with sweat, he was trudging through these itchy grasses in this unbearable heat trying to track an animal that, right now, he couldn't give a damn about. Matt had bricks in his boots. His tongue was furry. His safari hat dug into his forehead, making his head pound. He would have taken a short cut back to the vehicle, but they weren't allowed to separate. They were in single file. Gus was first then Julian, Sara, Dan and Lizzie and Alan. Katherine wanted to be at the front, but Matt couldn't keep up. Connie was at the back.

Gus gestured with his arm for them to stop. Obediently, they did. Here they were made docile and unquestioning, ultimately putting their lives in a young ranger's hands. Hysteria welled up inside him. He couldn't contain it. It came out in a snort that released the snot that had blocked his nose since dawn. Katherine immediately produced a tissue and passed it to him. Matt looked at her gratefully.

'Matt, are you all right?' she sounded concerned.

He laughed. It came out as another snort.

Sara barked, 'Shut up, Matt.'

Gus listened intently to his radio. He relayed that Ben had found a lone female nursing a one and a half year old calf in fairly dense bush about thirty metres ahead. 'There is no wind, eh? Softly, quietly. Try not to disturb anything.'

Adrenalin passed like a current along the group's line. Matt stepped slightly to the side to see if he could spot the female. She was unnervingly invisible, which gave his empty stomach a jolt. He could see more dense bush, more tall grasses. Where was she? It was hard to believe that such an aggressive animal was calmly chilling out here.

They stepped gingerly forward, lifting each foot with exaggerated control, up and down. He could hear the grasses crush and crunch under their boots. They sounded too loud to him. He started to worry about the noise they were making.

Gus's left index finger jabbed at the grasses ahead, slightly to the right of them. The two horns of the mother pointed out of the grasses about twenty metres away, exquisitely camouflaged. The sight of them made his heart race. It was thrilling. Christ, how could he have doubted it? Let a hangover ruin this moment, one of those 'life moments'. She was lying down. The curve of her grey beige back was visible, though not her calf.

Gus moved back down the line and spoke. 'She is nursing her calf. It is rare to witness this.'

Sara looked as scared as he felt, which was gratifying. Underneath their manoeuvred careers and controlling personalities these fierce women were ultimately little girls. What would Annabel do if she was here? Run. For once, he thought about his ex-wife with satisfaction.

He stared at the black rhino. They were small and compact, the bland colour of an anaemic elephant. It was unnerving being on foot, sharing the same patch of sand as them.

Gus stopped about twelve metres away. Matt could see the mother and calf calmly lying side by side. Nature was mocking him.

The mother bolted. She moved heavily, yet rapidly towards them. Julian, Lizzie and Sara stepped back simultaneously, falling against Dan and Alan in a desperate, crushing attempt to escape.

Gus spoke urgently, 'It's okay. Keep calm everyone. We've surprised her. She'll veer off, eh?'

They ignored him and continued to retreat. The line descended into chaos and they careered into each other. Lizzie swallowed a scream that came out as a sharp intake of breath. Gus squeezed her arm. He wanted to reassure her.

'We are outside her sight. She is picking up our scent,' Gus whispered urgently, 'And can possibly hear us.'

The thought of no longer being the trackers, but being tracked, silenced them. The group's desire to push and shove subsided as their instinct for survival was stronger. As Gus predicted, the mother galloped for another two metres before abruptly slowing down as if she were unfit and running for a bus, only to miss it. She trotted to the right of them and out of sight. Surprisingly, she didn't 'thunder' past. She barely appeared to move. Her legs appeared to be folded into her skin.

Matt thought of Kipling's 'How the Rhinoceros Got His Skin'. His mother had read the *Just So Stories* to him as a child. Life was beating him up, whichever way he looked.

Despite the intimacy he had witnessed, the mother had left her calf alone and exposed in the small clearing. The calf moved uncertainly forward on its own and looked at them. He couldn't see that far, but looked in their direction. It was difficult to feel afraid of a child, though as far as black rhino were concerned, that was a naive and reckless position to take. Still Matt felt sorry for this calf alone, possibly afraid of them. He was ashamed that they had disturbed them. Slowly, the calf disappeared after its mother.

Once he was out of sight, the group erupted. There was a burst of euphoria, the thrill at being metres from danger: excitement, pride, emotion, togetherness. Matt caught Julian's eye. 'Quite a tale for the office.' He nodded curtly, because that was what he was thinking, but he didn't want to countenance Julian in any way. Katherine pronounced that Connie would be a fool not to leave him now. Otherwise, what would he do next? Move his mistress back into their family home? He seriously wondered whether Connie would agree with that. He wasn't sure. Matt had no desire to judge Connie.

Gus instructed them to turn slowly round and walk back towards the vehicle. Ben joined them from his vantage point up in an acacia tree. He led them, while Gus took up the rear. Their obedience had been stretched to its limits and they slid back into pairs. Katherine went first and he had to keep up with her long stride; Julian and Dan, and Alan and Lizzie followed with Sara a few feet ahead of Connie, who was trailing at the back. Gus was politely hovering behind her.

Matt heard the snorting before he saw any movement. Immediately afterwards, when he was comforting Sara and Katherine, he had only one image of the whole scene. It was that image that he would replay, re-tell for years to come, to the point where he wasn't sure what he had seen and what he had embellished.

The black rhino bull had been hidden in the acacia bush behind the opening where they had first seen the mother and calf. He burst out into the space. His nostrils were flared, his head right down until it touched the ground, his tail was erect, his ears cocked forward, listening for human sounds. He couldn't see them, but he moved distinctly in their direction. No one moved out of line; every one of them looked to Ben, then Gus, then Ben again. Ben power-walked them towards a cluster of acacia trees. They squashed behind them, squeezed, as if getting even closer to each other might make that vital difference. Gus stood his ground, facing the rhino and shouting at him. He slipped his rifle in an easy movement from his back to his arm. What had he said? Three rounds in nine seconds.

The bull charged. He could only be twenty metres away from them now. They saw her in their peripheral vision. Connie. She hadn't followed the others behind the acacia bushes. She was standing out in the open behind Gus with her hands calmly together in front of her, like Kate Middleton's at an official function. There was no change in her expression.

Julian moved out from behind the bush, shouting, 'Constance.'

Ben grabbed his arm and jerked him back; Julian hit Ben, a feeble punch in the shoulder, but Ben was too strong for him. 'Let go!' Julian shouted his anguish in a long howl: 'Constance.'

Ben and Julian wrestled as the sound of the bull became more distinct; the ground shifted. He could only be a few metres away now. They heard the clack of a rifle bolt being slammed back. A shot. On top of it, another one. Then only the sound of the bull. And silence.

Sara was crouching down and weeping uncontrollably. Katherine looked blankly at Matt, before whispering, 'I have urinated.' He didn't know what to say. He held her tightly. No one wanted to be the first to look. Ben moved decisively out from the bush and they waited as long as they could before following him, except Sara who didn't move or stop crying.

Connie was standing beside Gus. They were both unharmed. Matt's relief was tempered by his dread of seeing one of these rare animals dead because of them, because they were keen to see it 'in its natural environment'. High-powered tourists, who need to track an animal to feel alive. He was deeply ashamed of everything. First surrogacy, now this crime on safari, Matt closed his eyes and then slowly opened them again and followed the others.

There was no dead rhino. No rhino at all. It had gone. Gus had apparently fired warning shots.

Connie spoke into the silence. Her mouth traced a smile. 'Well, Gus, you said to stand your ground. So I did.'

Gus was bright red, visibly shaken. His anxiety and stress seeped out of him in sweat around his neck and down the sides of his shirt. He didn't speak but stared at Sara, who was crouching on the ground.

The group erupted. Katherine stood behind him, clearly trying to hide her wet trousers. She whispered into his back, 'I mean, when that rhino came out of nowhere. How crazy was that? Matt, I thought "we are going to die".'

Dan looked an unhealthy shade of grey. Sara was wailing. Gus helped her back upright. Sara flung her arms tightly around his neck, a gesture so out of character it emphasised how shocked she was. Gus squeezed her back. Julian squeezed the corners of his eyes with his fingers, before moving slowly and deliberately towards Connie.

Only Connie looked calm. 'You better get out your species checklist, Lizzie. Two ticks for a charging black rhino, don't you think?'

Connie could cope with anything. She was stronger than she looked. Matt was humbled, yet again, by the strength of a woman.

Chapter 26

The charging rhino was a sign. Connie imagined Leo and Lou laughing, but like Flora, she firmly believed in the synchronicity of life. How else could one accept the decisions one made, for good or for bad? Last night she made love to Luke, accepting the obvious sign: Julian and Emma had acted despicably, leaving Connie and Luke beached and wounded. They were meant to seek solace in each other. It was clear to Connie. On the journey to find the rhino, Connie thought about her night with Luke. She had no idea what it meant in the wider context of their complicated lives, or how they would move it forward. But it felt right.

When the rhino charged, she felt she was being taught a lesson: she needed to stand her ground with Julian. Making love to Luke was only the first step.

Julian was taking the midday flight in twenty minutes. His tears and his bloodshot right eye moved her in spite of the deed he had done. She wanted to share her grief with him. She wept silently. They were slumped in wicker chairs in the staff-free airstrip reception. Gus sat far away in the vehicle, pale and quiet.

Connie stopped weeping. As she watched Julian, she thought it was only four days since they flew into Gae. It had been long enough for her life to unravel. Connie wasn't ready to leave. It wasn't the safari she would miss, it was the space and time to be with her close friends. It was inextricably bound with a nostalgia for her past before Julian, family and children. It welled up inside her. Of course, it would pass. She would unlock their front door and Leo, Lou, Flora and Hector would be there, demanding and wonderful. Her family life would greedily re-absorb her, though it would never be the same. A fact she was forced to accept.

Julian looked up. His face was tortured, drawing Connie back to their life. 'Are you going to divorce me, Constance? I won't leave you. I'll sleep in a tent in the garden, if I have to.'

Connie considered the question. If she divorced Julian, everything she stood for was over. Her children would lose their close relationship with their father; their family would be forever incomplete. Julian would move on and in with Sally and their baby. Yet they could never repair the damage. Their marriage was over. Connie had seen a path with Luke, however unclear. The answer was somewhere in the middle of the possible options. She craved order, but she couldn't pretend there was order any more. Her life was messy and imperfect.

'For now, I am happy for you move into the basement flat.' Connie couldn't quite bring herself to say Sally's old flat. 'Long term, I'll have to see.'

Julian was looking down at his knees, Connie coughed to signal her intention to speak. 'Were you ever planning to leave?' Connie heard a certain detachment in her question, which gave her strength.

'No,' he insisted hurriedly. His eyes blinked. Connie could see he was fearful of her. 'That was never the plan. Believe me. I made that clear to Sally. She is happy with that.'

'I can imagine,' Connie believed him, knowing Sally. She would demand nothing, create no issues. 'What exactly was the plan, Julian?'

She gave him space to answer. She had no desire to speak for him. Her anger wasn't vituperative. She was comforted by the thought of Luke.

When Julian failed to speak, Connie couldn't resist saying, 'Were you really planning to wait until she was in the delivery suite to say: "Sorry, forgot to mention, Sally and I are having a baby today." '

'Connie, it wasn't like that. I wanted to tell you. There was never the right moment.' He looked up at her for understanding. Madly, she knew it was the truth, however flawed.

'You are a coward, Julian,' Connie said.

At dawn, when she lay in bed talking to Luke, she articulated Julian's cowardice. She talked herself through the enormity of the situation and the possible outcomes. When he was sure that she had finished, Luke spoke surprisingly firmly. 'Connie, last night, I took a slim chance that if we made love again, it might lead somewhere. But I'm not expecting it. Okay?'

She had simply nodded.

'I thought you must have known and you decided not to say anything.' Julian's words dragged her back to their conversation.

'What a despicable excuse. You are a huge coward.' She wasn't hoping he would acknowledge his own cowardice. She had finally learned she couldn't redeem him: she had had four children in the belief that the largesse of their family love would outweigh his adultery. The children hadn't changed anything. His affairs had been largely nameless and faceless, bar the odd tabloid exposure. But she had to face that her complicity had led inextricably to Sally.

Julian's head was bowed. He was crying again.

'How long have you been sleeping with each other?'

She could let the question slip out between her lips. She smiled inside. She was strong enough not to tell Julian that she had slept with Luke. She didn't owe Julian any explanation, nor did she want to devalue what happened with Luke by exposing it to Julian's censure.

'Sort of off and on,' Julian said quietly. His head was bowed. Connie was gratified that he felt some shame.

'How long, off and on?' Connie asked.

'A few years.'

Connie reflected that it had taken this shocking thing to enable them to talk properly about his extra-curricular life. Connie wondered what they had been doing all these years. Mere couriers delivering packages of pointless words.

'What? Ten years?'

Julian looked up at her. She could see his surprise. He hadn't expected her to be this calm. 'About four or five.'

Her chest tightened into a knot that made breathing excruciating. 'You are in love with her.'

Julian shot her an assessing look. The question was calmly asked. It demanded the truth. 'I was. Yes, I suppose I was. I was sorry for her. She was desperate for a child.'

'I know. Of course.'

How many conversations had they had about poor Sally and her genetic alarm clock? Had Connie chosen to bury the truth she surely must have spotted? Had she been deeply complicit? Surely over the years, she must have seen what was between them? Had her brain chosen to block it out? Connie couldn't honestly say.

'You slept together in our basement?' The knife was deep in the folds of her flesh. There was no point pulling it out now.

Julian looked awkward. He could only offer her silence in response.

Connie had to repeat it. 'You slept together in our basement?'

He nodded bleakly without looking at her.

They were left with their great family, four children, which Connie calmly noted was much stronger and better established than Sally and her poor baby.

'What are the plans now?'

'I've said to Sally that I will obviously be around.'

'Be around? What does that mean exactly, Julian?' Connie sensed her strength. She could face this situation. Julian couldn't.

'I will obviously see her. Well, see the baby.'

'I'm confused. Spell it out for me: you are going to continue to have sex with Sally and see your child?'

Julian blushed.

'No. Not the former, obviously. See the baby.'

'Okay. No sex, just paternal visits.'

He paused, embarrassed. 'I mean, obviously somewhere else.' He looked up, hopefully, but with a naivety, which gave Connie even greater strength.

'Far away.' Connie concluded forcefully. 'North Oxfordshire is not going to be far enough.'

Julian nodded. 'Whatever you want.'

Connie couldn't stop. 'When are you going to tell the children?' Back to the children. Safe ground. Neither of them wanted to hurt the children. 'Leo and Lou will take it very badly. They are adults.'

Julian paled.

'Right, well, let me know when you have told them.'

He nodded.

It was like the end of a long meeting in an airless room. They were both drained. Of course, they would talk on and on about the situation. It would never go away. Sally and her baby had changed them forever. Right now, Connie was done. She looked at her watch. Ten minutes before he would board. She didn't want to hover, only to fake a wifely wave in front of Gus. She got up, scraping the feet of the wicker chair back along the decking. Julian mirrored her moves.

'Constance, I know you wouldn't believe me now, but I do genuinely love you.'

Connie sighed. 'Clearly, the love you feel for me is not the right kind.'

He looked suitably cowed.

Connie turned from where she was standing. Her boots comfortably sinking into the orange sand.

'Happy birthday,' he attempted a smile. 'For tomorrow, obviously.'

She held up her hand to acknowledge him.

'I have something for you, but I wasn't sure. In the circumstances.'

'Quite,' she said quickly.

She turned away, her phone bleeped. She swiped into her text messages.

Connie, I feel awful. I never wanted to hurt you. I thought you knew. Can you ever forgive me? Sally x

Connie deleted the message.

Chapter 27

After their insane experience, the group tipped in the bar: talkative and eager to relive their dawn duel with death, except Alan, who looked surprisingly sullen. Since they were safe, Lizzie noticed the rhino danger slipped easily into being a story that they would always remember, like their times together at Harley Place.

This holiday was the glamorous adventure that Lizzie believed that she always wanted. A dangerous experience, which confirmed that she was alive. Now she wasn't sure. She started thinking about her local friends Sasha and Julie and missing their straightforward personalities and lives.

When the others peeled away, looking exhausted, frankly – Connie with Julian to the airstrip, Katherine and Matt to their room, Dan and Alan to eat brunch by the pool – Lizzie was left alone.

She perched on a barstool with yet another coffee, glad to be on her own. Julian was gone not only from her head and also from Gae, and she was subtly different. She couldn't quite place it. She rejected the bowl of coconut balls. It was a rare moment of calm. It struck her like walking into a vast, silent room. It was an unexpected breathing space. Time to think.

When the rhino charged, the others had unravelled. Katherine had wet herself, Sara had wailed as if her career was over, but Lizzie had stayed relatively calm. She was surprised by her reaction, but also proud.

She finished her coffee and thought that she would go to her room and make a list of things she wanted to do as soon as she got back home. She passed Sara and Gus sitting on the sofa outside the sitting room, overlooking the pool deck. Sara looked miserable. She ought to briefly join them. As she sat down beside them, she saw that Gus looked as low as Sara.

Sara folded her arms tightly across her body and looked wary. 'Lizzie.'

'Is anything wrong, Sara?' she was obliged to ask.

'Nigel Sutton has confessed to Alistair Blunt. There will be a re-trial.'

'Did he kill Jade?' Lizzie quickly thought. 'Why would he tell a journalist?'

'He probably couldn't live with the guilt,' Sara said glumly, glancing at Gus.

'What does that mean for you?'

'I'm finished as a barrister – set to be disbarred.'

'Oh no, how awful.' She attempted a light joke. 'The husband did it in the bedroom with the pills.'

Sara looked at her blankly. Lizzie realised her mistake. Sara probably never played Cluedo on a Sunday night.

'I was thinking of Cluedo, the murder board game.'

'I know about Cluedo,' Sara snapped.

Lizzie was annoyed. Sara knew about everything, she was worldly wise, but what did she actually experience? If she had had more life experience, perhaps she wouldn't have made a mistake with this case.

Gus appeared to be trying to intervene, leaning towards her. 'Lizzie, you were brave this morning.'

Lizzie smiled, 'It was quite exciting, though I shall be quite happy to get back to London alive.'

Sara stared out darkly. It was unlike her. Sara was constantly listening, reacting, amusing and diverting.

For once, Lizzie felt less complicated than Sara – in fact, than the whole group. Matt and Katherine losing a baby; Julian's revelation about his baby; Sara and her teetering career; Luke's divorce from his wife, his custody of his children, and his obvious love for Connie; Dan and Alan's unhappy relationship. Her concerns about her job, buying a flat, even finding a boyfriend were less insurmountable than she had previously thought. She had envied them all, particularly Connie. But she didn't want the high drama of Connie's life. She checked herself. She wasn't smugly thinking her life was sorted, far from it. Still, she was luckier than she thought. Lizzie felt a lightness, which didn't depend on her friends or their moods.

Sara was marooned on the sofa. She could only talk to Gus because he knew the truth before Alistair exposed it. Lizzie was long gone, yet Gus said nothing. He didn't give her his probing look. In fact, he didn't look at her all. Sara was ashamed.

'What are you going to do, Sara?' he said eventually.

She hadn't thought about that, but looking at his expression she knew the answer.

'Of course I'm on the back foot, despite my good intentions. I need to go back. Confess all, before Joanne Sutton does,' she sounded neutral. Years of practice talking to clients. She was very good at it. 'There'll be a disciplinary hearing and, considering the profile of the case and Nigel Sutton's imminent re-trial, I will either be suspended or disbarred.'

'Are you sure?'

She smiled. 'I only understand the law, Gus.'

He gently returned her smile. 'It's the right thing to do, Sara. Then you can live with yourself.'

'Which is a good thing when no one else wants me.' She blushed. The comment was beneath her.

'You think that someone will only love you because you are a high-powered barrister?' He paused. 'You're harsh on yourself, Sara.'

'Not as harsh as other barristers will be.' She mimicked what she thought the other barristers might say. '*Sara Wilson went completely off the rails. Normally it's the client who is a nutter. Sad considering how hard she worked to become a great barrister.*'

'You are only human, Sara.'

'That's the point.' She tried to wave her free hand amusingly. 'I'll be buried. For once, Lizzie's spot on. I will end up a lonely lesbian in a Florida bungalow.'

'Only you're not a lesbian,' he swung back, smiling.

'A technical detail.'

'Sara. You've been having sex with the wrong people, eh?'

'Who is the right person?'

He stood up. 'Only you know that, Sara.'

What Sara wanted to say was, I am going back to get disbarred. Might you want me after that? Take me to your tower of integrity. Of course, she didn't. Life wasn't a Mills & Boon novel. It was a bloody 18-rated movie.

Luke felt terrible. He was getting something, perhaps even a chest infection. It hurt as he breathed. His head was throbbing. His muscles ached as if he had overdone the exercise. He barely moved from his bed after Connie left for the ride. She hadn't wanted to go, but they both decided it was best for at least one of them to show up.

Luke was ill yet happy. When he had woken to find Connie standing over him, he had made a snap decision. Of course, there was a distinct possibility she was only with him for comfort after Julian's treachery, combined with a deep-rooted sympathy for the wounds that Emma had inflicted. However, there was a slim chance she might still love him. He wasn't going to live with regrets as far as Connie was concerned. If they had only one night together, so be it.

Lying in bed, smiling to himself, he was relaxed for the first time in a long time. He had no desire to move, certainly not to run. He was going to take a break from exercise until he got home. It was too hot. He didn't need to do it. If he wasn't fit enough for the Iron Man, he could always drop out.

He wound the duvet around himself. With Connie, he felt emotionally and sexually alive, when he had thought that those parts of him had been suffocated. Even the thought of making love to Connie made him grin. She must be back from the airstrip. Luke knew Julian would have fought hard to keep her. Yet he was calm. He had made love to Connie. It was as great as he remembered. He could do no more. He understood the situation was outside his control, but it didn't make him panic.

He heard the outer door scrape on the stones. Matt or Connie.

205

He toyed with the odds of either. He was enjoying his game, when his door opened. He knew it was Connie before he rolled over to see her, standing with her back against the closed door. She stood watching him. 'Are you feeling better?'

He shook his head. 'Are you okay?' He studied her face.

'Yes, I am.' She gave her half-smile.

'Julian?' He struggled to say his name neutrally.

'Gone. Banished to the basement. Didn't tell him about us.'

Luke briefly weighed up Connie's reasons for keeping last night secret. On balance, he was pleased. Of course, he would have loved Julian to suffer, but it could mean that Connie was using him to get back at Julian.

'And Sally?' He said tentatively, aware how unpredictable pain was.

She walked straight up to the bed and swung her bag off her shoulder and crouched beside him. 'Banished further afield,' she paused. 'He has been sleeping with her for around five years.'

He took the bag out of her hands and held them.

She glanced up at him. 'You are thinking that I must have known.'

He didn't speak for a moment. 'I have never judged you, Connie. I'm not going to start now.'

She kissed him, before answering her own question. 'Did I see a look between them and choose to block it out because it didn't fit my narrative? Honestly, I can't say.'

'What are you going to do, Connie?'

She didn't answer. Instead, she bent down and dug a packet of Nurofen Extra out of her bag.

'I've already taken far too many codeine.'

She dropped them back into her bag. They looked at one another. Luke ran his fingers down the side of her face, wondering if he had the strength to make love to her again. She captured his hand and kissed it gently, before letting it go.

'Do you remember I showed you that photo of Gae in the forties?'

He nodded. 'The land was ravaged.'

Connie leaned her head against his arm. 'I found a notebook belonging to my grandfather.' She dug the book out of her bag.

Luke curled his fingers round her neck. 'Brilliant. What does he say?'

'I started reading it while we were camping. It's all about this being the last great wilderness and we need to protect and nurture it, leave it for our grandchildren.'

Luke smiled. 'How appropriate.'

'Is this boring you?'

'I'm not Julian.'

She blushed.

Luke quickly wrapped his arm round her head and pulled her face right up against his. 'I'm sorry, Connie. Very childish. Please. I'm interested and listening.'

'I just rang my mother to ask why he ended up here. And I told her about Julian too. She acted as if I were going mad.'

Luke smiled, imagining Connie's outspoken mother's reaction. 'I can imagine Felicity was *rather alarmed* in the circumstances.'

Connie gave a slight snort. 'Rather alarmed, yes, such a Felicity phrase.'

'How's Philip taking it?'

'Dad's devastated,' she looked up. 'I'm worried about him.'

'I'll give him a call later.'

'He said I should have married you.'

Luke managed a smile. 'Well, we all know that.'

Connie dipped her head. When she did that she always reminded him of a swan: breath-taking but sad.

'About your grandfather?'

'Oh yes,' she looked relieved. 'My mother reluctantly told me he came here because my grandmother left him for a pilot.'

Luke silently absorbed the similarities.

Connie nodded. 'Can I read you something?'

'Of course.'

'Okay.' She carefully flicked the pages through to one she had marked with a piece of torn paper. '*Mother Nature is a great healer: all she needs is time and space. There are plenty of both here.*'

Luke watched her silently. He could see where Connie was leading, as clearly as if she had written it on a white board, but he didn't rush her.

She glanced up at him. 'He went on to write: *I want to restore the Kalahari to itself.* Isn't that beautiful?'

'Yes,' he spoke quickly. 'And a perfect metaphor. For him and for you.'

She smiled, delighted he grasped her full meaning. Studying with Connie had been wonderful. They led each other to the right conclusions. They both got almost exactly the same high 2:1.

She flashed him an emotive look. It reminded him of when she spoke about her first dinner with Julian. Waiting for him to thrust certainty upon her, which he could never do. Though now, he could meet her halfway.

'Look, you don't need to be sure, darling. Try out the idea on me.'

'I was wondering whether I might set up a black rhino foundation,' she hurried on. 'Of course, I'm in London with four children, but they have long holidays. I don't know anything about it, but I can learn. It is one of the most extraordinary places on this planet. And I should continue my grandfather's work. Though I might be reading too much into it…'

He kissed her gently. 'No you're not. It's a great idea. I can see you running an animal foundation.'

'Really?' She looked at him critically.

'Really.'

'Luke, you're brilliant at business. Could you help me set it up? I know you're busy with your company, and Ella and Finn, of course. I mean, not full-time or anything. Just to get me started.'

He smiled. 'Definitely.'

'Thank you, Luke.' She kissed him and, as she pulled away her blue eyes, focused on his. He decided that she probably did love him. Whether it was enough to surmount her loyalty to Julian and the children, he wasn't at all sure.

'About us, Luke.'

'It's complicated,' he quickly acknowledged.

'Yes, it is. If we didn't have children…'

He stroked her hair, 'But we do.'

She was silent, watching him.

'Connie, we don't need to know where we are going, but what we feel right now. It is enough for me.'

He could see in her eyes that she didn't believe him. She knew him too well. She squeezed his hands. They sat there for a few minutes.

She moved suddenly to delve into her bag and bring out a clear tube.

'What is that?'

'Pure vitamin E oil. I use it when I burn,' she paused, 'It's amazing at healing scars.'

Luke couldn't speak. She took off her canvas shoes, slipped off her trousers and carefully climbed over him and into the bed. She lifted off the duvet and turned him gently on to his stomach. He didn't stop her. He felt the extreme coolness of the gel as she applied it to his back. He felt it soaking into his burns and the scars from his stitches, making him aware of how dry and itchy they usually felt. She got him to move to face her. Lying on his left side, she squeezed the gel gently along the front of his hips. She ran her fingers along the stitches to help the liquid soak in. He watched her, amazed at himself. He was no longer wary of her touching him. She stretched over him to put the tube down on the table. She lay down on her side, close to him. She was smiling. He watched her watching him, until she fell asleep.

Chapter 28

Torches cast vermillion shadows on the rugs unfurled over the bronze sand. The dark side tables were mesmerising in candlelight. Sofas and throws had been transported here to create an intimate sitting room, but no one sat down. Mile upon mile upon mile of dunes radiated around them to a horizon that was limitless in its reach and possibility. The group was trapped by the weeping beauty of such an openness. They wanted to absorb it and for it to absorb them.

Luke placed his weight on to a director's chair. The cream canvas bowed down to compensate for his weakness. He painfully stood up and struggled towards the bar. He glanced at the square dining table glistening with the full tableware they had at the lodge. Imagining the human toil involved in transporting this entire dinner party here on to the dunes made his chest tighten again. He slumped back on to his chair.

He was happy, though shattered. Lying in a cool bath earlier in the evening, he had unpacked his thoughts. Julian was banished to the basement, though he might well climb back out into the house. For now, they were separated. Their divorce was incidental to Luke, if Connie was emotionally and physically free from Julian.

Connie slipped into the khaki director's chair beside him. He had carefully avoided her, knowing the group would instantly realise what had happened. He didn't mind whether they knew or not, though he sensed Connie would.

'It's unbelievably beautiful, isn't it?' she said softly resting the palm of her hand flat on top of his. Her warmth seeped into his skin.

He took her hand and placed it on his leg. 'I love it here, Connie.'

'So do I.'

They smiled at each other. He was buoyed up by her public show of affection.

'Are you feeling better?'

Connie was the only woman who had truly cared about him.

'I'm fine.' He didn't want to talk about feeling ill. It was banal and irrelevant in the circumstances. All he wanted to do was enjoy being with her. He leaned over to wrap his arm around her. It hurt to do so. He winced. 'How are you feeling now?'

'Surprisingly good.'

He leaned his head close to hers. He felt a stray hair touch the side of his face. He moved it carefully back behind her ear. She gave him that dreamy smile.

She shifted back and down the chair and looked out at the view. 'How could you and I not be okay out here?' Connie turned towards him.

'Exactly. What the hell.'

'What the hell!' she grinned.

He grinned back, but grimaced as his chest clenched. 'You and I should make that our motto.'

'A motto for my forties.' She quietly turned to him. 'Can you believe that I'm going to be forty tomorrow? You will be in June.'

He nodded. 'I feel old and young.'

She turned to him. 'Yes, that's it. We should be old enough to know what we are doing. Only we are still beginners.' She sighed. 'Though I'm happy being forty.'

Luke thought about it. 'Yes, so am I.'

Connie rested her head under his neck. Her chest gently pressed against him. Her weight hurt. He almost asked her to move.

'I've known you for twenty-two years. Isn't that incredible?' She sighed. 'Such a long time.' She looked up at him. 'I could never become as close to someone new.' She kissed him. Her smile, her lips, her fine neck, those bare collar bones were moving against him. Finally, they parted. Luke knew what he wanted to say.

'Connie, I fell in love with you at the first Freshers' Week dinner. And I never stopped loving you. Why I didn't tell you, I'll never truly know. But I love you even more now.'

'I loved you, Luke,' She smiled gently. He loved her smile. 'And I still love you.'

Connie kissed him again on the lips. It was always Connie. She stood up in front of his chair. He would have stood up too, only he was feeling too weak. She gave him that mysterious smile, which he now could interpret.

Dan had spent years considering nature and plants. Landscapes. Yet he had never fully appreciated one until now. The quiet majesty of these dunes filled him with joy. He was happy and free of the nagging sense of melancholy that had been haunting him. It made him feel warm and loving towards Alan. Dan had had his doubts, but they had a wonderfully loving and stable relationship. Sara joined Lizzie and Connie, leaving the two of them alone. Dan put an arm round Alan and drew him close. 'It's amazing here, isn't it? Can you believe this place? The whole trip has been incredible.'

'Yeah, if you enjoy dicing with death in the desert.' There was no mistaking Alan's tetchy tone.

Dan didn't want to spoil this rare moment, but he sympathised. 'It was terrifying this morning, wasn't it? I think that Gus knew what he was doing.'

'Like hell he did. He looked as shit-scared as I was.'

Dan nodded, his mouth tightening. He wanted to divert Alan away from yet another post-mortem on this morning and draw him towards the horizon, their future, wherever it was.

Alan was having none of it. 'Connie's a good friend, and I do buy that, but it's been a waste of a shed load of money and annual leave to boot, if you ask me.'

Alan was speaking in a stage whisper that made his complaints obvious to the girls a few metres away.

Dan didn't reply. He turned back to stare at the sky. It was a painting in a profusion of fuchsia, flamboyantly touched with blue and purple. He wanted to absorb it, draw its beauty into his being. He wished he had brought his sketchpad. He had thought there would be nothing to capture at sunset. How mad. He turned to share his feelings with Alan. 'I'd love to paint this sky on a large canvas for our sitting room.'

'Yeah.' Alan eyed the sky sceptically.

The girls were bending down, flashing infrared torches and giggling loudly about the scorpion hunt they were going to have later. Dan closed his eyes and opened them again. It made the colours burst brighter.

'Dan, look…' Alan sighed.

'I understand, Alan. Don't worry. It wasn't a great day, I can see that.'

'It's not the blinking day or holiday, though it has made me realise. Seeing you with your complicated friends…' Alan's left hand was flapping. 'I am sorry, but I don't want my life to change. I like it exactly the same. No upheaval, no drama except on a box set. A couple of nights' clubbing, a couple at the gym and a couple of takeaways from Poppadum, that's me.'

'While I've been feeling unsettled. I wondered whether I wanted to buy that land and create "roots". It's probably a bit of a mid-life crisis.'

Alan frowned, as if even referring to middle age put him out of sorts.

'It wasn't you, Alan, that was the problem, it was me. In my head. We are similar.' He touched his hand. 'A box set and a Moroccan vegetarian curry,' Dan forced a smile. 'That's me too, isn't it?'

Alan didn't smile back.

Dan pushed on. 'We are close; we are right. It wasn't you. It was my dissatisfaction with myself.'

'I'll never lose a spot in my heart for you, Dan. You are great, Dan my man.'

He stared at Alan. He no longer looked like the sullen teenager he had been for the last year.

'I'm sorry, Dan. I want out, that's the long and short of it.'

Dan felt a desperate lurch, which he quickly identified as fear. He didn't want Alan to leave, for the worst reason. He didn't want the instability. He had been prepared to live on with him indefinitely, even though they didn't want the same future or life. He wanted to buy that land in Tuscany. He wanted to move on and create something lasting, somewhere he was proud to belong. Why hadn't he been brave enough to follow his instincts? Alan hated confrontation more than he did. Yet he was prepared to go it alone. Unlike Dan. He had to be pushed. He was a coward. He needed his friends, or madly even Alan, to make him brave.

'Sure, Alan. I do understand. It's the right decision.' He took a deep breath in. 'Very brave, Alan.'

It was the truth.

The shadows darkened into silhouettes. The group gathered round the square dining table. The meat had been grilled on a long barbecue, a discreet distance from the table. The smiling staff had put in dark earthenware beside the pap and pumpkin. Connie was sitting squashed between Matt and Katherine at one corner of the table. She was replaying her kiss with Luke. Their reignited love could survive when they were back in their daily lives. Practically, she didn't know how it would work. But she was sure she was meant to be back with Luke. It was the synchronicity of her life. Somehow the hurt she felt about Julian and Sally would ease into the status quo. One got used to anything in the end.

'Gus, what's it to be tomorrow? I'm not sure that you can top walking into black rhino.'

'Well, if the wind's right, you have your balloon ride, eh?'

'Hey! I had completely forgotten about it,' Katherine looked thrilled.

Maybe life did work out for the best, however unclear it was at the time.

'In the meantime, safari party people, we have scorpions,' Sara paused. 'Now I am sorry to disappoint you, but they don't charge. Though I promise they bite.'

Director's chairs bumped back over the sand. Gus and Sara led the others back towards their 'sitting room' and beyond to the raw thorny slope. Alan and Lizzie went first, immediately followed by Katherine and Dan. Connie gave Luke a quick glance, hoping to catch his eye. He was asleep. He clearly wasn't well. She wondered whether she should ask someone to take him back to Gae, but then she would rather go back with him later. She didn't have the energy to crouch low looking for a scorpion and she relished a moment with Matt alone.

'What a mad day, Mattie,' she smiled.

'Scary to the sublime.' Matt tried to shift, only he was constrained by the narrow director's chair. 'After a night when Luke nearly finished me off.'

They both smiled and contemplated Luke. He looked peaceful.

'He hasn't changed,' she said with an easy smile. She floated on a lake of possibility.

'No. He hasn't. Nor have you two together. I saw you earlier.'

Connie blushed. 'Matt, I can explain.'

He leaned against her. 'Don't worry, I think that I was the only one who did.'

She smiled. 'Maybe that's the problem. I'm not bothered.'

Matt raised an eyebrow at her. 'Sara's always spot on. She told me something was going on between you.'

Connie smiled.

He touched her arm gently. 'Not surprising, Connie, in the circumstances, for both of you.'

She looked over at Luke. 'You know, Luke had a horrendous time with Emma. Believe me.'

Matt nodded vigorously. 'Yeah, I've worked that out, though he doesn't want to tell me exactly what happened.'

'It's too awful and too personal for him to share.'

'Except with you.'

Connie registered the point. 'I don't have the answers, Mattie. Strangely, I'm all right about it.' She paused and looked at him. 'Do you disapprove?'

'Me? No, Connie. God knows you both deserve to be happy.'

Connie smiled.

'Are you going to divorce Julian?'

She sighed. 'He's going to move to the basement. I'm taking it one step at a time.' She touched his shoulder in appreciation. 'I have no desire to destroy my family in the process.'

'You have four kids to think about, I understand.'

She chose her words carefully. 'Katherine is strong too. She seems to be coping with the news about Isobel.'

Matt nodded silently.

'What about you, Mattie? How do you feel now?'

'What about me?' There was a hollow echo in his voice. 'Coming up against a rhino puts your life in perspective. I have Katherine: she is beautiful, wise and lovely. And she really does love me. It's not ideal, but it's more than enough for me.'

Connie was silent as she considered what he had said.

'Katherine doesn't want to try again. The surrogate thing was tricky from the start.' Matt spoke quietly. He sighed and pulled at his handkerchief in his shorts pocket. 'I don't know, Connie. I hated the whole process too. If we had got what we wanted in the end... who knows?'

They were both silent, distracted by the hooting of the others.

'Scorpions,' she grimaced, 'Too much for me.'

He didn't seem to have heard her. He was staring at Luke.

She followed his eyeline. 'He's not feeling well. It's probably flu. Let's leave him.'

She touched Matt on his shoulder to draw him back. He ignored her. He lurched precariously round the table until he landed in a heavy squat beside Luke's chair. He awkwardly re-adjusted into an uneasy crouch. Connie couldn't read Matt's movements and expression.

'Connie, he has stopped breathing.'

Chapter 29

Connie tried to resuscitate him. She used every ounce of her strength. She fought to bring him back to life. She could give him air; she could save Luke. She kept trying, again and again, until she was oblivious. It was as blinding a tunnel of physical endurance as childbirth. After a while, she wasn't aware of herself physically or mentally. The doctor arrived with oxygen. Matt gently tipped her back on to her knees, but she refused to move further away. Minutes later, the doctor stood up and told them what he thought had happened. A myocardial infarction, probably caused by coronary artery disease, which could have been exacerbated by sudden and extreme exercise, though he made clear that only the post-mortem could be conclusive. And he pronounced Luke's death.

Connie sat on her knees beside Luke's body. She didn't move. She could hear the others talking, but she couldn't make out what they were saying. She sat watching Luke. She was focused on this task, because it was important. As the others moved around, back to Luke and away again, she stayed where she was. Only she was too late to protect him. Always too late.

She reached for his hand. She lifted up her shirt and pressed his palm to her stomach.

Dan was beside her. She saw the knee of his jeans. 'Connie, we are going to get Luke back to Gae.'

He talked like a nurse, explaining the practical details the doctor glossed over. She heard him, but she couldn't respond.

'Connie?' Dan paused. 'They are going to make a bed for Luke in the goods vehicle. You can go with him, if you want.'

Connie wanted him to go away. Leave her to Luke. Leave them together. He didn't move.

'Connie, sorry. Someone needs to call his parents and the children.' Dan struggled to contain himself. 'And Emma, I suppose…'

Connie spoke sharply. 'Not Emma.'

'Sure,' Dan spoke hastily. 'But we need to call his parents right now. Matt's prepared to make the call.'

Connie slowly turned to him. He was crying.

'I should call them.'

She saw Dan look at somebody and Matt descended down to her other side.

'Connie, darling,' Matt's voice was unstable. His face was wet with tears. 'It's fucking horrible. You've gone through hell in the last hour, I'm not sure that, understandably, you're up to call. God, I don't want to have to speak to Tina and Michael but I will. Why don't you leave it to me?'

'It's my call to make.'

Matt and Dan moved simultaneously up and away from them. They were left together again. Connie and Luke. As they were meant to be. She bent gently down over his chest and wrapped her arms around him.

'Connie, Matt has the number in his phone. Are you sure that you can do this, sweetheart?' He squeezed his fingers into his eyes.

She nodded vigorously. She spoke softly to Luke, 'I have to go and talk to your parents now. I'm coming back.'

Dan and Matt helped her to her feet. She took the phone from Matt and walked to the edge of the living room. She sat down in the director's chair, where Luke had been before dinner. Strangely for him, his glass was only half finished, resting on the arm of the chair. She felt repulsed by it and turned to Matt's phone for comfort. It rang and rang. It was after midnight, and Tina and Michael were over seventy. She kept ringing. No answer. There was an automated voice: *We cannot connect your call. Please try later.* She ended the call and returned to the number again. This time it was as if Tina was beside the phone.

Tina's voice tinkled through the darkness. '01364 714—' Connie didn't hear the rest of the number, which, anyway, she still knew by heart. 'Hello.'

Matt and Dan were right. She couldn't do it to them. They were such good people. Luke was their only son.

'Tina, it's Connie.'

'Connie, hello!' Her enthusiasm punctured Connie's numbness. 'How is the Kalahari? Oh and happy birthday. I can't believe you are forty, makes me feel old. I remember you at nineteen.'

Connie was shaking. 'Oh Tina.'

She fought to hold in the tears. She bit her lips furiously. She had to be strong for Tina and Michael, for Ella and Finn. It was all she could do for Luke now.

'Connie, what's wrong?' Tina's voice sounded scared.

Connie clasped her mouth. How could she make her suffer like this?

'Tina.' She was sobbing too much to speak.

She heard Tina move away from the phone. There was silence for a moment. She sniffed violently several times to hold it in.

'Connie, hello, it's Michael. Tina's at the other end. Please tell us what has happened.'

She breathed in sharply, 'Luke has had a heart attack.'

'No.' Tina's voice seemed to disappear from her.

'I'm so sorry, Tina, Michael. He's dead. I'm so sorry.'

Tina was wailing; Michael was silent.

'Thank you for making the call.' He said eventually. 'Can't have been easy.'

'I wanted to be the one to tell you.' The tears flowed. She couldn't stop them. 'Michael, I wish I was with you.'

'Thank you, Connie. I don't know what to say.' Michael's voice was formal. He didn't do personal conversations. Here was the cruelty of life forcing him into an alien role. 'Especially after yesterday.'

'Sorry?' Connie couldn't follow.

'Luke called us yesterday.'

'Oh,' Connie was nervous about where this was leading.

'He told me what happened with Emma,' Michael coughed. Connie knew he was hating every minute of it, but he needed to talk. And she was, perhaps, the only person he could confide in. 'He told me, because he had confided in you, and it made him realise that we needed to know. He had to be brave enough to tell us. He said we needed to understand why he had the grandchildren.'

Connie struggled to think what she could say. Michael didn't deserve guilt on top of grief.

'Emma hurt him physically,' she said carefully. 'But she couldn't destroy who he was. Luke was unchanged by her.'

Michael coughed. Then Connie realised he was crying into a handkerchief or something to mumble the sound. She didn't say anything. She waited for him.

Finally, he spoke. 'I'm not sure whether it's the truth, but thank you, Connie.' He paused. 'He also told us about the two of you.'

'Oh, Michael, what must you think of me,' Connie continued rapidly. 'If it's any consolation, I always loved Luke.'

'If it's any consolation, he did too.'

Connie wiped her face. She didn't know if Michael was now speaking the truth, or was he simply comforting her as she had comforted him. But she gratefully accepted it.

'Michael,' she paused, 'I abandoned him, us. I am responsible for the fact he ended up with Emma.'

He sighed. 'Oh Connie, don't punish yourself. You were both too young to be serious about each other.'

Connie didn't believe that. 'But I'm not going to abandon him now. I'm not leaving Africa without him.'

'I don't know what we are going to do.' He sounded frail and lost. 'We need to tell the grandchildren. Then we'll have to stay put to be here for them. Anyway, I'm not sure that I could make it over.'

'Absolutely not. You must stay at home,' Connie hoped she sounded reassuring. 'Luke would have wanted you to be there for Ella and Finn. It's the best thing you can do.'

'Yes, you're right,' he sounded as if he gathered courage from the thought of them.

'I'll bring Luke home to Dartmoor.'

'God bless you, Connie.'

Chapter 30

The wake was Sara's idea. Her mother and her best friend Sandra had held a wake for her auntie Val. Sara wouldn't have suggested it if Luke had died in his bed in Battersea. London would have constrained her taste and emotions. Out here, it was only right that the group should watch over their closest friend. They were his family. In the morning, he would be gone from them – his body was being flown to Jo'Burg for a post-mortem. Sara hadn't expected the others to embrace the idea. She was quite prepared to stay up alone with Luke.

As they arrived at Gae, following the vehicle carrying Luke, Sara spoke carefully. 'I think that we should all stay with Luke tonight.'

Matt started to cry. Katherine held him in her arms with a tenderness that Sara envied. Lizzie was silent, staring at the vehicle ahead.

Connie was in the other vehicle with Luke. Sara was shocked and hurt, she couldn't begin to imagine what Connie was feeling. She walked slowly to join her. She was fearful of seeing Luke again. She didn't look at him.

'Connie, I was suggesting to the others that we stay with Luke tonight. But would you rather be with him alone?'

Connie didn't look at Sara. She was crouched on the floor of the vehicle beside a stretcher, which was placed in the empty back of a storage vehicle. She was holding his hand. 'I'm not leaving him, but I would like you there.'

The reserve staff were desperate to oblige in the circumstances. They understood their need for the wake, but were keen to quickly isolate them away from the few other guests. Sara, Matt and the doctor shifted the sofas in Luke's sitting room until they pressed against the large wardrobe housing tea and coffee, a kettle and an iron, and the bookshelf leaving a large space in the centre. A dining table was found, carried down the brick path from the deck by two staff and covered with white tablecloths.

The doctor and Matt lifted Luke from the wheelchair, which they placed him in to get his body from the vehicle to his house. Connie covered him in a throw, while Sara lit candles around the room and turned on two low table lamps. Connie opened the curtains though it was too dark to see even the outline of bushes or animals.

Sara was shocked when Connie climbed on to the table beside Luke. She curled beside him underneath the throw with her arm over his body. Her eyes were wide open, but she didn't speak or cry. Lizzie looked like she might be sick. She sat next to Dan, who squeezed her hand and wiped away his tears with his free hand. On the other side of the room, Matt and Katherine wrapped their arms around each other.

In the silence that settled on the room, Sara watched her friends. Connie had such strength, it radiated from her, even now. Matt had undoubtedly lost his best friend, but he loved Katherine. Lizzie would weep and sentimentally re-tell everybody about losing Luke. Dan would process it and move on. Alan was nowhere to be seen, which hardly surprised Sara.

What about her, Sara wondered? The others believed she had Northern grit, but that was rubbish. She was soft like egg yolk, the mere touch of a fork and she burst. She had no brothers, no sisters, no father. The loss of Luke drew her back to her perennial loss. She closed her eyes.

She didn't know any more if she made it up. She had never discussed it with Mum. It was too cruel to ask her. Her dad in his grey ill-fitting pin stripe with the shiny knees, his blond hair gelled back, dressed up for his job at the bank, on the tills, as he used to say. His long legs forcing his knees up over the minute pine table fitted

222

between their cooker and kitchen cupboards. Every morning he had three slices of toast with a thick layer of butter and marmalade. They never talked at breakfast time. Her mother hovered, serving them both. Sara usually had her head in a book. She probably had that morning. She needed to believe she did. It somehow excused her from not realising that this moment was upon her. He finished his toast and tea. Did he kiss her on the forehead, as he usually did? When she was a girl, she believed that he said, 'I will never stop loving you, Sara.' Of course, he didn't. It hadn't been a movie moment. The camera didn't pan to his pained expression as he left his wife and daughter forever. He simply left.

She found tears coming. She shifted on the arm of the sofa, trying to tear herself away from the past. She rigorously never ever thought about it and certainly didn't talk about it, even to the group. The past was the past. Lots of people had had difficult childhoods. The important thing was what you did with your life.

Matt gently unwound himself from Katherine and reached for her hand. His tenderness overwhelmed her. She sunk into Matt's shoulder. He hugged her tightly.

These friends were her precious family, whom she had somehow taken for granted in the last ten years, imagining they would always be around. She had superficially replaced them with her fellow barristers in Chambers. Charles Fahy, head of Chambers, became a modern father figure: a career mentor. Yet when she called him, as she must do today about her breaches of the Code of Conduct, she couldn't imagine telling him about Luke's death. How could she share with him what Luke meant to her? What this week meant to her?

She wept in Matt's arms.

Dawn drew in the scene outside the veranda doors. The light paled to grey blue; an impala stretched to graze on a fresh patch of sour grass; a trio of tiny brown birds performed the salsa; several African sunflowers yellowed into view.

Connie was asleep beside Luke. They looked like they were a couple in bed together, which made Sara weep again. She moved to lean on Dan's shoulder. Dan appeared to be asleep sitting up. Katherine's tiny form was curled up on Matt with her head in his lap, her arm across her face. Lizzie and Matt were awake.

Sara had grown up with the myth that a wake was about watching for the dead to wake up. She didn't feel that now. As she watched Luke, she could see his features wax away; his expression was blank and his form was no longer defined. Luke was leaving them. Luke, who was generous, warm, honest and an embracer of every tiny corner of his life: love, marriage, children, career and physical and mental challenges. He was the epitome of the modern man with his own Internet company and his Iron Man challenge. Yet Luke was pounded out of here, after his efforts.

Life was continuing to emerge on the other side of the window. Daylight highlighted the grasses; the white butterflies flickered into view. This must have been what it was like for Joanne Sutton. Despite her husband's killing her only child, the light glistened through her curtains, and in the bleaching morning, she could believe for a moment that none of it had ever happened. None of it was real.

Sara knew that she would never again put her existence on hold for a case. How could she after losing Luke? Seemingly healthy, handsome, energetic Luke. She could never take her own life seriously again. Her time was precious. She had forgotten that somewhere along the line. Most likely, she would never again stand up in court. She couldn't imagine what would replace it. How she would fill the void. What else had she ever done? Or achieved? She couldn't ride, play the piano, paint, sing or even swim. She got up. Her hips were stiff. She was freezing, despite knowing how hot it must be outside. She couldn't leave. She caught Matt's eye. He seemed to have the same need to keep watch. She couldn't move in case. In case she missed this moment which, for all its awfulness, meant she belonged.

Chapter 31

When the phone rang across on the other side of the sitting room, it startled Connie. She lay beside Luke, allowing herself to believe it was the night before. He would turn to face her. Those piercing eyes would watch her. She heard Matt speaking into the receiver. She wanted to block out the world outside. She heard Matt move towards her. She ignored his approach and closed her eyes, willing him to leave her alone.

Matt touched her hair. 'Connie, it's Lou. Why don't you take it in the bedroom?'

Reluctantly, Connie nodded and without thinking walked into Luke's room. It was intimate to her: the bitter lemon of his deodorant; his BlackBerry half buried under a copy of *Men's Health* magazine; the clutch of lime-coloured running tops temporarily dumped in one corner; his professionally laundered shirts folded individually into plastic covers above a combat-coloured range of desert boots. She stopped in the doorway, wanting to close it and seek the comfort of Matt and Katherine's room. She looked at the bed. It was exactly how they had left it. She knew if she lay on it, she would smell him, feel him. She stood trapped in the doorway, until she allowed herself to be drawn back to his bed. She lay on his side, squeezed the pillow and wound the duvet around her.

She remembered that Lou was on the phone. She cautiously picked up the receiver from the wooden beside table.

'Lou,' she said for her own affirmation. The thought of her daughter was unreal. She was utterly disconnected from the part of her that was a mother.

'Mum? I thought we had been cut off.' Lou sounded too loud. Connie was unsure of how to speak to her. She was tempted to tell Lou about Luke, but she couldn't. How could she share with her daughter, however grown up, what had happened?

Lou knew Luke as a family friend. How could Connie share his importance in her life, before Connie became a mother. The only side to her that Lou knew.

'Lou, how are you?' Connie wondered how she could follow it. What day was it? Friday. What did Lou have on Thursdays? Rowing. 'Did you have a good session on the river?'

'How do you think I am? Are you completely stupid? Fucking hell. Whatever.' Lou's vicious teenage words slashed across her thoughts.

'Lou, please don't swear. There's absolutely no call for it,' she said automatically, though she registered her mistake.

Luke was gone, making Julian's baby next to irrelevant. What had Luke said about the pain Emma had caused? It was all relative. You get used to anything in the end. Hearing his voice in her head made her lips tremble.

She struggled to think what words she could put together that might reassure Lou and encourage her to end the call. What would Luke do? She could hear him talking to her. Tell her the truth, Connie.

On their last day at university, she was almost packed and still he didn't say goodbye to her. He avoided her. She fussed, putting the last of her things into her car, waiting for him, but knowing he wouldn't come. Finally, she walked slowly back to her car. There was a card slid under her windscreen wiper. *Be honest, be true to yourself. It's all I ask. Lx*

She struggled to breathe. A wave of panic enveloped her.

'You know about Sally's baby,' she managed.

A choking feeling constricted Connie's chest and neck.

'Yeah, Mum. Dad has been honest with us.'

She heard the insinuation. Connie hadn't been honest with Lou.

She hadn't. She had denied the pain of putting up with Julian's affairs. She had produced a puppet show of a family. The story itself was false.

'I am sorry, Lou.' What had they done to deserve Julian's philandering and the harm it would do them now and, undoubtedly, in the future? Would Lou ever find a Luke? If she did, would she recognise him?

She was sorry for the children, but not for herself. Her breath was trapped between her heart and her head. She had loved Luke. A part of her never stopped loving Luke. She was heartbroken. This is what that word meant. How could Luke die? Luke, who had suffered, who had Ella and Finn, and Connie. How could he leave her? She was alone for the first time in her life.

Connie paused, drawn to Luke's T-shirt that she had shoved between his pillow and duvet earlier. She tucked them under her head.

Once Connie would have said it was inappropriate that Lou had told Rolo. How could she say that now? She had confided in Luke and the group.

The only option was to talk to Lou as if she were an adult.

'Lou. You have a great father. He is brilliant, charming, loving, generous and a wonderful family man. And he loves you, in particular, a great deal,' she sighed with exhaustion, wishing again she could put the phone down. 'He isn't the faithful type, as you know. It's harder this time, because Sally was part of our family. And there is a baby involved.'

Lou was silent. She wondered whether she was on the right track. It was difficult to tell with teenagers. They wanted to be treated as grown-ups, but when you did, they were too easily and emotionally effected by everything.

She needed to conclude the conversation. She breathed in to get the air to do so. 'We are incredibly lucky to be alive.' She was choking, fighting the tears as if she were fighting to keep Luke alive. 'We have to appreciate the wonderful things that we do have as a family.'

'The wonderful things we do have as a family? Christ, you're not in bloody Sunday school.'

Connie couldn't speak. She was crying silent tears. She held a hand over her open mouth as her body let go.

'You say he's not the faithful type. What you mean is he's not faithful to you?'

Connie squeezed Luke's T-shirt against her and tried to breathe more easily. She inhaled his smell. She couldn't speak.

'Mum, are you listening to me? For God's sake. Are you there?'

'Well, he is married to me.' The thought made her want to cry again. She was nearly there. She almost walked away with precious Luke. His was the most generous type of love. He had loved her enough to set her free, allow her to leave without guilt. He loved her for who she really was.

'That's a cop out, Mum.'

Why had she not predicted this? Lou would never let Julian fall from grace. The only person going down in her estimation was Mum.

'It's not intended to be.'

'It's your fault, Mum. You dropped the ball.'

She heard the click she had wanted. Though Lou was no longer on the line, she held the phone to her ear. *You dropped the ball*.

She wanted to sleep, she wanted to dream of another time and take Luke back there.

Chapter 32

Matt was tempted not to wake Connie. She looked happy asleep in Luke's bed, but the pilot and medical assistants had arrived from Jo'Burg and the stretcher was waiting to transport Luke. They wanted to cover him. He shuddered. It felt like moving Luke's body was on a par with committing a crime. Matt wanted to leave Gae with Luke, accompany his body to Jo'Burg. Connie wanted to come too, but the reserve staff and the doctor made it clear this was not possible due to the size of the plane.

He had just phoned Emma. She didn't deserve an earlier call. Emma probably led Luke to his death. The only reason Matt called her was that she was still Luke's next of kin on his passport. Doubtless, an administrative oversight by Luke, but under South African law she was required to give consent to a post-mortem because of the sudden nature of Luke's death. He reluctantly agreed call her back when he knew more.

The bland voice at the end of the out of office emergencies line at the High Commission in Pretoria insisted Luke would need a South African death certificate following the post-mortem examination.

'We want to bring him home,' he said more emotionally than he intended to this woman, who had an Eastern European accent, possibly Russian. 'We want him to have a British funeral.'

She was silent. It was impossible to tell if she had heard him or not. He was about to repeat his last sentence, when she started speaking. 'We can help you find an international funeral director, who would need to prepare the body for repatriation.'

His stomach lurched, before he asked the next, obvious question. 'What does that mean exactly? Prepare the body for repatriation?'

'The body needs to be embalmed.'

His shock turned quickly to anger. 'That's barbaric. With all due respect, we are in the twenty-first century. I can't believe that is necessary.'

She didn't reply. She waited until she was absolutely sure that he had finished, before continuing, 'Then the body would need to be placed in a zinc-lined coffin, before it could leave South Africa.'

He was silent, lost in the horror of transporting a body. He wished he could smuggle Luke back. It was easy for them to leave the UK on holiday. He sensed he would struggle to get Luke home.

'Alternatively,' she continued brightly, 'you could organise a local funeral.'

Connie was clear that Luke would want to be buried in Dartmoor at his parents' farm. It was obviously what his parents wanted. Matt agreed with her. Connie promised his parents she would not leave Africa without him. Matt had to be back home for Isobel's funeral, but he planned to return and stay until he could help Connie take Luke home. It was the right thing to do. He knew it. He hadn't broached it with Katherine yet, but he was determined that, whatever she said, she wouldn't change his mind. However hard it was going to be, he wanted to be there for Luke.

'To conclude,' said the voice, 'you would need a certificate of embalming, authorisation from the South African authorities to remove the body, after the autopsy. It would take some time.'

He understood her to mean weeks, but maybe it was months.

'The British Consul would be able to help with this documentation.'

He managed a hollow laugh.

'The deceased's travel insurance should cover the costs, including repatriation.' She paused before adding, 'Though it's worth checking the small print.'

It seemed she was reading from a pamphlet.

'Once back in the UK, you would need to see the registrar in the district where you wish the funeral to take place. He or she will need to issue a "certificate of no liability to register", which they can only do when they have seen the South African death certificate.'

She coughed or maybe she had too large a gulp of her coffee. 'Is there anything else I can help you with? Bereavement counselling?'

His voice shook. 'No.'

And now he was in Luke's bedroom. He hated waking Connie when he knew that she would open her eyes to more pain. But he had to. Matt gently nudged her. She rolled away from him. 'Connie, wake up. They are taking Luke.'

Connie sat up. She struggled to her feet and into the sitting room. The medical assistants from Baragwanath Hospital, where pathologists would do the autopsy, were covering Luke's entire body with a heavy white sheet. Connie gasped and pressed both her hands over her mouth, before reaching underneath the sheet for his hand.

The group were all together. Luke was lifted carefully on the mobile hospital bed. Matt wanted to speak to Luke, to the others about Luke, before he left them, because they would never see him again. They would only stare at the lid of his zinc-lined coffin and try to recall his handsome boyish face, his warmth and honesty, his friendship, his undoubtable will, his fighting machine of a body, before the embalmers had got to him. The stretcher was wheeled off the wooden decking on to the sand before the top half was slid into a seatless vehicle. Connie quickly folded back the end of the sheet. There Luke was. Or a glazed outline of the body of Luke.

One of the assistants said, 'Madam, please.' The other touched Connie's arm for extra emphasis.

Connie ignored them. 'Bye, darling Luke.' She kissed him on the lips, willing as if he could be brought to life by the kiss of the one he profoundly loved.

Katherine squeezed Matt's hand tightly.

As they slid the flat bed of the hospital trolley into the vehicle, Matt wept. They were silent tears, anything else would somehow have been wrong. They all trailed through the orange dust after the slowly departing vehicle, until they had seen it curve twice and out beyond their horizon. Matt and Katherine stood together, lost in their own thoughts, unable to decide what to do next. Matt no longer had the energy to pack and rapidly leave. He wanted to lie on a sofa. 'What are we going to do?' Matt felt desperate and lost.

Dan was the first to respond. 'Let's go to the bar.'

Matt was thankful for the suggestion. It was a destination, a place to rest together away from their rooms, which eerily reminded him of Luke's wake. Matt and Katherine led them on to the decked path and back inside. Katherine and Connie ordered a couple of pots of coffee. They settled close to each other, needing intimacy and a couple of throws, which they wrapped around themselves.

Katherine sighed, 'Connie. It's crazy but I wonder if you and I might order something stronger?'

Matt was pleased to notice Sara smiled. He waited until they got their drinks.

'To our dearest Luke. He was a great mate to us all,' Matt paused. 'He was an eternal optimist, an eternal romantic, a lover of life.' He sighed. 'To Luke,' clinking his glass against Dan's cup of tea. 'And to seeing more of each other, before it's too late.'

He gulped the contents of his glass. It provided pain relief. Perhaps that was what drove Luke to drink so heavily. The desire to blank out the bits of his life that didn't match up to the perfection he so desperately wanted to believe in. Katherine got up from where she was sitting beside Dan and sat gently on Matt's lap.

'Sweetie, you okay?' She murmured, her hair drifting over his face, 'That was lovely.'

He wrapped his arms around her, drawing her to him. 'Thank you, Katherine,' he squeezed her gently.

'Matt, sweetie, listen, I am sorry about the things I have said in the past about Luke.' Her forehead wrinkled and her eyes were full of tears. 'I have been thinking about it. I mean, how I could judge him? He had a family and friends.'

He hugged her. 'Luke was my best mate, and the only thing I can do for him now is come back to South Africa and help Connie bring him home.'

Katherine was silent. She was probably thinking about Isobel. Their own grief, their own lives. He didn't know any more which was more important.

'Let's both come back,' she said gently.

He felt her concern, her strength, her love. He wanted to weep.

Connie wandered up to them and perched on the arm of the sofa. 'Am I interrupting?'

'No.' Katherine was effusive in her concern, 'Connie, please come sit with us.'

'How was Lou?' Matt asked.

'She put the phone down on me,' Connie bowed her head, 'She blames me for Julian's baby. Apparently, I dropped the ball.'

'Oh Connie, she's a teenager. Don't take it to heart,' Katherine clasped her hand.

Connie shrugged and shook her head. They would survive not having a child and move on. What about Connie? What was she going to do without Julian or Luke?

'You know, I'm not rabid like Sara,' Katherine stated. 'A career isn't the answer for everyone. But I do think, Connie, you could use a cause.'

Connie was silent. She looked deflated. And Matt was anxious for her.

'Outside of your family,' Katherine insisted.

He touched Katherine's hand gently. 'This is not the time, Katherine.'

'No Matt, it's okay. She's right.'

John, the balloonist, wandered over to them. He adjusted his faded blue cap. Ridges of wrinkles landscaped his deeply tanned face. He looked like an old sailor found in some random bar in Barbados. His ragged but ruddy health didn't fit with their grief. Sara eyed him with suspicion.

Once he reached the centre of the bar, John neutrally announced, 'Wind's perfect this morning.'

Surely he had already been paid. Why couldn't he leave them alone?

No one said anything.

Gus coughed and folded his arms carefully across his body. 'It's awful to lose Luke like this.' He made eye contact with them. 'You are all hurting. If you want to rest here together and talk about Luke, it's absolutely okay.'

Gus seemed to be gauging the mood of the group, trying to be sensitive to their reaction.

'Or you can rise up into the sky, over the Kalahari, over the wildebeest, over the land, where you have been happy together with him, and say a proper farewell to Luke.'

Sara looked at John again in a new light. Less beggar and more saviour.

'The choice is yours, eh?'

Sara looked to Connie. Whatever she wanted, Sara would make happen. Connie didn't say anything. Sara was worried that Gus's thoughtful speech would go unrecognised.

'I don't know about everyone else, but I don't think that it makes much difference.' Dan stared at John, as if he were expecting the answers to be buried in the crevasses in his face. 'Everything has already changed.'

Sara waited for him to continue. He didn't.

Connie spoke. 'Luke would have wanted us to go. Shall we?'

Chapter 33

The sky filled the space. It was that unblemished blue that Connie remembered on the day they arrived. Two solitary acacia trees marked the horizon. Otherwise it was bountiful grassland, which whistled to greet them.

Her grandfather wrote about his balloon trip over the Kalahari soon after he bought the hunting lodge. The worn red and plain wicker basket jolting along on the trailer in front of them might have been the one he flew in. It was faded, yet solid. It couldn't be further from high-performance ballooning. John swerved his white truck off the road across a wide, grassy plain. Despite the apparently perfect wind conditions, there appeared to be no rush. John and his son Graeme, a teenage Jimmy Carter before the sawdust was airbrushed off him, and Dominick, a chunky black helper in his mid-thirties, slowly unhooked the basket, pushing and pulling in hushed tones, before sliding it off the trailer and lifting it down on to the ground. They surveyed the basket and the ground around them like a family faced with IKEA instructions. John inched the vehicle further forward, before they all moved the basket twenty feet in front of the truck's bonnet. A four-cornered metal frame was assembled over the basket to support the propane gas cylinders. They tied one end of a grey karate-style belt around the front bumper and the other to the bar in the basket.

Connie watched carefully. Focusing on their preparations was reassuring. Life and its tiny details were happening around her. She was alive, if numb.

He grinned. 'Our umbilical cord in case the balloon takes off too soon. With only one of you on board.'

'Right,' she nodded.

She thought about what that would feel like. Alone in a balloon crossing Africa. The way to go. If only Luke had known that this was it. If only she had known.

As John laboriously unscrewed a Thermos flask of tea and slowly sipped from the metal cup, Graeme and Dominick started to unroll the balloon. If it were possible, it looked more worn than the basket. The wide blue stripe, bordered by red, green, yellow and black, had lost its lustre long ago. Stretched out on the grass, it looked similar to a parachute paraded for toddler entertainment. John slowly placed his cup on the bonnet of his truck and wandered over to the basket. Graeme helped him tip it on its side. The balloon was dragged towards it and attached to the basket. Then the gas canisters were lit.

The whooshing sound burst into the stillness. The others, who were hovering round their safari vehicle, moved forward, drawn to the noise that marked the real start of their balloon trip.

The fabric started to billow off the ground. It got slowly fuller and fuller. It was mesmerising. A flame tore through the fabric, leaving a charred hole in the material. John looked up at the flame, before nodding and waving an arm towards her. 'It's okay. Not a risk, eh.'

She couldn't explain why, but she trusted him and the balloon, which was this vast half cuboid starting to rise off the ground. John, Graeme and Dominick moved with surprising speed and energy to right the basket. The flames were visible. John shouted and waved frantically for them to come.

They ran, even Matt. They jostled, trying to get into the basket. The tall sides forced them into high leg lifts. Katherine pulled Matt's arm as he nearly ripped his trousers getting in and then landed on Katherine. Gus and Ben climbed in, as they had two spare spaces. The balloon was tipping a few inches off the ground. John firmly instructed them to crouch down below the height of the basket, in a contorted brace position. She looked across the small space at Sara, who was squashed on the opposite side with Gus. Matt was holding Katherine; Alan and Dan were wedged in the other corner. They felt every jolt. Her legs were shaking. The physical exertion released the tight grip of Connie's grief. She was forced to breathe properly and in that breath found some energy that had eluded her since Luke's death.

It was moving but not straight upwards. The balloon seemed to curve rather than lift. When John instructed them to get up a few minutes later, Connie didn't realise that they were off the ground. Then they moved quickly up like a puppet controlled by strings on high. They rose and rose.

Sara stared down. Already the scene was bleaching out, the vehicles were shrinking. Sara had never seen the earth from this perspective. She let out an exhalation, 'Oh.' It wasn't a word, rather a feeling. Gus reached for her hand.

The vehicle shrank first, then the acacia trees, before the land itself seemed to separate from them. The horizon elongated, as the ground became less familiar, more lunar. A suggestion of elands came into sight and quickly disappeared. The mountains rose to greet them and then vanished beneath them.

'There's Mozambique,' Gus pointed beyond the hills.

John grinned. 'We have ended up there, when the wind's changed.'

Connie felt she could end up anywhere.

Dan could only watch the tracks, now faint pencil lines, turn from orange to yellow; the grasses faded from familiar green to invisible beige. The odd tree or bush looked like a tiny pom pom on a hat. The sun flooded the scene with a yellow wash, leaving dark stripy shadows. He was drunk on its beauty.

Matt held Katherine close, as they both stared out of the balloon. It was absolutely silent as if someone had pressed the pause button on human life. Matt daren't speak. It would destroy this moment of utter peace.

Connie felt as if she were in a space capsule looking down on the earth. A herd of wildebeest dotted the scene, mere scratch marks across the burnished landscape. The reality of existence was here, not the knotted ball of her own pain. She remembered what had happened to her grandfather. Up here, he had seen the majesty of this beautiful land. He had written with certainty that the Kalahari would give purpose to the rest of his life. It must have made his wife's betrayal petty and insignificant. There was no greater healer than Mother Nature. All she needs is time and space. To restore you.

'Connie, thank you.' Lizzie was the first to speak.

Sara spoke quietly, 'Thank you to Gus for persuading us to come up here. We needed it.'

Matt added, 'It's a fitting goodbye to Luke.'

Connie couldn't speak. She would never be ready to say goodbye to him. He would always be with her.

They were silent for the next ten minutes, which seem to pass too quickly, before John explained that they would need to crouch down in the basket to land. It could be quite rough, they might ride over trees and land in a bush. Connie bent her knees as far as she could and placed her arms over her head. They hit the ground fast. They tore through trees, which scrapped the basket, covered the balloon and poked through the gap in between. The balloon was moving rapidly, tearing through every bush in its path. Connie's legs knocked together against Lizzie, Matt, Dan and Sara's. They were a jumble of shaken limbs. Finally, it stopped moving. They were miraculously on the ground.

Chapter 34

Connie, Dan, Matt, Katherine and Alan had already boarded. After blowing her a kiss, Lizzie disappeared into the plane. Staring at the desolate airstrip, Sara wondered if she had made a mistake extending her trip, even by twenty-four hours. She wasn't ready to face Charles, Pete and the others yet. What would she say to John? Her junior would be appalled, immediately concerned for his own safe passage far away from her. She needed to prepare to face them. Yet she was already lonely without the group and feeling low about Luke again.

'Sara, shall we be getting back, eh?' Gus wrapped his arm gently around her.

She considered his touch for a moment. She wished that she had flown home with the others. She needed to be with her friends. Since Ben wasn't there, she sat in the front passenger seat. It was rude to sit in the back like the bloody Queen. She heard a text ping through from Connie. She opened it, eager to hear from her.

Gus is in love with you, Sara. Be honest, be true to yourself. It's all I ask. xxx

She tried to hide her excruciating embarrassment. 'The whole world has gone mad, Gus. Homeward, eh?'

She felt him, before she saw him coming. It was a swift sidewards lean. He didn't touch her anywhere except her lips. She was an observer no longer in control: her mind was still and her body active. She felt the deep tenderness in his kiss and she knew in her gut and in her groin that she wanted him. As she shifted forwards, kissing him back, he pulled away. Without a comment, he turned on the ignition and started driving.

Fear flooded through her. Her deep-rooted fear of rejection. She never trusted men. She hated herself and Gus for cornering her. Losing Luke had made her vulnerable. Gus had taken advantage of her grief.

Neither of them spoke for the next ten minutes. Time dragged. She stared fixedly at the horizon, willing the lodge to come into view. When she saw it, nestling in the mountains, she sighed louder than she had intended. Gus didn't radio in to say that they were nearly back. There was no member of staff waiting with chilled towels.

When he stopped the car, she struggled to get back to normal. 'I'll see you to ride out this evening.' She turned to go.

'It'll be one of the other guides. I've got four days off.' He didn't make eye contact.

'Good,' she was desperate to escape. Strangely, she thought of her mum. *'Best face, Sara. Always your best face.'* Sara forced herself to stay. 'Going anywhere exciting?'

'Down to Cape Town tomorrow.'

'Isn't that a long way to drive?' Count to three. Her pride would be intact.

'Sara.' He turned away. She heard the admonishment – he could obviously tell her conversation was merely an attempt to save her pride.

'Keep an eye out for road kill, eh,' she flung at his departing back.

She turned down the path to her room. Only it wasn't her room, it was the room she had shared with Lizzie and the evidence of her friend's disorganised departure was everywhere. Lizzie's sheets were half coiled on the floor. The things she had left behind: a tube of toothpaste on the bathroom floor, a hair brush thickly entwined with her frizzy coils, and a lipstick without the lid were depressing reminders of the group's holiday together. On top of the sheets was a Post-it note. Sara picked it up. It was barely legible. Sara was one of the few people who could decipher Lizzie's scrawl:

Things to do:

Call Michael Stubbs about possible job.

Call parents. Ask them for help with mortgage.

Find Internet dating site.

Do 5:2 fast diet.

Buy new clothes.

Sara couldn't believe how much she already missed Lizzie, let alone Luke. She must pull herself together. She made a snap decision. She would settle on to the wicker sofa on her terrace and read. She was done with safari rides. She had brought three books and she hadn't touched them. She needed to escape in a great novel. Then she would feel strong enough for her conversations with Chambers. Work calls, sleep and back to London. She wouldn't drink for the rest of the holiday. She had overdone it. Detox and refocus. It made perfect sense.

Sara had a nagging feeling, an itch she couldn't locate. She knew it was about Gus, but she refused to explore it. She read until six in the evening. Famished, she ordered poached eggs and toast for supper and ate them in her sitting room.

She couldn't put off calling Charles. It wasn't just that he was her head of Chambers, she owed her career in large part to him. Not recognising her landline number, he didn't answer his mobile phone. How typical. He always screened his calls. Only it irritated Sara now.

'Charles.' She coughed. 'It's Sara. Call me back.'

Her mobile rang. It was Charles, of course. She immediately heard the concern in his voice.

'Sara. Thank God, I've got hold of you.' His phone voice had a Shakespearian rasp to it.

'Charles, what can I say?' Sara was about to say sorry, but she checked herself. She forced herself to switch into Chambers speak. 'It was a stressful case load, media pressure, internal jealousies, you know the score.'

'Quite. Exactly.' He sounded pleased with her answer. 'Sara you are a brilliant barrister. I believe that. This is a fucking disaster. Pardon my French. The only answer is plead emotional stress, pile on pressure. You know the thing: harrowing family heartbreak mirroring your own story can get to even the toughest woman.'

'Charles. I'm not playing the girlie card. Or delving into my family background.'

'Sara, listen to me. You don't have a fucking choice.'

'I do. I'm going to tell the truth. I should have alerted Stephenson; I misled my client. End of story. If I get disbarred—'

'Sara. You need to get your arse back here. Get yourself back into Chambers super bloody early Monday. We'll thrash this out.'

'I haven't got the energy to thrash it out, Charles. Are you listening to me?'

'Sara, I know you better than you know yourself. You're one of my best. This isn't like you. You're exhausted. This case was huge. I understand all that. But you need to get yourself back into your battle gear. Okay? Let's do it.'

Sara was silent. She didn't care anymore. After Luke's death, it no longer mattered. Charles took her silence as acquiescence. He relented.

'Look, get some sleep. I know this is stressful. Julia sends her love.'

Sara imagined his sleek wife Julia beside him on their sofa, stroking his paunch with her manicured nails.

'Come for dinner Monday night. Okay, Sara?'

Her audience was over.

'Bye, Charles.'

Sara hadn't the energy or desire to speak to Pete or John. She was drained. Her sober resolution wavered. As she closed the door to the bar, she saw too late that the only occupants were Gus, Kimberley and another ranger. They had the only three high stools next to the mahogany bar. Gus ignored her. The other ranger immediately stood up for her.

Kimberley urged. 'Hey, Sara. Come and join us.'

'No thanks. I'm grabbing something to take to my room.' She tried to sound in control, but she heard her own vulnerability. So much for her resolve to detox.

While she waited for the barman to appear, Sara played the bar as if it was her Steinway at home. Why did Gus kiss her and then pull away? She batted back the hurt. What was the point of trying to analyse men? They were all shits in the end, which is why she was lucky to have such great friends.

Where was that barman? As she waited, she glanced at Gus. He was wearing a checked blue shirt and earth-coloured jeans. He looked good in casual clothes, in a way that someone like Julian never could. No longer encumbered by his shapeless safari shirt and thick trousers, she was forced to recognise that he had a strong body, not too bulky. Listen to yourself, Sara. She tightened her orange silk wrap over her breasts.

'More Marilyn than Moss,' she flippantly snapped around Chambers, 'Real curves and breasts: only real men need apply.' It always got a laugh. His Jess was probably some skinny bird. He didn't fancy Sara. It had probably been no more than a dare from another ranger, or worse, a sympathy snog. Christ.

Her confidence re-surged as Kimberley and the other ranger moved to a sofa. Gus got up to follow them. Before he could, she tapped him as lightly as possible on the shoulder.

'Gus. Quick question.' She tried to sound matter of fact.

Gus looked levelly at her. 'Sure, Sara.'

She almost asked, 'Why did you stop kissing me?' She was being ridiculous. He was the bloody ranger, who probably slept with every singleton who came through the safari. She had a lucky escape; she needed to get back home. Her cleaner would have been. Everything would be spotless. She could face her new reality much better from the security of her home.

'Forget it.'

Her canvas wedges unevenly hitting the path. She was too agitated to go back to her house alone. Dan and Alan's door was half open. There were no new guests. Sara settled down on their sofa. She lay there thinking. Even Dan and Alan had split up. It proved how impossible relationships were. Only Matt and Katherine were truly happy together, but even they were locked in their own grief. It was safer to be alone, to avoid pain. Sara knew that.

She didn't have any clarity on relationships. She couldn't think straight. She kept thinking of Luke. He was full of energy, despite the shit time he had had with Emma and losing Connie. He ploughed on until his death. Where did it leave her? Depressed and lost.

The whole of her life had been a branding exercise. Since university, she had been better at packaging her life than Lizzie and

Connie. That was all. Her life was an empty Shard building. There was nothing of significance inside. A soaring significant edifice on the London landscape, yet one vandal had thrown a rock and the glass had shattered.

She didn't have the strength to worry her way through another complex set of strategic moves to fight her potential disbarment. She wondered dispassionately if she would even turn up to the tribunal.

She reluctantly returned to her room. Gus was sitting on her doorstep, his face shadowed; his knees awkwardly up near his chin. He didn't look comfortable, but he didn't get up.

She wished there was an easy way of getting past him into the house, locking the door and curling up into a deep, long sleep. She wanted to escape her unravelling mind.

'What did you want to ask me?'

'Why did you stop kissing me?'

'You've lost a great friend. You are stressed out because your career is falling apart. You are going home to months of disciplinary hearings. And you are on holiday, far from home. I've been an easy shoulder to cry on. No more. Who knows if you will allow yourself to see what is between us. You'll return to your life in London. Happy or not. You have no intention of coming back.'

What Gus was saying was logical. She wasn't a barrister for bloody nothing. She didn't reply 'you are right', because it wasn't the truth. She could easily come back for him. He was the closest she had got to wanting someone.

'Then why did you kiss me?'

She saw in his smile her own desire. 'I'm not a saint, Sara. Despite what you may think.' He sighed looking away from her. 'You are beautiful, sexy and incredibly smart. A big softie to boot. And I'm a man.'

She tried to imagine any other man being able to deliver that line without making her cringe. Failing, she allowed herself to glimpse the possibility.

Gus stood up. He was too close. He inspected her. 'Look, I better go, eh.'

If a bloke said that to her in London, she would have known that it was an elaborate ploy. The bloody lot of them were into games that confused and angered her, which is why she resorted to one-night stands. 'You get what you get and you don't get upset.' It was her line. How many lines did she have? Too many. All meaningless.

She couldn't extricate herself from Gus. The fear returned. Only now it was the fear that he would go straight to Cape Town. If he lurched right that moment. If only she was brave enough to say please don't go. She studied the grasses behind the path. She convinced herself that the huge disappointment she could already feel physically weighing her down was irrational.

'Goodbye, Sara, take good care. I'll be watching for you, eh.'

She heard his feet pad the path. She moved her eyes to watch him go. He kept walking. He would soon be out of her sight.

'Gus.' He didn't seem to hear her. 'Please come back.'

She started running. In the seconds it took her to reach him, he had turned round. She was afraid he would be gloating, but his face was awash with emotion. He was a proper person. How could she have nearly missed it?

'I don't want you to go.' She was calm.

He kissed her and this time she kissed him back. She drew him to her with the intensity of her feeling for him. Her fingers blended with his hair. Gus gently peeled his mouth from hers. But he didn't let go of her this time. She watched him openly. Those thoughtful green eyes, his gentle intelligent smile. And the glimpse of his chest above his top button. He put his arm around her waist as they walked back to her house. He didn't pause in the sitting room. As he moved the two beds together, his smile spread into a grin. Sara folded her arms around him, slowly undoing his buttons from behind. He turned swiftly round and drew her tightly to him, pressing his body against hers. His soft smile flicked to desire. His hand moved down under her blouse and into her bra. As his fingers skimmed her left breast, he murmured. 'God, I've been desperate to do that.' He undid her blouse and unclipped her bra. Then he paused. He was staring at her breasts.

'More Marilyn than Moss.' Sara said shyly. She wished she had stepped through the doors of her expensive gym. 'And only Marilyn if you're shortsighted.'

'Sara, I've been avoiding the pool in case I stare at you.'

Then his hands were on her body, his breath on her neck, his eyes burning into her, his mouth on hers. She was completely lost in him.

Afterwards, they lay twisted together, looking at each other. Neither spoke. She gently ran her finger from under his thick fringe along the side of his jaw to his mouth. His green eyes became part of hers. She was going to drive with Gus to his farm and his family. It was the only thing she wanted to do.

Gus raised himself on to one elbow without moving away. 'Tell me about your dad.'

Sara sighed. 'What do you want to know?'

'You told me he left when you were six.' He kissed her.

She looked quickly at him, before dropping her gaze. 'I never stop thinking about him. Yet I never talk about him. I have this picture of our last breakfast together, but I have probably imagined it.' She gave a rueful smile. 'My mum's amazingly strong, but she never talks about him either. It's like this weight we both carry around, which we have never shared with each other or anyone else.' She didn't want Gus to feel sorry for her. 'Probably more info than you wanted.'

He didn't say anything for a moment. Sara reflected that it didn't feel awkward. It wasn't a silence that was begging to be filled.

'You need to trust me, Sara,' he said quietly.

'I've been single for two decades. I have made a concerted effort never to trust a man, but somehow I do trust you.' She managed a smile.

Gus gently took her face in both his hands 'Sara, promise me now, you won't panic. You have nothing to fear with me, eh? I fell in love with you the moment I saw you at the airstrip. I thought you looked like Grace Kelly with your string of pearls close to your neck and your cream silk blouse.' He grinned and stroked the side of her cheek. 'Only smarter and funnier.'

He had no fear. Sara was in awe of his honesty.

'I went back to Gae and I called my parents. It's happened. I've met her. I ended it with Jess. She was expecting it. It was a relief for both of us.'

'You were that sure?' she whispered.

'Yes. I realised when I saw you that I never loved her.' He kissed her, before frowning. 'This is going to make it harder for both of us when you leave tomorrow.'

'What? I'm not going to leave now. Not after this.'

He stroked her hair. 'Sara, if you run away with me now, it won't work, you know that. You'll always wonder what would have happened if you had faced the music in London. It will be unfinished business. I don't want us to start our life together like that.'

She jerked her legs out from under his, moved to get out of bed and away from him. He was quicker than she was. He grabbed her and turned her back round to him, tightly squeezing her to his chest.

'Hey stop, where are you going? Listen to me, Sara,' He lifted her chin gently making her look at him. 'I am never, ever going to let go of you.'

'Where will you be?' She clung on to the practical details.

'You have made me realise it's time for me to get back home. I need to get stuck back into the farm.'

Her disappointment was irrational. He couldn't come with her to London. She couldn't ask him to sit around in her house for two months. What man would do that? Let alone Gus.

He smiled gently. 'Sara, I'm going to go to drive you as far as Jo'Burg and see you on to your plane.'

'What a concession,' she tried to smile. 'Are you sure?'

'Yes,' he pulled her close.

'You're prepared to let me go back to London alone?' She was sure. 'Do I have to beg, Gus Hamilton?'

He looked genuinely confused.

'If you are leaving Gae anyway, why not have a break in London? You could sightsee, maybe you can look up friends there? In a couple of months, the tribunal will be over. We could come back together to your farm.'

One night of intimacy had her planning out their lives together. It wasn't rational. So what? She thought of Luke. He didn't get his chance to be happy with Connie. The least she could do is snap up her own happiness.

He was grinning. 'Is that a serious suggestion?'

She nodded vigorously. 'Then we can see where we are.' He was about to speak. She had to get in a last pitch. 'Look I'll even cook. And I hate cooking. Failing that I'll order great takeaways. We can explore at weekends. I won't drag you up north to meet my mother or anything like that.'

'Why not? I want to meet your mother.'

'You are an endangered species.' She paused. 'I won't bore on about the case or my legal career. We will have fun. Really.'

'Really? Don't make too many rash promises Sara.' He laughed.

She couldn't bear it any longer. 'Well?'

'The answer was yes a week ago.'

Chapter 35

Connie knocked on the door. She wondered if she was interrupting anything, but Sara would hardly have acted on her heavy hint. She would have only mocked poor Gus more. Connie knocked again.

'It's open, silly. I'm not planning to lock you out. Yet.' Sara swung the door open. 'Connie. What the hell?'

Connie smiled nervously. Her plans didn't seem strong enough to withstand Sara's scrutiny. 'I'm taking a break from Jo'Burg for a night. I am not allowed to see Luke and I feel closer to him here.'

Sara led her by the arm through the glass doors on to the terrace, squarer than the one outside Julian's and her little house. The table was a mosaic of suncream, notebooks, a pen, two dirty plates and two glasses. Connie was about to enquire about the user of the other glass, but any insinuation would ruin their precious time together.

'You're not packed yet?' Connie realised that she always focused on domestic details.

'I've extended my holiday by another night,' Sara stated. 'I don't want to miss Isobel's funeral, of course.'

'I've spoken to Matt at length,' Connie hurried on. 'He understands that I cannot even briefly leave Africa without Luke.'

'Of course he does,' Sara sounded reassuring. 'What's going on? Talk to me now, Connie.'

She forced a smile. When had they last sat around talking, the two of them together? She was always listening to Sara's wit but never properly looking at her. She was beautiful: her delicate white skin, shining green eyes, bony collarbones extending across her broad frame like a hanger for her deep curves. Strong, clever and beautiful with a certainty about her place in the world that Connie profoundly envied.

'Okay. I will make it easier for you. I've relied on "us" being the constant in my life without appreciating how much I love you all. You are my family.'

Connie was moved. Sara never talked about her feelings. Connie wanted to tell Sara what she felt about Luke, but she didn't know where to start. She expected Sara to speak, but she watched Connie attentively. Her legs were crossed and she was leaning forward, resting her elbow on her top knee and her face in her hand. She realised that this trip had been great for Sara, at least. And for her? If she could somehow make sense of it, perhaps there was hope.

'Luke and I. We made love.' As she spoke, she saw him naked before her, physically and emotionally. 'I couldn't help it, Sara. Why shouldn't we be together?'

Sara didn't say anything.

'When I kissed Luke, I remembered the beautiful, happy past I had, and I felt there was another future for me and for Luke. For both of us.'

'Go on, Connie,' Sarah said.

'I feel this physical and mental ache for him. I don't think I'll ever get over this sense of emptiness,' she sniffed, and delved into her bag for a packet of tissues. 'I know you are going to say I'm being self-indulgent. I keep thinking about what you said to me when I dumped Luke for Julian. "Your problem, Connie, is you can't be on your own. What's wrong with your own company for a change?"'

'Oh please, Connie, don't quote me.' Sara looked mortified. 'That was twenty years ago. Anyway, I say things that sound great but I don't think them through. It's hard to love someone. It's a cop out to be on your own.'

Connie spoke quickly. 'It's a cop out to hide behind your children, your housekeeper and your friends. Unlike you, I've always had a mortal fear of exposing myself. I'm not good at anything, except keeping the peace.'

'Connie that's not true.' Sara reached forward to squeeze Connie's knees. 'Did you know about Sally? I promise not to comment.'

'I genuinely don't know. Maybe on some level I did. I never let myself think it.'

'And Julian?'

'Banished to the basement. There he will remain, I think, for the foreseeable future. Who knows. It's probably the best option for all of us. If Luke was alive, it would have been different. I'd have been forced to boot him out eventually. But with Luke gone…what's the point of denying the children easy access to Julian? What's the point of destroying our family life?'

She looked up to give Sara a chance to have her say. Instead, she gazed at Connie without judgement.

'You know, half my life is inextricably linked to Julian. In a strange way, he is still in my life, even if we will never be intimate again.'

Sara was silent, but watchful.

Connie breathed in. 'It means my focus is no longer my domestic groundhog day. In a way, that is a great thing. It leaves a gap in which I can do something.' She tried to feel energised if only for Luke. 'I am going to do something, Sara.'

Connie sat up, tense about trying out her idea on Sara. 'I talked to Luke about my grandfather and his vision for the restoration of the Kalahari. I know I want to play my part and set up a black rhino foundation. Luke thought it was a great idea. I want to do it in his name now,' she said quickly, holding her hand up to stop Sara from interrupting her even though it was unnecessary. 'I know what you are thinking, Sara.' She sounded sterner than she intended. 'It's not a placebo for an abused wife. No. I want to set up a proper body using my political connections, with proper funding, putting political pressure on the South African government to act against the poachers, lobbying European powers to exert pressure and expose their crimes to global media. I have the connection with my grandfather, which will buy me some right to interfere. And I will be continuing his work.' She hesitated. 'I know, you're probably wondering how I'll manage it with the children. They have such long holidays and I want them to be involved. This was their great-grandfather's old lodge. I want them to experience it and to understand the commitment to something bigger than their individual lives. To the planet, ultimately. Much bigger than my petty concerns.'

She paused. She wondered if it sounded ridiculous and impractical. She nearly asked Sara. She was guaranteed a truthful answer. She didn't. It didn't matter. She was going to do it anyway.

She added hastily, 'Obviously there are practical considerations as well: I need a good name, logo, website. I need to find out what other organisations I can work with, which politicians are already campaigning on behalf of endangered wildlife. I realise that there is a lot to do.'

'Connie, didn't it feel good to get all that off your chest?' Sara's hug enveloped her. She squeezed her back. 'God, I love you.'

'It's not a crazy idea?' Connie allowed herself to ask.

'No. Even if it was, it doesn't matter. It's your idea. Every decision you make leads you somewhere else.' She laughed. 'Did I just say that? It's bloody brilliant, Connie.'

'What's bloody brilliant?' Gus rounded the back of the wooden terrace. He wasn't wearing his uniform. Two glasses, two plates and his feet planted territorially on the veranda. Connie tried to catch Sara's eye.

'Connie is back for a night, as you can see. She's going to set up a foundation to save the black rhino, dedicated to Luke.'

Connie blushed. 'Very idealistic. You know much more about the subject than I do, but I'm planning to come back once—' Connie felt the loss of Luke yet again. 'Once we have buried Luke in Dartmoor.'

Sara and Gus spoke at exactly the same time. Sara: 'It's really important work.' Gus: 'I'd be happy to help you.'

He flopped on the sofa beside Sara, his knees bending towards her, his arm stretched along the wicker edge until his fingers reached her neck. Neither looked at each other. They didn't have to.

'I'm not the only person with news,' Connie smiled encouragingly.

Sara feigned nonchalance. Gus allowed his hand to slip on to her neck. 'You haven't told Connie? Are you hiding, Sara Wilson, eh?'

Sara burst out laughing. Connie hadn't heard her broad, relaxed cackle for a long time. Sara slid her left hand on to his leg. 'Of course not. Connie was the first to know.' She winked at her. 'Weren't you?'

Sara leaned forward and grabbed her phone, scrolled through her messages and lifted the phone to show Gus. Connie was mortified.

'What Connie doesn't know is that I had to beg you to come with me to London.'

Gus laughed loudly. 'You can imagine that, can't you, Connie, eh? Sara with her hands wrapped round my trouser legs. On her knees.'

'It was worse than defending myself in court.' She looked happy. 'I really did beg.'

'Well, you were silly,' he grinned. 'You only had to ask.' He kissed Sara on the lips.

Connie looked away. She was shocked. She had never seen anyone kiss Sara. Let alone with such possession. There seemed to be a part of Sara that only Gus could wheedle out of her.

Sara nudged Gus. 'You're embarrassing Connie.'

Gus looked briefly at Connie. 'No, I'm not.' His eyes were inextricably drawn back to Sara's. 'She is shocked that you have given in to your feelings for me. Too right, Connie, eh?'

Connie realised that Gus understood Sara in the way that she did. It made her feel close to both of them. She smiled. 'You must have drugged her.'

'Excuse me,' Sara retorted. 'I can't believe you said that. For the record, I did all the leg work. Utterly humiliating.'

'Gus, are you moving to London?' Connie was in awe of Gus and Sara's decisiveness.

Sara jumped in. 'Not moving, staying until I'm through with my disciplinary tribunal. We've got the rest of our lives to work out the petty details.'

Gus's whole face lit up. He seemed delighted by her every word. 'Sara's declaration of love. I'm down there with petty details.'

In the glare of their elated, new love, Connie felt a sense of hope. Life was moving forward inexorably even if it was painful in so many ways. She had had the most amazing week of her life with her dearest friends. She had had precious time with Luke, before it was too late. She would never regret that. And she would always love him. She was closer to Matt, more intimate with his relationship with Katherine. Dearest Dan was on his journey to the peace he deserved. She would be a large part of his move to Tuscany, because they had shared his decision together. Perhaps the group's next reunion would be a working holiday on his new land. Or out in Africa with Gus and Sara. The idea made her smile. She was going to miss them so much. But at that moment, sitting on the terrace with Sara and Gus in the sinking light, she didn't need more.

Acknowledgements

I am deeply indebted to Hilary Reyl for her tremendous literary smarts and constant support, my awesome agent Caroline Michel for being an unwavering champion, my editor Justine Taylor for her inspired notes and my dynamo publisher, Stephanie Duncan, whose creative brilliance and hard work has propelled *Unpacking* forward.

I am grateful to Christoph Brooke for finding me a writing room with a view in his hotel, The Elephant; High Road House for saving my corner table; Elin Davies for filling the gaps left by the book. And Bob Marshall Andrews QC for bringing Criminal Law alive.

Thank you to Cyrus Jilla for the privilege of such a unique view of the Kalahari, the Tswalu game reserve, in particular, guide Adrian Bantich for sharing his knowledge and passion for the wild-life and the bush. Trevor Carnaby's *Beat About the Bush* was invalu-able; *The Wildlife of the Southern Africa* by Vincent Carruthers was a great help.

Lucy Yago Briggs and Francesca Brill for keeping my creative heart beating even on a dull, wet night.

Camilla Cavendish, Anna Cotton, Charlotte Emmerson, Jose-phine Frampton, Katie Gagan, Charis Gresser, Kate Harri, Kate Holroyd Smith, Judith Howard, Anthony Howell, Becca Metcalfe,

Nina Omaar, Denise and Mark Poulton and Sara Williams are the stars in my constellation.

At the heart of the clan, Harri Pritchard-Jones for all his love and encouragement.

Never least, so much love and gratitude to Guto, Ben, Cal and Amelia Harri. For being everything.

A NOTE ON THE AUTHOR

Shireen Jilla was a journalist before she turned her hand to fiction. *Exiled*, a dark psychodrama set in New York, was published in 2011. *The Art of Unpacking Your Life* is her second novel. She lives with her husband and three children beside the river in west London.

www.shireenjilla.com